The
Yazoo
Blues

GEORGE ANNAND

MEMPHIS

TENNESSEE

MISSISSIPPI

DE SOTO

MARSHALL

Ashland

BENTON

TIPPAH

Hernando

Arkabutla Reservoir

Coldwater

Holly Springs

Ripley

Tunica

Coldwater

TATE

Senatobia

UNION

New Albany

ARKANSAS

TUNICA

Helena

PANOLA

Tallahatchie

Sardis Reservoir

Sardis

LAFAYETTE

Oxford

PONTOTOC

Yazoo or Moon L.

Batesville

Yazoo Pass

Tallahatchie

QUITMAN

Yocona

Water Valley

Coffeeville

CALHOUN

CHICKASAW

Clarksdale

COAHOMA

Charleston

TALLAHATCHIE

YALOBUSHA

Skuna

Pittsboro

Mississippi R.

Tutwiler

Lambert

Webb

Coffeeville

Arkansas R.

Sumner

Yalobusha R.

Grenada

N

BOLIVAR

Glendora

Philipp

Schlater

GRENADA

W E

WEBSTER

Barrows

Sunflower

Whaley

MONTGOMERY

S

Clear Cr.

Shaw

Sunflower

Itta Bena

GREENWOOD

Sandy

Carrollton

Chester

Deer Cr.

Indianola

Moorhead

Rising Sun

Winona

CHOCTAW

Greenville

Steele's Bayou

Sidon

CARROLL

Itta

HUMPHREYS

Cruger

Tchula

ATTALA

Louisville

WASHINGTON

Belzoni

Murphy

Lexington

Kosciusko

WINSTON

Midnight

Black

ARK. LA.

MISS.

Mayersville

Sunflower R.

Yazoo R.

Tallahatchie R.

HOLMES

Eden

Tchecha Cr.

LEAKE

NESHOBA

ISSA QUENA

SHARKEY

Benton

Big Black R.

Satartia

Canton

Redwood

MADISON

LOUISIANA

WARREN

VICKSBURG

JACKSON

LA. MISS.

HINDS

The Delta

The Yazoo River

The *Yazoo* *Blues*

A NOVEL BY

JOHN PRITCHARD

NewSouth Books

Montgomery | Louisville

ALSO BY JOHN PRITCHARD

Junior Ray

NewSouth Books
105 South Court Street
Montgomery, AL 36104

Library of Congress Cataloging-in-Publication Data

Pritchard, John, 1938-
The Yazoo blues : a novel / by John Pritchard.
p. cm.
Sequel to: Junior Ray.
ISBN-13: 978-1-58838-217-7
ISBN-10: 1-58838-217-6
1. Rednecks--Fiction. 2. Delta (Miss. : Region)--Fiction. 3. Mississippi--Fiction. 4.
Satire. I. Title.
PS3616.R5725Y39 2008
813'.6--dc22

2008023749

Design by Randall Williams

Printed in the United States of America
by the Maple-Vail Book Manufacturing Group

TO MY BELOVED CHILD,

MY SON, JOHN HAYES PRITCHARD III

Most Mississippians like to think of themselves as the last of the semi-rugged individualists. Some of them may be. But the majority are bred to the bone with conformity and anti-intellectualism. They like to think they are "rebels," but they grow up in and are nurtured by an authoritarian society in which there have not been very many rebels at all since the earth's very first Scotch-Irish, Adam and Eve. Indeed, the young men—and women—of my time would not have thought it strange in the least to say "Yassuh" to a fence post.

— *Owen G. Brainsong (deceased), Superintendent,*
Mhoon County Consolidated Schools,
St. Leo, Mississippi

Isapuntak laua. [Choctaw/Chickasaw]: "There are many mosquitoes."

— *Byington's* Dictionary of the Choctaw Language,
Bureau of American Ethnology, Bulletin 46
See also Chickasaw: an Analytical Dictionary,
by Pamela Munro and Catherine Willmond

CONTENTS

FACILITATOR'S PREFATORY REMARKS

My name is McKinney Lake. To clear up any ambiguity about the sound of it, I am a female, and I am just a bit younger than Junior Ray. Further, in the spirit of full disclosure, I must warn the reader that something may now have begun that was never intended by the publishers of Junior Ray Loveblood's first interview, which was conducted by Mr. Brainsong's nephew. That interview, which became the controversial book, *Junior Ray*, was—so I am told—meant mainly to gather information about our peculiar part of the nation and to provide background and substance for young Mr. Brainsong's philological and anthropological contributions to his peculiar corner in the field of Southern culture, by locating, examining, and organizing the "notes" of Leland Shaw and by paying attention to Junior Ray's extended account of their acquisition.

The project was a success, and that should have been the end of it. But, as a result of the attention the work received on publication, Junior Ray decided he had more to say and became almost immediately fired up to "talk another book." In truth, he was enjoying his fifteen minutes in the spotlight. However, Mr. Brainsong's nephew informed the publisher in Montgomery that his intense exposure to Junior Ray had affected his *Weltanschauung* as well as his health and that both his therapist and his Unitarian minister had recommended that he diligently avoid any further connection.

So I was asked by Junior Ray—after someone put a bee about me in his bonnet—if I would function as his facilitator on a second book. His publisher approved, and I said I would give it a shot.

My principal responsibility was to record what Junior Ray said and to offer suggestions from time to time, but I have decided to serve the reader as well by injecting perspective and, I hope, clarification through footnotes where needed. Though do not expect me to do so with young Mr. Brainsong's eloquence.

I SUPPOSE JUNIOR RAY can be considered part of an "oral tradition" for the simple reason that he doesn't actually write anything, nor is anyone who knows him certain that he could.

Since failing to kill Leland Shaw and subsequently retiring as a deputy, he has become obsessed with two things. First, the Union forces' failed but utterly fantastic Yazoo Pass Expedition in the late winter and early spring of 1863 into the watery Hell of the Mississippi Delta—our odd, *oval-shaped alluvial plain*, in Mississippi's "forehead," between an area of the state just below Memphis, at Walls, Mississippi, on Highway 61, and the mouth of the Yazoo River just above Vicksburg. Junior Ray has developed the amazing notion that he is now "a historian" and an expert on that particular Northern naval operation—complete with ironclads—in the backwaters of the Mississippi Delta during the Civil War.

Secondly, but more or less simultaneously, with Mad Owens's self-inflicted love affair with Money Scatters—a famous exotic dancer from Tchula, Mississippi, and a former Memphis policewoman, who, as part of her deep concern for the happiness of all mankind, traded in her gun for a g-string and her badge for a splendid pair of extraordinary tits. Through his considerable imagination, Junior Ray has combined the story of that 1863 naval warfare fiasco with his contemporary account of Owens's "exploration into the swamp of love," much as William Faulkner paired *The Old Man* and *The Wild Palms* into a single volume, though not exactly.

I have known Mad Owens all my life, and rather well, even though he is much younger. I should mention that he and I are double-fourth cousins once-removed, which, down here, is pretty close, considering the large number of fifth, sixth, and seventh cousins we all have. It's like Sicily.

To the average reader Mad may appear to possess almost no sense of emotional self-preservation or practical sense about anything. But Junior Ray Loveblood, in spite of his violence and profanity and sledge-hammer insensitivity, has developed a solid affection for Mad. I suppose you might call it paternal or avuncular. But the truth is Junior Ray has always held a soft spot for underdogs and the innocent, except in the case of that little episode with Leland Shaw.* One reason Junior Ray might feel that way about individuals who are at some sort of legitimate disadvantage is that, in them, he sees himself. It's just a thought. But I've thought about it a lot.

I WENT TO SCHOOL with Junior Ray. He and I are near the same age and have been friends, in a way, since the day I entered the second grade at Mhoon County Consolidated. Junior Ray was in the second grade, too, for the third year in a row (though they moved him up later that year), where he bullied the life out of some of the softer little town boys who were scared to death of him. He was tall, loud, often barefooted in the winter, and had muscles in his arms as hard as golfballs.

At that time, Junior Ray survived in a life the rest of us could not have imagined. He obviously wasn't much of a student, and because his family didn't yet have running water and electricity, he always smelled like a coal-oil lamp. But he was especially nice to me, called me strawhead, and threatened anybody, young or old, who did not show me the most extreme courtesy. I've always loved him for that. In my view, and I am sure in yours as well, nobody should demand one hundred percent perfection out of anybody

---

* A delusional, shell-shocked WWII veteran whom Junior Ray wanted to shoot, as described in his previous "memoir."

unless they can demand it of themselves. The point is, you ought not to throw somebody away just because once in a while they may seem like a monster. What kind of world would that be? We'd be without friends and have to avoid mirrors.

STILL, AS A WOMAN I must seem an unlikely choice for the job vis-à-vis the book's language and subject matter. But most people locally would not think it a bit strange. I expect they have always understood whether they wanted to or not that I never let *woman-hood* stand in my way when it came to claiming my *indelible* right to *this* short, manifold segment in the process of *Time* and to *this* place in the mystery of *Space*. That's all any of us ever have. Nor would I believe they could accuse me of ever letting my status as a female block the road for anybody else.

Even so, I am a Delta girl through and through. I did not see the allure of screwing sheep on the levee, but I knew the boys who did it and even went out with them one night, the time the whole flock ran over Brantley Duckworth when the game warden, Mr. Briarfield, showed up and threw his spot on the home team, most of whom were just standing around while Brantley attempted to bridge the chasm of the species.

He was then knocked flat into some sheep . . . "do" . . . when the lambs got spooked by the game warden's light and the scattering heroes, who—I along with them—fled to their fathers' cars and sped across a field toward the gravel road that would take us back to town, leaving Brantley in pursuit, hopping like a kangaroo on the turnrow, his breeches down around his ankles and the rest of him shrunk up to nothing as the game warden's truck with its spotlight followed him at about one mile an hour and then turned off to the right, back toward to the levee, and left Brantley, the Don Juan of Livestock, standing out there in the Mhoon county darkness, rejected by sheep and man alike.

So, yes, I know all about that and because I do may be why when my name came up Junior Ray didn't bat an eye—as he most certainly would have if I'd been one of those Chi Omega "Oouu-oouu-oouu!" sorority types who went to Ole Miss, whose blouses never wrinkled, and who only *did it, and said they didn't,* real quick in the dark. Thank God some of them grow out of it and become human beings. Still it is no wonder those boys went out to be with the sheep. It was a relief from all the vivacity.

JUNIOR RAY PRETTY MUCH reports on things the way they are, but like the rest of us he sometimes tells them the way he wants them to be. I figured I had a firm obligation to the reader to keep Junior Ray in the ballpark of accuracy as much as possible. So, I have injected two or three cents worth from time to time throughout this second helping of Junior Ray's "talking" contributions to the development of American literature.

Though the contents of this book are neither always fiction nor always fact, what Junior Ray has to tell us is nothing more—and nothing less!—than an autobiography. I mention this at the outset because the question of plot arose, and though I was convinced the issue was beside the point, I had no solid answer until I realized that Junior Ray is not merely an informant reporting an oral history but is, himself, all the elements of drama and fiction and, likewise, those, too, of a basic and recognizable reality within a subset of the human condition peculiarly bound up in a single, overwhelming persona.

Indeed, Junior Ray is plot, he is place, he is time, and above all he is character as well as theme. In terms of point of view, even I can see that he falls into the category of "limited all-knowing narrator," although he would most likely not accept the "limited" part, even if he could admit he were. I finally understood, as Alfred Hitchcock might have put it, that Junior Ray is his own MacGuffin

. . . you know, the thing in a story that's the whole reason for the story in the first place.

I also want to inject this: I happened to be home in St. Leo during the time Junior Ray and that nitwit Voyd Mudd were chasing around after Leland Shaw. I was here the day Lawyer Montgomery, Sheriff Holston, Atlanta Birmingham Jackson—with her "entourage"—and Boneface (thank God for him) were gathered over at Miss Helena Ferry's house. I remember it all because I was just across the street inside the new office of the Mississippi Power & Light Company, where I had gone to pay Mother's utility bill, and I saw the whole thing in progress through the plate glass window, on the east side of the building.

People were well aware of what Junior Ray had been up to, and they were not going to let it happen. After the first two weeks of Shaw's disappearance, almost nobody was buying Junior Ray's crappola about public safety and "protecting folks." Impenetrable as guys like Junior Ray are, you can usually see their insides on their outsides, like projected images of themselves moving in the opposite direction. It's what I call "the good ol' boy giveaway."

It's just that some of them you like, and some you don't, in spite of all the reasons you should or shouldn't. There are people who are bad all over and others who are bad only here and there. But when part of an avocado is rotten, it's still perfectly possible to appreciate the part that's not, depending on whether you like alligator pears in the first place. It's up to you, of course.

That's my story. You must continue now with Junior Ray's . . . just the way he told it.

—McKinney Lake, *St. Leo, Mississippi*

The
Yazoo
Blues

CHAPTER I

God invented Cusswords — Bible Books — First & Second
Befukatheez — The List of Saint Pisstofus — Majorettes and
Mallards — A Cussin CD — Mad Owens — Litter-ture — The
Hot-Tamale Nigga — Pelicans — Okra Winfrey

S umbich, you won't believe this, but somebody'll walk clear across the street just to come up to me and say, "Junior Ray, you ass'ole, why do you have to use so gotdam much profanity in that book you wrote about us?"

I look at that coksukka hard with my right eye, and I tell 'im: Listen, goat-dik, I didn't write the sumbich, I talked it, but the fukkin fact is God invented cusswords. He invented them sumbiches just like He invented everything else—I mean, if you believe in God—and I don't—but I'm just saying, if you're one of those cobuptheass pekkaheds that always wants to let folks know you got to go to church on Sunday and sing all them draggy-ass songs in praise of a fukkin figment of your or somebody else's gotdam imagination, then you don't have no choice but to agree with what I just said: namely, that Godalmighty, Hissef, invented cussin'.

Plus, you have to agree, too, that if what you're singing all them hymns to needs all that dumbass praise, your ass is in more fukkin trouble that just the possibility of goin' to Hell—which I have no doubt is probably somewhere over across the river in Arkansas.

I tell 'ose sumbiches to look at it thissa way: If God is God and He's perfect, then He can't make no mistakes. Plus, if he's tee-totally-ass good to the bone, then He can't do nothin' bad—or I guess I ought to say *wouldn* do nothin' bad, because otherwise you'd be strappin' Him down, puttin' limits on His power, so to speak, and of course, bein' God, He's about as un-fukkin-limited as you can get. Otherwise I can't see no sense in Him wantn the job.

So, whenever a sumbich comes up to me and starts in about my gotdam profanity, I just use *philosophy* on his ass and tell him he can go fuk a truck tire.

I coulda been a preacher. And, even though it ain't no longer Bible days, if I had my way, I'd put special cussin' books in the Holy Bible. I'd add those sumbiches, and right off the bat I'd have *The Book of First Befukatheez*. Then, naturally, I'd have to th'ow in a follow-up and call it *The Book of Second Befukatheez*. And both of *them* would come right after *The Hoodoo Hex of Saint Damyoass* and *The List of Saint Pisstofus*. I'd slap 'ose muthafukkas right up at the front of the whole deal.

Some smart-mouthed sumbich said there weren't no saints as such in that part of the Bible. Fukkim. There will be in mine. I ain't waitn around for Jesus and nem to come up with the gotdam saints. Besides, can't nobody understand half the shit in the damn thing nohow. *First Befukatheez*, though, would be clear. It'd open right up with, "Holy Shit! Behold!" Then it would go on and get better from there.

Just like you, I expect, I have heard plenty of Bible talk and know how they said things back yonder, stuff like: "Lo, what cometh up the roadeth, muthafukka?" and other such old-timey googah. It wouldn be hard to make any of it sound bible-y, just like the names of the new books themse'ves: *Befukatheez I & II*. You can't hardly tell the difference in the way that sounds and what's in the original Bible. Specially in the one them fukkin Cath'lics uses. Oh Hell-o Bill, I seen it! Miss Helena Ferry's sister Peekie showed it to me. She'd done been a lot of things, but by then she had decided to be a Cath'lic and thought I might want to consider joinin' up myse'f. I told her, "No, ma'am, thank you," and I said I hated church worse'n I hated niggas and bankers—but I didn't mention planters cause she was one of em—and I guess, because she was, she give me a sharp look and said, Now, Junior Ray, you mussn speak like that about *our darkies*," even though she knew sure as shootn-sherry I didn't have none.

But now they was one wild-ass book in the front part of that Cath'lic Bible she showed me that stuck out in my mind. It was called the Wisdom of Sirach, Son of Jesus. Kiss my ass. If there wuddn no saints in that part of the Bible, there sure as shit wuddn no Jesus neither. So how'd that sumbich get in there? That's why I say if them Cath'lic muthafukkas can do it, I guess I could too. Plus, I do like the way the names of my new books *sound*, and for all I know that's how the whole thing was wrote up in the first place. I can just hear all them old scribes and Pharisees and fukkin apostles settin' around sayin', "Hey, muthafukka, what about us callin' thissun *Abbadisticus*?"

"Fuk yeah, Mozayuh," anothern'd say, "And let's line that coksukka up between the *Song of Shazamoab* and the gotdam *Letter of St. Boogaloo to the Baptists!*"

"Suiteth the shiteth outta me-ith, sumbich," the first one might answer, and that's how it all coulda went—all the way up to and be-fukkin-YOND the *Chevrolation of Saint Cleatus the Frogburp*.

I expect I might have to put some thought on what else to include. I can hear a preacher right now, drummin' up the spirit and getn into it, sayin', "Now, brothers and sisters, please open your floppy-ass Bibles to *First Befukatheez*, chapter 4, verse 6:

"And the Lord did have pity on the po' sumbich who had tore up his life beyond recog-fukkin-NITION, and the Lord sent-eth forth His angels to flap down and give the miserable muthafukka a gotdam bath and a bottle of Mad-dog 20-20, so he—the aforesaid muthafukka—could get through another day of his knee-walkin', dirt-likkin' life up and down Highway 61 as well as on the nasty-ass streets of Meffis, especially after he'd done gambled away all his money at the casinos, and had drank up and pissed away every last no-count gumbo acre of buckshot bean-land his granddaddy left him until he, the dikhed in question, flat fukkin didn't have nothin' to say for his sorry sef but half a lung, a lump of charcoal for a liver, a pulse, and a twenty-year-old piece-a-junk-ass Cutlass Supreme."

But, like I say, anytime some of these sumbiches around here get all righteous and green-p'simmon-lipped—I'm talkin' about *whenever* these muthafukkas jump all over my ass about "the language" in my fukkin books AND about me bringing up the sheep screwin' and all—I just look at em and say, "You little diklikkers, yawl woulda done it with rats if they'da been tall enough." Or, I'd add, if they'da been majorettes. Bygod, you can hear em howl all the way to *Itta Bena.*

Anyway, I expect even old God Hissef couldn't do nothin' to suit sumneez sumbiches.

But, hot-da-um! *Majorettes.* I didn't never love football, but I *sure as Shubuta** wanted me one nem majorettes.

Back when I was in Mhoon County High School, for a while, the dumbass little football team was called the Mallards; though, later when all the greenheads was just about shot out, some of the men in the town—the *Boosters*—wanted to switch and call the team the Gadwalls, but them lesser ducks didn't pass the taste-test one bit, so it wuddn long before the team said to fuk *that* noise and went back to callin' theyse'ves, once again, the Mhoon County Mallards.

However, when all them planters begun to use chemicals to keep the Johnson grass from growing between the rows, some sumbiches on the St. Leo Junior-ass Chamber of fukkin Commerce piped up and said they wanted to call the football team the Herbicides. That didn't catch on neither, and so they stuck with the ducks.

* A small town in southeast Mississippi, definitely not in the Delta.

I remember thinkin' to myse'f at the time: Well, hell, what's the matter with callin' em the Hoe Hands? I didn't say nothin' about it because hoe hands, black *or* white, was about to get just about as scarce as mallards was; plus, very few of them little diklikkers that suited up on the high school football team had ever knowed anything about choppin' cotton. Not *all* of em, but a lot of em, was just a buncha townfukkas and one way or another was hooked into them planters.

Finally, though, later on in the 1960s, the niggas come in and took over the public school, and the whites, natchaly, went off and built their own prissy-ass school, which they decided to refer to as a *academy*, so now if you want to know the truth, I don't know what none of em call their gotdam teams. Fukkum. I don't keep up with it. Plus, I don't know what a bug-bumpin' *academy* is, unless it's to make them chillun talk right, walk right, and don't ast no questions.

Anyway, a lotta these old goat-pokers want me to use words nice *people* uses and would want to read—to other fukkin nice people I guess—but my question is what do nice people say when they want to call somebody a muthafukka or a coksukka, or even just a plain old sumbich?

I sure as hell don't know. I ain't growed up around no nice people—I try not to hang around with none, and if there *are* any out there somewhere, they can kiss my four-wheeler. Fuk them sumbiches. They ain't as nice as they think they are nohow.

Oh, I know them planters is *supposed* to be nice people. Double-fuk them coksukkas, and the gotdam bankers too. Some of the lawyers is all right, though. I'll give their ass a slide.

The long and the short of it is I like cussin'. And I like listening to it as much as I like doin' it. Shoot, I wouldn mind having me one nem CDs with nothin' but cussin' on it—so I could stick it in the stereo and play it, and I'd just set there and relax.

Some nem sumbiches—out in California, I think—has CDs
of birds fartin', fish jumpin', and leaves falling, or the sound of
waves, like in the *GuffaMexico*, which I am about to get to, and
they play em at night to go to sleep by. But I—me, personally—
I'd be happy layin' there in the dark with the window unit on just
listening to some muthafukka cuss—real soft, of course, I guess
you might even say *gentle*—in one nem Skyway-Hotel-Peabody,
uptown *radio-announcer* voices?*

Or I can see puttin' a cussin' CD on my alarm clock thing:
"Good morning, sumbich. It's time to drag your mean-old worthless ass outta the bed, and go fix some gotdam eggs."

THERE HAS BEEN A lot of yip yap about me having had Shaw's
notebooks and, now, also about me having a good bit of the
stuff Mad Owens wrote during the time he was pussywhipped
by Money Scatters and afterwards when he tried to lose hissef in
the GuffaMexico, way-off down there on the fukkin Mississippi
Guffcoast, out at the ass-fukkin-end of just about ever'thin', on
Horn-gotdam-Island.

Bygod, next to Arkansas—and to the *Yazoo Pass, in the Mississippi Delta, back in 1863*—that place was as close to Hell itse'f as
a sumbich like me would ever want to get.

People say, "Junior Ray ain't got no business havin' nothin' to
do with litter-ture. I just say fukkum. I *am* a *historian*—and that's
what this book, right here, is about—so I don't see why me havin'
that other crap around—like Mad's poems and the book he wrote
down there at Horn Island on the beach, in the fukkin sand†—is
so unusual.

---

* In the Upper Delta, during the 1940s and '50s, people listened late at
night to their radios, and heard an announcer from one of Memphis's principal
stations say something like: "And now from the Skyway Ballroom High Atop
Hotel Peabody, we bring you Les Brown and his Band of Renown."

† Mad wrote it out on something else first.

If a sumbich is a historian, that's part of what it takes to be one. Besides that, in Mad's case, he knew I would hold on to all the stuff he handed over to me and that I would not let nobody fuk with it unless he give me the word. And in this case he give the word to me *and* to McKinney, who has already introduced herself to you and who thinks as much of Mad Owens as I do.

McKinney Lake is my *fa-fukkin-cilitator*—or whatever you want to call it. The publisher decided we'd call her that because this book ain't really an actual re-search interview like the first book was, with young Mr. Brainsong who wanted to find out about the Delta and get hold of Leland Shaw's notebooks. He didn't want to do it no more, so McKinney agreed to help me while I *talk the book*. For one thing she's *from* here and knows damn near as much as I do about the place. Plus I've knowed her since we was both pretty young and went to Mhoon County Consolidated. If all women was like McKinney, there wouldn be no problems in the fukkin world. Plus, people would think a whole lot better of women in general. You'll see what I mean directly.

Anyway, I got all of Mad's litter-ture in the closet under the stairs wrapped up in my waders, right where I kept Leland Shaw's notebooks. I don't wear the waders no more, cause I don't go walkin' out th'oo the sloughs, like I used to, to hunt ducks. If I want a duck, I know a dozen muthafukkas that'd be glad to get rid of some they've got, which they shot mostly in Arkansas, just so they could make more room in their freezer for other things, like okra . . . and their special chili, which nine times out of ten is made with squirrels and raccoons.

Wouldn nothin' surprise your ass down here—they was a nigga one time who made hot-tamales, like you'll find in all 'eez Delta towns, and, Oh Hell-o Bill, people couldn stop talkin' about how dee-fukkin-licious them hot-tamales was. Well, the sumbich was makin' em outta mink meat.

He was trappin' the mink, like a lotta sumbiches did in those days, right on the west edge of town all down along the Sugar Ditch and selling the hides to old Fess Bright who'd ride the train to Meffis and sell em to a dealer on South Main. Fess was white of course.

I found it all out one time when I knocked on the hot-tamale nigga's door to ast him if he knew who kilt another nigga the week before in the alley behind the Palace Thee-ater. And that's when I saw what he was usin' and knew what it was cause I seen the skins and the heads as well.

I never said one word about it. And I wuddn gon' fuk up the deal he had goin' with Fess. It coulda gotten complicated. He gimme the name of the sumbich that stabbed Bob Irwin's top tractor driver, and I figured me not sayin' nothin' about him usin' mink meat from the side of what was at the time the town's sewage ditch was one way he and I could continue to have a workin' relationship, which, as you know, in law enforcement, is real fukkin important. Plus, I had free hot-tamales anytime I wanted em.

Speakin' of cookin', after that first book that I done with young Mr. Brainsong II, it wuddn long before I noticed that books that has *recipes* in em do pretty well because women seem to go for em. So I decided to th'ow in two or three of my all-time personal favorites,* just in case. I had McKinney put the first one of em at the end of this chapter.

But now, back to the ducks. Fuk wadin' around in a swamp waitin' for those little skimmers to decide to fly over on their way to the South Pole or wherever it is nature tells em to go—plus I don't think very many of em has flew over Mhoon County since the day Voyd pulled out a thing he ordered from a catalog, put it

---

* This is one of Junior Ray's greatest fictions. He has never cooked up anything in his life except in his imagination, and the reader is advised to proceed with caution.

in his mouth, and said he was gon' show me his "feeding call."

Whatever that little sumbich told them ducks they was gon' have for breakfast must have changed their mind forever about settin' their formerly unsuspectin' duck-butts down in Mhoon County. Well, that and the fact it's been so hot and dry.

I used to get a kick out of watchin' nem good-tastin' little gliders come into the slough on a cold-ass morning, just at first light, when the water was froze over. They couldn't tell it was solid, so when they landed on the ice, they'd go "Whump" and skid a few feet. I promise you those little "scofers" actually looked surprised, if you can imagine what a surprised duck might look like when the sumbich discovers things ain't what they was quacked-up to be. That's a joke, sumbich. But the ducks slidin' in like that wuddn. They really did it.

Even though they ain't none much no more around St. Leo, ducks is still serious business down here. People have the impression they's all these rich-ass doctors out there somewhere—mostly in a lot of landowners' dreams—and the idea is that when these doctors ain't busy as a coonass eatn crawdads, they're killin' ducks.

It's like, "Oh, doctor, please he'p my ass!"

"Sorry, son, you look exactly like a duck to me, *Blam*." And then of course the dumb muthafukka's family gets the *bill*. That's another joke.

Anyway, McKinney loves the you-know-what outta Mad's poems. Personally, I think poetry is fulla shit—*but*, I don't think McKinney is, *so* if she likes Mad's poems, then I know there's something to the sumbiches, because, as I have indicated, McKinney ain't just any lillo gal—or wuddn, when she *was* a gal—plus, she lived a long time up the country in New York City at a place called The Barbizon, whatever the fuk that was.

Even though I never saw much need of travelin' anyplace, I do think it's good for some people. And I have to admit, I did 'sperience some things when I went down to the GuffaMexico to visit Mad on that datgum island that I wouldna come up on no where else: like water you can't see across, jellyfish, and stingarees. I would say pelicans, too, but we got them muthafukkas hanging out around the catfish ponds here in the county, along with the gotdam water turkeys.* Although, as somebody pointed out, our pelicans up here is white, and down there they's a good many brown ones. But as far as I'm concerned a fukkin pelican is a pelican; I don't give a shit what race he is.

Speakin' of that, I know there's a lot of people that call me a racist. Fukkum. I ain't. I'm just a sumbich that uses the kind of words people don't like to hear because the words ain't long and wiggly they way they want em to be. I mean, I don't have anything especially against most Pekkawoods, Niggas, Greasers, Chinamens, Jews, A-rabs, Eye-fukkin-talians, and them gotdam Cath'lics, nor boy nor girl Queers, neither. Anybody that knows me, knows me damn well and maybe better than I know myself. Yet I do admit I have said some hard things about Planters and Bankers. But, them, and all the rest of those sumbiches I just mentioned—every fukkin one of em—I reckon they can take care of themse'vs without frettin' over the likes of me. And if they can't . . . then can't nothin' in this world ever help em.

---

* Cormorants.

🌸 OKRA WINFREY 🌸

Take a pound and a half of fresh—or frozen—okra, whole or cut-up, along with lots of white and/or yellow onions and canned whole tomatoes, which you can mush up as you go along. Add some chopped, tender, white celery shoots from the inside of the stalk, but th'ow away the leaves.

Dump it all into a big-ass skillet with a little olive oil—not too much because there's gon' be a lot of juice from the stuff you've already th'owed in there—then cook it for a good while, stirring it around every now and then. Add a lot of garlic. Use the powder.

Later, after it cooks down, and when you feel like it, add two pounds of fresh, peeled shrimp, and some nice big scallops. You can use frozen crawfish meat. But be sure the crawdads are Americans and not those gotdam Chinese-ass muthafukkas. You can't tell *what* them sumbiches might be! Plus, if you want to, you can use chicken, but I wouldn because it's too fukkin ordinary, and you'll want to avoid *that.*

Mix it all up, and let it simmer on low heat—and even though it duddn take a lot of time to cook shrimp, make sure the shrimp gets down in there and rubs up against the other stuff for at least fifteen minutes, after which, cut the fire down and keep everything simmering, with a top not on all the way (so some of the steam can get out), for a fairly long time, maybe an hour or two—or more—on real low-ass heat. And don't mess with it.

Then cut off the stove, unload the whole thing on top of some of that unpolished brown rice from Arkansas, and eat it—with, of course, salt and cayenne or, you know, salt and . . . Crystal Pepper Sauce.

CHAPTER 2

*Junior Ray Reflects on the True Nature of Time — He and Voyd
Deal with a Nekkid Fat Man — And a Large Snake
— Slab Town — Mr. Reitoff*

ersonal time?! What the fuk do you mean *personal time?* All
time is personal," I told that dumb muthafukka. Course, he's
my supervisor, and I ought not to talk to him thatta way,
but the silly sumbich went to some kind of management school up
the country, in *Pennsylvania,* I think, and it gave him a fukked-up
sense of reality. He believes there are several kinds of time: personal
time, company time, sick time, and vacation time. Oh, yeah, and
down time. What an ass'ole.

Like everybody else that come here with these casinos, he's a
Yankee, and those sumbiches NEVER know what time it is. And
yet that's all they think about. They're down-to-the-minute kind
of people. The trouble is they handle time like it was a handful
of chips—stackin' it up, countin' it out, and tryin' to save some.
They don't realize time ain't in no danger and that it's *them* that's
runnin' out and that they, themse'ves, is only a moment, kind of
like a raindrop.

My supervisor's young, but I don't think any amount of time,
personal or otherwise, is going to improve him. Also, he's one nem
fly fishermen, if you know what I mean. But I don't hold that against
him too much. I don't give a damn if he cornholes armadillos as
long as he lets me take off when I need to, within reason naturally.
All in all he's not a bad guy, just a little silly.

The thing is I've got to go over to Sledge. You remember I've told
you about my girlfriend over there. Anyway, she's having a big do

for her daughters and her grandchildren, and she especially wants me there, so I can talk to her oldest daughter's middle boy about a career in law enforcement. She says she thinks he's got what it takes and that he's a lot like me. I didn't touch that.

But I will say one thing: Being in law enforcement most of my life taught me a shit pot of a lot about what's what. I guess I seen just about everything you could think of and then some you couldn, like the man with the snake up his ass.

That situation come about late one summer night out on the Cut-Off* when Voyd and me was patrollin' that part of the county, and we heard there was a party out there. Other'n we just wanted to make sure hadn't nothin' got out of hand, we didn't particularly think much about it because bunches of Meffis folks had parties out there all the fukkin time, and this was long before there was any casinos.

Anyway, just as we topped the levee there at the Tippen place, here come the biggest, fattest sumbich you ever saw, nekkid as a porkchop, his hands clawin' at the air in front of him, runnin' up the levee on the road from the other side straight-ass into the head-lights of the patrol car. I slammed on the brakes, cause I thought that coksukka was gonna dent up the grill, and I didn't want no more of that kind of shit to deal with that month. But, he swerved off to his left and come hollerin' like a muthafukka by Voyd on the passenger side.

"Gotdam," said Voyd.

"Gotdam," I said back. "We better turn around and see what the hell's the matter with that sumbich."

We woulda radioed for some help, but in those days there wuddn nobody to radio *to* but us—well, we could've *called up* the highway patrolman on the phone, but there wuddn no phones, neither,

---

* An artificial ox-bow in the river created by the U.S. Corps of Engineers in 1942, with TNT.

where *we* was. Plus, Voyd and me was on his shit list for a number of reasons, and he said if we called him one more time, he was gon' tell Sheriff Holston we didn't know our butts from a soupbowl and get us fired. Well, get *me* fired—hell, Voyd was basically just *ridin'* with me and, even though he'd been made a *constable,* wuddn, like me, a real full-time deputy on the county payroll.

So we knew we had to handle the situation ourselves. But, you know, there's just something about a six-foot nekkid fat man runnin' around in the dark out in the middle of nowhere that turns your blood to Kool-Aid, especially when we saw he had a snake up his ass—we never did get to the bottom of *that.* That's a joke, muthafukka. Well, it is and it *iddn.*

Anyhow, there we was. And there *he* was, with a live snake wavin' out of his butt. So I said, "Go apprehend the suspect, Voyd."

It didn't make no difference that Voyd wuddn a real deputy. There wuddn nobody out there that time of night on the levee in the fukkin dark except him and me and that huge sumbich runnin' up the road with the tail of a big snake whippin' thissa way and that around his backside, either tryin' to crawl in or crawl out; we couldn't tell which. Plus, when we run up on this sumbich, or vice versa, we never did make it 'cross the levee to check whether there was any kind of party over there.

"Go appre-fukkin-hend him yourse'f," Voyd said. "I ain't goin' nowhere near that coksukka—what kinda suspect is he anyhow?"

"I don't know," I said.

"If he turns sideways," said Voyd, "maybe we can *shoot* the gotdam thing."

And I said, "Voyd, you couldn't hit your own dick with a brickbat, much less a gotdam snake flappin' around outta somebody else's butt, and I ain't gettin' nowhere near him neither."

"Well, I don't reckon we can just go home and not do nothin'," Voyd more or less suggested.

"No, we gotta do *somethin'*," I said. But right then I couldn for the life of me come up with what that might be, so Voyd and I just followed along behind the nekkid fat fellow with the snake stuck up his T-hiney, a-wavin' back and forth like he had a long-ass tail.

Fortunately, the sumbich stayed on the gravel and didn't cut out across no fields. It looked to me like he was goin' to run hollerin' and carryin' on, jibber-jabberin' all the way back to St. Leo—which would have been an award-winning achievement that, for him or, I guess, for most other three-hunnuhd-pound white men dancin' around in their birthday suits with snakes in their ass, I could not bring myself to feel overly optimistic about.

The truth is I was kind of hoping he might just die with a heart attack, and then Voyd and me coulda come out the next day and *discovered* him. Maybe by that time the snake woulda been gone.

Also, the snake wuddn no skinny blue racer. We decided it was a king snake—which was the good part, though it don't speak well for that type of snake. Yet it was good for the suspect because, as you know, king snakes ain't poisonous. But Holy Shit it seemed like the thing was big-around as a Mason jar and longer than Burl Ives's belt, at least a third of which was hidin' up *inside* that goggle-eyed sumbich who was busy tryin' to outrun hissef, the snake, and his own ass-end after twelve o'clock at night on a country road. Speakin' as a law-enforcement professional, I don't know who had the most to worry about, him or the rep-tile.

I wouldna never thought, at the time, things would turn out okay in the end—that's a joke, too; wait a minute, I got to burp— but they did.

Finally the nekkid fat man reached around and grabbed the snake and pulled it out of his ass. He stood there in the headlights of the patrol car for a second or two holdin' the po' snake up in the air in front of him while he was still screamin' and sayin' words neither Voyd nor me could understand, and then he th'owed the thing off into a bean field. Voyd said, "Thank you Jesus," and I said, "Fuk yeah." But I spect the snake was more relieved than me and Voyd was.

We crammed the terrified Meffis sumbich in the back seat, and hauled his ass on in to the little hospital there in St. Leo. The next day, Doc McCandliss said he ain't never seen anything like it. He said the fellow had some "rips" in his rectum, and that if Voyd and me hadn't told him what had happened, he'da thought the sumbich had been captured by the Turkish army, whatever the fuk that means. Doc McCandliss further stated it took a long time to calm the man down, but that after he did stop shakin' and started makin' some sense, the sumbich swore to Doc that he did not know how the snake got up his butt.

He was a Meffis fellow, natchaly, and claimed he had gone to sleep on a couch outchonda at his trailer, which was up on pilings like a buncha them others there by the Cut-Off, cause the water can rise awful high in the spring, and that before he lay down on the sofa-bed he had done took hissef a nice hot shower, and he thought he'd just lay there on top of the sheets and look at the TV for a while. But, because it was already late when he got to the Cut-Off from up in Meffis, and even though it was warm that night but not especially humid, he said he didn't want to crank up the air conditioning till he really had to, and he thought he could catch a breeze comin' through the screens. It seemed like a pretty good idea to him; plus, he was glad at last to be down there beside the peaceful waters of the Mississippi River Cut-Off outside St. Leo and not still up in the city with all the noise and dangerous robbin' and rapin' and carjackin' and senseless-ass killin' in addition to all the other everyday *crappage* that goes on there.

Anyway, he told Doc he went sound to sleep and was dreamin' he had done found the love of his life. Doc says the fellow did not go into no detail about what that was, but that, after layin' there for a while, the sumbich said he begun to wake up a little and to feel like somethin' wuddn right, and it was at that point he discovered he had a snake up his butt.

After that, he said he didn't remember a whole lot until Voyd and me picked him up in the patrol car. I believe the sumbich. I wouldna wanted to remember none of it neither. And now, he said to Doc, he seriously thought he might want to sell his trailer and not never come back down to the Cut-Off or anywhere in the whole fukkin Delta no more as long as he lived. And I wouldn neither if a snake had crawled up *my* ass.

Over the years I've thought about this more'n once, and, frankly, when you take into consideration where he was and what things are like down here, there ain't no need not to give him credit for what all he said. You know, you get in them woods over there across the levee, and *anything* might happen to you. I don't care if you *are* up in a trailer on twelve-foot pilings. I wouldn doubt nothin' nobody said about stuff over in there. And even though now some of them woods is all done up like Lost-fukkin-Vegas, the *real* reality behind the bright lights is that them casinos are gamblin' with somethin' a lot wilder than a king snake on a couch; those muthafukkas is shootin' craps with the Mississippi River.

THAT REMINDS ME THEY was another time, way back before that, when Sheriff Holston telephoned and woke my ass up one morning about first light, on December 22nd, 1964.

Now, right here, hold your potatoes, and don't fuk with me. I aint *forgot* about gettin' to the part about how I became a historian and come to know all about the Yankee blue-suits' Yazoo Pass Expedition, but there's still some more important background information concerning my life in law enforcement that I have to tell you about before I can get to the real, old-timey historical part. Which is where I'm headed.

I guess what you don't know—cause you're not a historian—is that background *is* what *is*—it's the onliest thing that is definitely set and done while the rest ain't nothin' more'n pure-dee speculation, or hope, or wish, and such diddlyass crap as that. But the past is *it*, sumbich. It's the fukkin frontier. It ain't what *was*, it's what *am*. And without it, you and me and every page in this book wouldn be nothin' but a blank.

So when I answered the phone, Sheriff Holston said: "Junior Ray, meet me out at Slab Town quick as you can." Then he hung up. Sumpn bout it give me one nem feelings like you get when some muthafukka in a movie is hangin' by his fingers off a window ledge on a tall building or if you was settin' in a bathtub and some sumbich dumped a bucket full of fishin' worms on you.

I called Voyd—this was not long before he got to be a constable, but technically, I guess you could say from a common law standpoint, he was almost as official a law officer as I was, but not quite. Anyway, I picked him up in his yard and seen Sunflower peekin' out the window. She'd done pushed the shade to the side, and I just barely made her out. But I spied her. And I knew she was sayin', "Junior Ray, you gotdam muthafukka," under her bad-ass-big-thinga-bobbakew-before-she-went-to-bed breath.

I can't help it, but I always think about Sunflower and the crap she's pulled on Voyd like the time he didn't know where she was until a deputy up in Meffis called his house and told him Sunflower was in jail for bein' "intoxicated in a public place." The public place turned out to be a lover's lane out on the east outskirts of the city, where she was settin' in the back seat of a brand-new used Lincoln Mark VIII with a Meffis Cadillac salesman, who I guess was givin' her a test drive.

It was after dark, and a Shelby County sheriff's officer come up on em and shined his light inside the vehicle. And there they was, both of em, her and the salesman, bolt upright and ram-rod

straight, drunker'n jaybirds eatin' hackberries, and it wuddn just
that neither of em could walk a straight line—what it *was* was that
Sunflower had *both* her legs jammed down in just *one* leg of her
Capri pants.

Po' ol' Voyd. I truly do feel sorry for the sumbich. Hell, he's
my friend.

Anyhow, we scratched off with the blue and red lights blappin',
hit 61, and drove south and then, not far below the bridge at Broke
Pot Mound, we turned straight east toward what folks called Slab
Town, which was not no town at all, just one lillo country store
built on a slab—instead of up off the ground like most things
down here are—and *another slab,* with nothin' built on it, right
next to the store, both of em facin' a gravel road that runs east and
west, from Askew to where it hit the levee at Yookaloosa* Brake,
and vice-versa. Of course, there wuddn much at Askew neither,
and even today there ain't nothing to see a-tall when you get to
the levee. Shoot, the gravel don't even go up onto the levee, the
whole thing just turns into a rutty little dirt road at the base of it,
from which, if it ain't too wet, you can go up on top of the levee
and ride north till you come to Austin or south till you get to a
blacktop road that'll take you back to 61 by way of Dundee. Either
way, you ain't been nowhere.

But at Slab Town, there wuddn but about six houses and an
old caboose fixed up to be a fukkin Sunday school. The houses,
if you wanted to call em houses, was strung out along the north
and south sides of the gravel road, goin' east, between the piss-ant
store and the caboose, which wuddn no more'n three-tenths of a
mile total.

Now, don't get me wrong. These raggedy sumbiches livin' out
there wuddn no niggas. They was white.

Anyway, Voyd and me come roarin' up and seen Sheriff Holston's

* Choctaw/Chickasaw: yuka (slave) + loosa (black) = Black Slave Brake.

big-ass Ford parked on the side of the road on the other end of the bridge, with *his* lights all goin' so there we all was, out in the middle of nowhere with our lights and all, makin' quite a sight. And Voyd and me still didn't know what we come there for. But as we slid on up beside Sheriff Holston's official vehicle, we knew something was mighty wrong.

"What the fuk!" Voyd said. And when we got out of the patrol car and walked up to where Sheriff Holston was standin' in the middle of the gravel, we got the picture: There wuddn no Slab Town there.

Over in a little field knee-high in dry grass and cuckaburrs, across from where the store had been, we seen Preacher Flickett. He lived in St. Leo and was one nem Piscob'ls. Anyway, he was standin' in the weeds with his face turned up toward the sky and his arms helt up like he was fixin' to catch something.

"He's not going anywhere, Junior Ray," Sheriff Holston said, "but why don't you walk out there and see if the minister would like to come on over here and rest for a while inside your patrol car." I done what the sheriff ast me to, and Reverend Flickett didn say a word or do nothin' impolite whatsoever. He just walked beside me back to the car. Voyd, who was standin' there by it, lookin' like he'd been hit in the head with a REA* light pole, blinked two or three times, closed his mouth, and opened the back door. Brother Flickett got in, and that was all there was to it.

The long and the short of it was that the Shepherd had blowed up his flock and had wiped out the whole so-called town. He done it with dynamite, which it turns out he had collected over a period of time from one planter's commissary here and from another's pickup there. It was a wonder he didn't blow hissef up months before that night.

---

* FDR's Rural Electrification Authority, which finally brought electricity to the Delta in 1935.

What it was, he had been goin' out in the county to some of the wilder places and preachin' and teachin' his Piscob'l shit, which I am told is mostly sort of quiet and dignified and not rockin' and rollin' like what some of them other stump-jumpin', Bible-thumpin', more holy-rollerish sumbiches would th'ow out back then to them beat-down po' whites who lived half-out in the middle of the gotdam woods and who musta thought, somehow, their pitiful-ass souls had a chance of goin' somewhere besides Hell—which, frankly, compared with how they lived, woulda looked like a stroke of good luck and mighta seemed no worse than a day choppin' cotton.

It was the same with Elvis. He thought that house of his was a mansion. It ain't. It's just a house.

Anyway, Reverend Flickett, the Piscob'l sumbich, felt like he wuddn gettin' nowhere with the clientele. He'd tell em they better shape up, and they'd just set there and yawn. But then he seen the light, even if they didn't. He was gon' have to scare the shit out of em to get em to take his Piscob'l ass seriously, even though, somebody said, he didn't really want none of them cootie-bit muthafukkas *ever* to decide to join up and become Piscob'ls. And the more he tried to do the right thing but, you might say, with the wrong objective in mind, the more confused that pitiful muthafukka become. Personally, I'll lay money he meant well, but you know yoursef, whenever anybody says some sumbich "tried to do the right thing," it normally means he was dumber'n shit and had fukked up real bad.

The story come out bit by bit. He had begun to tell those transplanted hillbilly muthafukkas that the end of the gotdam world was comin', and just to th'ow em into high gear, the sumbich put a date on it: December 22nd, 1964.

So the coksukka kept on warnin' em: "The world is goin' to end—on December the twenty-second in this the year of Our Lord, nineteen hunnuhd and sixty-fukkin-four!" And then, the word was, even though the Reverend Flickett was a Piscob'l, he neverthe-fukkin-less tried his hand at shoutin', and they say the sumbich would drill his beady eyes into them pekkawoods and holler, "Repent! You sorry sonzabitches!"

People all said that for a Piscob'l, he was more like a Baptist. The Baptists, natchaly, said, "Bullshit," that he wuddn no such a thing. Personally I don't give a fishfuk. I'm just tellin' you what happened and what I heard.

Anyhow, apparently late—*late*—in the middle of the night, the one that was gonna come up the morning of December 22nd, 19 and 64—he got a coil of electrical wire, some blasting caps, and all the dynamite he had collected and hid away underneath the Piscob'l Church in St. Leo, and very syste-fukkin-matically made nine bundles of nine sticks each. He later told the doctor at the state insane asylum down at Whitfield he called em his "Triple Trinities." After he stuck the blasting caps in em, he attached thirty-five to forty-foot wires. Then, in the dark, without no lights, he drove slowly down the gravel road, stoppin' in front of each lillo shotgun, where he'd dismount and ever so tippy-toe cast one nem bundles of dynamite up underneath the house, leavin' one end of the long wire next to the road—or off in the ditch beside it. And since the store was built on a slab—instead of up off the ground like the houses was—he couldn th'ow nothin' under it, so he broke the glass in the front door and lobbed the package inside; after the blast there was gotdam baloney and potted meat and and vy-eena sausages and them real red, strung-together weenies all strowed out fifty fukkin yards in ever' direction.

Anyway, when he had done th'owed the dynamite inside the store, he drove back down the road and hooked all the wires from the bundles to one long-ass, main wire, one end of which, when he had drove off far enough, he looped around the negative pole on his car battery.

I don't know if he waited a little bit and thought about it or what, because I don't know when he got finished puttin' everything together, but about the time the first feelark* farted or the first goose honked, Pastor Flickett, you might say, completed the circuit, and the world ended *sho-nuff* then and there for Slab Town.

I heard the boom way-ass up where I was in St. Leo, but I was so sleepy I didn't pay it no mind. I thought it was a freight train pickin' up cars off the side track.

Dundee Hamlin not only heard the boom, he seen the flash. The way he told it he'd been up all night wonderin' what was goin' to happen to his "way of life" if it was ever a nigga on the Ole Miss football team. I guess, if the sumbich had a mind left, which he don't, he'd know now. He's in a nursin' home down in Clarksdale. I seen him about a year ago. He looked like a little piece of paper.

Anyway the thing rattled Dundee's windows and shook his wife's teacups around, so he phoned up Sheriff Holston, and you know the rest.

I know, though, to Dundee Hamlin, the loss of Slab Town wuddn nowhere near as bad as the possibility there'd ever be niggas on the Ole Miss football team.

Of course, they was thirty-three people kilt—eighteen of em children of one size or another—and seven dogs, plus a barrow hog that happened to be inside one of the houses so he wouldn get stole. It was a fukkin mess.

But I'll say one thing about that Piscob'l preacher. You could go to the bank on what he might tell you. Plus, it's a funny thing—after the story of all that come out in court, nobody at all, not even the kin of the Slab Town dead, wanted to put him in the gas chamber. Seemed like everybody just got to thinkin' about other things, so they sent his ass off to the crazy house at Whitfield, and, unless he died, I guess he's there to this very fukkin day, standin' in the grass

* field lark

with his eyes on Heaven and his arms helt up like he's gon' catch something. Maybe he will.

AND IN ALL OF it, didn't nobody even once think the niggas had done it even though there was one family of niggas just a little bit north of what was the store, livin' in a dogtrot that didn't get blowed up, on a turnrow runnin' alongside a little bye-oh.* Didn't nobody—nobody at all—think niggas had kilt all them unfortunate muthafukkas. And I can see why, too. A nigga wouldn do something like that. The thing about niggas is, they may be niggas, but they ain't crazy like white people. You can pretty much always trust a nigga not *never* to do something like blow up a row of houses on a gravel road, but you can't *ever* be sure about a white man, and if you've got one that believes in virgin births, risin' from the dead, and God punishin' two nekkid people for wantn an education, you need to watch his ass ever' minute of the day.

Another thing about niggas is them sumbiches'll agree with you all fukkin day long, with a gotdam endless-ass string of *sho-dos*, *awhn-haws*, and *ay-mens*, and then not go out and do a thing about none of it. In one way, I guess, them sumbiches have become experts on how to manage a white man, not that you're gon' find a whole lot of white men who'll agree with that, but it's still the gospel fukkin truth.

Niggas. I've tried to figure it out, but so far I ain't come up with nothin'. What is it, I ast myse'f, that makes them so different? And no matter how hard I try to think it out I don't never get nowhere at all.

For instance, I can't name nothin' they do that we don't. They knock up their girl friends, we knock up ours. They shoot craps and kill each other, and we do, too. When we was little, we played baseball, and so did them sumbiches. Hell, we played it together. I

---

* bayou, bayous.

can't think of one thing they do or did that we don't do or didn't—
except maybe two things, and one is that they are better at singin'
and don't look like they've been dead a week when they do it, like
we do, and the other thing is, and I can vouch for this, they didn't
fuk as many barnyard animals as we did. Or possibly do.

Now, them white-ass Baptist muthafukkas'll talk to you all
day long about how God is love and that's why he kilt Jesus, just
to show how much He loves ever' body, and them whites'll get all
misty-eyed about bein' saved and how they're filled with the joy
of the Holy Spirit and all—and also how it's better to give than to
take-the-money-and-run kin'a shit, and after they're thoo, you'll
find out them sumbiches hate ever' thin' that walks and don't talk
like them.

BEFORE THE TRUTH HAD got out, Miss Ellen Fremedon and her
brother Granville swore it was the Communists that blowed up Slab
Town. So did the president of the Rotary Club, Lofty Thawtts, who,
if you want to know the truth, had been hipped on that subject ever
since I could remember and who was the one way back yonder that
got the high school to make us all sign a gotdam loyalty oath.

I recall I swore I hadn't never been a member of the W.E.B.
Du Bois Boys Club. I was damn sure of that. And I still don't know
what the fuk it was.

Miss Ellen Fremedon, though, and her brother Granville was
definitely a couple'a cases. They was twins, and they lived together
down south of Clayton. And here's the funny thing: Granville was
a little bitty fukka, skinny as a willow switch, but he could eat like
a fukkin Massey-Harris combine gobblin' up a bean field.

People talked all the time about how Miss Ellen would fix him
whole chickens and whole pies and whole cakes, and Granville would
down them muthafukkas like they was peanuts; yet, he never gained
a pound. Doctor Austin once said Granville was an "anomaly." I

never knew what Doc meant by that, but Granville *was* a white man, and I don't think there was no foreigners in the family.

It was something to see that skinny sumbich eat. I seen him scarf down a *en*-tire turkey once—plus all the dressing and the candied yams and a whole bunch of mince-meat pies, all of which was enough, somebody said—and I believe it—to feed two Ole Miss guards and a tackle.

As far as I know he didn't even sneak a poot after that. But later, maybe ten years later, Miss Ellen's housemaid found him dead, settin' at the dinner table with his arms down to his side and a whole sirloin steak hangin' out of his mouth just like he'd swallowed all of a beaver except for the tail. He had apparently picked the thing up in both hands, chomped down on one end of it, and blowed a blood vessel at the same time. If that *is* the case, I hate to think of what's gon' happen to me.

Anyhow, at first there was some talk about the communists and how none of em believed in God and such. Then, wouldn you know it, when it come out a preacher done it, didn't nobody want to believe that. And it took a while for that *to take*, so to speak.

But when it did, most people was certain it had to be the Piscob'l fellow because, unlike the rest of the churches in St. Leo that crowded in so many fukkin people of a Sunday that it just about butt-sprung the walls, them Piscob'ls only had about *twenty-five* sumbiches who went to their church, which was just a lillo thing settin' back up under some white oaks on a side street in the middle of town.

Plus, as everybody said, too, them Piscob'ls drunk real wine when they had their "Lord's Supper," unlike the fukkin Cath'lics which I hear drinks blood with theirs. It's no wonder those few pope-ass sumbiches didn't even have a church in all of Mhoon County and had to go outta town ever' Sunday if they wanted to endure settin' in one. They *looked* Cath'lic, too, if you know what I mean.

Well, that's the kind of stuff you deal with in law enforcement. I just wish there was more of it.

A MINUTE AGO I mentioned old Lofty Thawtts. Lofty was one of these men that always seemed like one thing but was really not like anything you could ever imagine. For instance, there he was, back yonder, the president of the St. Leo Rotary Club, a position obviously in which a sumbich is supposed to have a lot of fukkin sense. But hang on, *Sloopy*. Lofty had his house and his land *and* his fukkin car and ever'thin' else insured by a company that called itself a Christian insurance company—*The Resurrection Insurance Group,* I think it was. Anyhow, years and years later, it come out that not a crow-fartin' thing he ever put in a claim for was honored because *the Group* told him, no matter what he filed for—theft of his pickup, a grease fire in his kitchen, some sumbich in a house across the road from his woods gon' sue Lofty's ass because a bullet from Lofty's brother-in-law's thirty-ought-six went through the neighbor's bedroom wall and into the pecky-cypress-paneled den where it kilt the cat sleepin' on top of the color TV—no matter what it was, them sumbiches up in Chicago, at *The Resurrection Insurance Group,* told him wuddn none of it covered cause it was all a act'a God. And, Lofty, that dumb-ass old Jesus-bit sumbich, just shuffled his feet and said, "*Yassuh.*"

But the *most Loftiest* thing of all was what I learned from Mr. Reitoff the CPA down at Spaniard's Point. Lofty got in trouble with the government for cheatin' on his taxes. Mr. Reitoff had to come up to the courthouse with Lofty and talk to some serious looking muthafukkas from the IRS, and they spent a long-ass time in the big room the Board of Supervisors uses when they meet.

I don't suppose Mr. Reitoff woulda told personal stuff about Lofty to just anybody. But me, bein' a' officer of the law and all— for some reason people just seem to tell me whatever's in their heads—I guess Mr. Reitoff felt like it was okay to say sumpn. He was maddern a wet cat too when he said it. Anyway, he died some years ago.

Plus, too, like Jesus, he was a Jew. However, I have to tell you, with all these preachers and people around here that are waitn for old Jesus's *Second Comin'*, I guaran-damn-tee you a whole helluva lot of em would rather look up in the sky and see Mr. Reitoff floatin' down to save em.

Anyhow, we was outside the City Barber Shop, and he said, "Junior Ray, I told Lofty not to do what he did, and I'll be damned if he didn't go right straight out and do it, and I had already done up his taxes and had signed my name on the form!"

"Well," I said, "whatever it was, he sho made you mad." I really wanted to say, "What'd the old fuk-bump do?" But I figured Mr. Reitoff was just about to come out with it anyway. And he did.

"Junior Ray," he said, "I'll swear and be damned if I've ever had to deal with anything like this in all my professional life! It was a case of *double* fraud, pure and simple, and because of the position he put *me* in, I'll never know why I even tried to help him after he was caught." Mr. Reitoff went on to say that Lofty tried to "deduct" what he'd been spendin' up there in Meffis on those old whores at the King Cotton Hotel fore they tore it down and, after that, in the *Out-n-Inn Minit Motel* over on Brooks Road. Old Lofty wrote it all in under "Medical Expenses" and said it was for his "mental health." Hell, it's a wonder the old sumbich didn't catch hissef some germs big as a gotdam lizard.

It was easy to see Mr. Reitoff's point'a view and why he was upset. Yet, I could see Lofty's side of it, too. The thing is, knowin' the world as I do, it ought not to surprise no one that there's whores walkin' up and down Brooks Road or anyplace else, but it sho oughta surprise a sumbich, if he got a good look at em, that anybody would ever go buy anything from em. Anyhow, as much

of a dikhed as I always thought Lofty was, I felt sorry for the po'
bastard, cause there he was livin' all alone and all and gettin' old,
and pretendin' to be sucha upstandin' muthafukka. It had to be
hard on him.

He was lucky, though, that Mr. Reitoff talked to the I-R-S's.
They let Lofty off with a warnin' that if he ever tried anything like
that again, they was gon' see that he went down to the federal pen
at Maxwell Air Force Base in Alabama, and I think that scared the
shit out of him, especially the part about goin' to Alabama, which
is funny because all his life he'd been worried about goin' to Hell.

His peabrain grandson went to college down at Wetland State
outside of Rollin' Fork and near bout got th'owed out cause they
caught him drunk one night on the new football field tryin' to
mow the astro-turf.

Things go where they go, and it don't never stop, does it?

I ran into Lofty a while back. I'da thought the sumbich'd been
dead by now. He's *got* to be up in his nineties, or over a hunnuhd,
hell, I don't know. Anyway, when I come up on him, I said, "How
yew, Lofty?"

He didn't blink or mumble a fukkin word, and he didn't look
at me, neither. But when I passed him and he was about a foot
behind me, I heard him say: "My stool is firm again."

And I thought, damn, for ol' Lofty, dead'd be a step *up*.

CHAPTER 3

The Yellow Dog — Moon Lake — Sno-Cone —
The Yazoo Pass Expedition — A Historian Is Born

I know you might think I'm lyin', but I ain't never been to no univers'ty or nothin', yet I know one gotdam thing: Them tootie-frootie professors over at Ole Miss ain't never seen a sumbich runnin' around at night with a snake up his ass.

On the other hand, to give credit where credit is due, there *is* a chance some nem five-star Four-AitcH'ers down at Cow College in Starkville has. That's because *anything* havin' to do with farmin' or with nature in general—and of course arithmetic—I'll bet you those muthafukkas have seen it, or, if they ain't, they sure as hell *know* about it. They are way more *progressive*, I guess you'd call it, than them *hoddy-toddies* over at Oxford. I'll put my money on the Bulldogs* any day.

But you know how women are, over in Sledge or anywhere else. They think they know you, and they don't know the gotdam half of it . . . and wouldn't believe it if they did. I guess if a man growed up thinkin' about brassieres and purses, he wouldn't know much neither.

If you ask me, the only time a man and a woman are anywhere near in the same world is when they're connected *you know how.* Their heads are probably still in two separate places, but their bellies ain't. Hell, a whang is a whang, and a snatch is a snatch, and there

---

* Mississippi State University's football team.

46

ain't no way you can dress em up to look like little philosophers.

Anyhow, Sledge is one nem little fallin'-down, broke-dick Delta towns over there along the Yellow Dog.* And ever' time I go over there, I think about three things. One has something to do with the *nature* of all them little towns along the Dog; another is how there used to be more woods and now there ain't hardly none; and the third thing I think about is the Coldwater River and the *Yazoo Pass.*

I guess I knew about what every other sumbich down there in the Delta knew about the Yazoo Pass and the Yankees: namely, not fukkin much, at least not till some years ago, when Voyd and me was down by Uncle Hinroo's—which iddn what it used to be, which was a tonk, but now it's a place where you can take your mama or where you'd go eat supper if you couldn get in Katherine's—down on Moon Lake, and that ain't got nothin' to do with Mhoon County, because it's a whole nother fukkin word entirely. Plus, Moon Lake ain't even in Mhoon County. It's south of Lula, in Coahoma County.

Course they say, back in the twenties, before my time, Uncle Hinroo's was the Moon Lake Casino, and then it was the old Elks' Club or vise-a-fukkin-versa, but in my day it was just a juke joint,

---

* The Yellow Dog is a branch of the Illinois Central Railroad that runs north and south through the Delta. It crosses the Southern Railroad at Moorhead, Mississippi—"Where the Southern cross the Dog." The origin of the name, Yellow Dog, is obscure. Speculation includes a reference to "yellow dog" scab labor and the one my father offered, which is that the nickname Yellow Dog is derived from the short-lived "Yazoo Delta" line, which later became the "Yazoo & Mississippi Valley Railroad" and was owned by the Illinois Central, which after a time bought the Southern as well. Somehow, those tracks that angled off to the east from Lake Cormorant, Mississippi, and then went south to intersect with the tracks of the Southern RR at Moorhead, came to be known as the Yellow Dog Railroad. My dad was from out of town, so that may lend some extra credibility to what he told me. Add to the pot the old story about W. C. Handy listening to a man at the train station in Tutwiler, Mississippi, singing about going to "where the Southern cross the Dog," which W. C. handily turned into "The Yellow Dog Blues."

and that was that. If you went there, you was real lucky if "Sno-Cone" Cohee didn't beat your ass—for the same reason some other world-famous sumbich said he climbed a gotdam mountain: cause the sumbich was *there*.

But all that's in the past, and Sno-Cone is dead. Some puny little fukka one night had enough of the "*Snoke*" kickin' the shit out of him, so without sayin' a datgum word, he went home, got his twelve-gauge, loaded it with *double-ought*, and then he come back, walked up behind the ol' Sno-Boy, stuck the barrel up his butt and pulled the trigger.

Bad as Sno-Cone was, I didn't never think he deserved that, but you just can't go on and on beatin' the shit outta people for no good reason and not expect something to happen to your ass.

Not much happened to that little fukka that killed him, though. Sno-Cone had too many people in the right places that was glad he was gone. Still, I noticed a long time ago that, personally, I always got kind of sad in the picture show whenever the monster got killed. That's because I understand those sumbiches. They ain't necessarily *bad*, they're just monsters, bein' what they was meant to be and doin' what they was meant to do. Hell, you wouldn have no show without em. Plus, things—and people—that are too nice and too peaceful tend to piss me off.

Anyway, we was down there, lookin' around, reminiscin' like a muthafukka about the old days when, like I just said, Uncle Hinroo's was a place you could get caught dead in if you called the wrong sumbich a *son of a bitch* and he *was*. Then sumpn catches our attention, and we look down the road, and there's Ottis* Alexander just standin' there on the bridge goin' over the Pass, right there at the curve, in front of the old bait store where you used to be able to rent a rowboat, which is closed now because all them farmers and lake-house owners killed all the fukkin fish with sewage and crop

---

* pronounced "Ahdis"

chemicals by letting it all wash into that beautiful-ass lake without giving a single ballscratchin' thought to what they was doin', or bygod I know they wouldn have done it.

But they did, so there ain't no fishing, and no boats to rent neither, down there no more. Well, I expect there's *something* up under the surface of the lake, probably just a' crawlin' along through the mud on the bottom. I wouldn want to see it. No sir-fukkin-ree. It gives me the creeps just to think about it, and I guarantee you it *ain't* one nem two-hunnuhd-pound alligator snappin' turtles. Actual alligators of course are only a once-in-a-while thing at Moon Lake. They generally start gettin' common about eighty miles down the road . . . although, as I said, occasionally, one'll pop up around here, in Mhoon County—even though there's always been some since anybody can remember over at Hinchcliff and all in nem sloughs around Marks and Lambert, and, I hear, down at Stovall as well—over on the Old River—and those big-ass muthafukkas builds nests and lays eggs and the whole fukkin alligator thing, plus those sumbiches get to be over thirteen feet long, and they can move quicker'n a lunchtime fuk and will flat come up after your ass if you mess with their nests. Here, let me get my billfold out—I got a Kodak of one. I call em *polar-gators* because these muthafukkas I'm talkin' about live on the absolute furthest mos' northern edge of their gotdam range, although I do hear you can find em up even higher, all the way up to the top of North Carolina on the East Coast. Well, I ain't never been there, but I saw a thing about em on TV.

Anyhow, these sumbiches is some serious lizards. One of em over just east of Belen bit the shit out of a friend of mine's truck. Tore that muthafukka up. He had to explain five times to the service manager at the dealership what happened. A lot of people who live in town don't know what the fuk's out there around em. And if they did, they'd think they was in Jurassic-ass Park.

But, about Moon Lake, the good news is I'm told the fish are comin' back, which means, I guess, so will the people. I don't know what they'll do about that other thing down there on the bottom. It'll probably stick its head up one day and eat a bass boat and some muthafukka from Meffis.

ANYHOW, WE SAID, "HEY, Ottis! What the fuk are you doin'?" And he said, "Well, Junior Ray, I'm thinking about the Yazoo Pass."

He was standin' *right over* where the Yazoo Pass, itself, goes east out of the lake. And I did never know till that very day, talkin' to Ottis, that the Pass comes *into* the lake way on around to the right—if you're lookin' out at the lake from Uncle Hinroo's or the bridge over the Pass—and down toward the levee and that, back before the Civil War, durin' high water, river boats used to use it *all the time* to get way back up into the Delta so, as Ottis put it, they could "serve the plantations." In a way, Moon Lake is just a kind of wide spot on the Yazoo Pass, if you want to think of it like that. And I do.

"But," said Ottis, "the state built a levee in 1853, and that cut the Pass off from the Mississippi River and vice versa. The levee blocked the entry to the Pass, so, after that, them steamboats couldn use it no more to serve all them isolated plantations back up in the Delta. You see, before the levee cut off the Yazoo Pass from the Miss'sippi, all them riverboats had to do—durin' high water—was steam out of the Mississippi into the Pass, chug up and across Moon Lake over to where the Pass went out, and then they could go east into the Coldwater, on into the Tallahatchie, and, after that, into the Yazoo at what would later be present-day Greenwood. Plus, in so doin', they could cover a helluva lot of the Delta—and come right out into the Mississippi again, just above Vicksburg! . . . which was *why*, in 1863, the Yankees thought about usin' the Yazoo Pass durin' the Vicksburg campaign."

"But further," I said, catchin' on real fast, "them sumbiches had to blow the levee first."

"Natchaly," Ottis said. "And they did it on February the third. Lieutenant-Colonel James Wilson said it was like lookin' at Niagara Falls, and it took four days for the water in the river and the flood on this side of the levee to even up. That musta been sumpn to see."

"Oh," said Voyd, which meant he wuddn really listenin'.

But I was. It turns out that Ottis had got hissef all involved with this one *tee-niney* episode of the whole Civil War. He'd even gone over to Ole Miss and took a buncha college courses on the history of the War Between the States, till finally, so the story goes, the professors had to just say to him one day that if he was goin' to go to school there, he had to take courses in other stuff, too, but he wouldn do it, so that was that. Them sumbiches over at the uni-fukkin-versity was too smart just to be inter-rested in one little ol' thing about something. And they didn't see how this one teeny-ass little piece of history could be worth some muthafukka devotin' a whole lifetime to it. But, hell, it was *his* life, and, Chr*EYE*st, it *was* history!

However, to them pasty-lookin' little diklikkers over there, un-less it's some useless de-tail *they're* interested in, they're not gonna have shit to do with it. Hell, one nem coksukkas wouldn even get in the car with Ottis and ride over to Moon Lake to take a look at the Pass. He "didn't see what purpose it would serve" because, in his view, "the 'episode' was such a minor event of the time and had little to do with the outcome of the conflict."

That's what *he* thinks. If he believes that six thousand* Yankee

---

* One authority claims 4,000, others 4,500, 5,000, and yet another that there were 6,000 army personnel and does not mention how many men the navy employed on the expedition. Junior Ray's penchant for excess attracted him to the higher number. And, yes, it is true that Junior Ray has a "z-rocks" to prove what he wishes to exist; it is also true his "z-rockses" reflect the imperfection of serious scholars and the nature of history in general. Junior Ray has said: "These

soldiers and sailors in thirty-two* fukkin steamboats—which, accordin' to Ottis, "Each was supposed to be just under 180 feet long
but at least one of em, *The Rattler*, was two hundred feet long,"
and that ten of em, leadin' the way, was fukkin battleships: namely,
"two r'nclads, six tin-clads, and two steam rams"—if that goggle-
eyed, pipe-puffing muthafukka thinks all that ordinance, smokin'
and churnin' across Moon Lake, is a "minor event," I'd sure like
to have tickets to a major one. That just goes to show you, *readin'*
too much'll fuk you up.

Anyhow, after listenin' to Ottis, I got a brand new slant on things.
Next to planters and bankers, I'm about to add a whole new group
to the All American Ass'ole Association, and that's them fukkin
professors. Hell, Ottis woulda made ten of them sumbiches.

Course *some* reading is okay, and one of the major facts I got
from Ottis, who got it from James Truslow Adams's book, *The March
of Democracy*—which is a multi-fukkin-volume set of books—was
that the North had nineteen million white men available for duty,
and the South only had five million. He said they woulda had five
hunnuhd thousand more, but that number was mostly them hillbil-
lies over in the mountains who for one reason or another decided
to fight on the side of the Yankees.

As it turned out, *only* about 1,750,000 diklikkers in the North
signed up, whereas some 800,000 Rebs—near one-fourth of the
available white men—enlisted, so that you could say almost all the

---

fukkin sumbiches who wrote those books can't say the same thing twice, and it
ain't even Bible times. I'mo do what I was advised by a cheap-ass bottle of scotch
whiskey I bought once. Them bottle-labels all say 'By appointment to his fukkin
majesty the king or the queen or the kiss-my-foot, but the bottle I bought said,
on that little wavy thing down at the bottom of the official coat-of-fukkin-arms:
'You be the judge.'"

* Twenty-three may be a more accurate number. Studying his "z-rockses,"
I have found only two figures for the number of army transports, 12 and 13,
which, when added to the naval portion of the operation, would come out about
23, excluding the two coal barges.

worthwhile sumbiches in the South were out there puttin' their ass on the firing line. In the North it was a different story altogether. They didn't ante up but about two-nineteenths of their men, and 100,000 of them was niggas. I mean, what the hell. Them Yankee ass'oles didn't stand to lose nothing except a few fukkin states which they didn't give a shit for nohow. At least, as I understand it, those *abo*-whatchamacallit-*litionist* coksukkas up around Boston didn't. Them sumbiches hated the fukkin planters worse'n I do and woulda been just as happy to have seen em all th'owed smack-ass into the Guffa-gotdam-Mexico.

As I INDICATED, OTTIS didn't much give a shit about anything else as far as the War Between the States was concerned, and that greatly disturbed the good doctors over at the University. They wanted him to be more interested in the *"economic aspects of the period and the wider scope of the war."*

Fuk that. I'm with Ottis. I want to hear about the shootin'. Who cares about all that other dull-ass crap? Plus, I ain't never been to Virginia and I ain't plannin' on goin'. Appa-fukkin-mattox, Bull-ass-run, or any of them other places ain't nothing to me—and they didn't set Ottis's hair on fire neither.

I wanted to know what was goin' on *then* where I am *now*. Gotdam—when Ottis described it, I could see it! And I wished to hell I'da been there. I wouldna cared about no slaves—my people didn't own none—and I sure as hell wouldna been fightin' for them rich-ass planters. I'da done it just for the fukkin fun of it and because them Yankee sumbiches didn't have no business comin' down here in the first place. Fukkum.

The truth is, the so-called "Old South" wouldna done me no good a-tall. Them planters run it, and the slaves run them, and both of em looked down on my kind as nothing but scum. Well, some of us was—and still are today—because we never learned there was any other way to be, or if we did, we didn't give a shit. In fact, Mr. Brainsong said we was that way when we was still back on the border between England and Scotland—and that a bunch of us, back then, went to Ireland but was asked to leave, so then we come over here and kept on bein' what we was. Looks to me like that's kind of a fukkin *heritage*. But it's not what I want to talk about, and Mr. Brainsong is a whole nuther subject hisself.

Anyway—to make a long story somewhat longer—and I don't know why Voyd and me didn't already know all this—Ottis had done got to be the *leading* datgum authority on what was officially called the Yazoo Pass Expedition. One reason was that he lived right next to the Pass at Moon Lake. The other reason is that almost nobody in the rest of the South, and America, too, had ever heard of the thing.

Plus, we learned something else. The Civil War is not called the Civil War! Ottis says the *official* name, in the Liberry of Congress, is the *War of the Fukkin Rebellion*.

Stop me if I get too technical. You see, this Yazoo Pass stuff kind of got me all fired up about history. Particularly when you realize that they was some pretty big names involved in the thing at the time. 'Course, for the most part, they was all Yankees, but they was big-ass names none-the-fukkin-less. I'm talkin' about Admiral Porter, General Quimby, and Ulysses S-hole-fukkin Grant hisself, and he was drunker'n Cooter Brown a large part of the time. Hell, his fellow officers on one occasion had to keep him locked up in the bottom of a riverboat till he sobered up so none of the enlisted personnel would see his knee-walking se'f and lose faith in his fukkin "ability to lead," and all that crap. I think that happened down near Yazoo City somewhere. But you couldn never tell when he was gon' start chuggaluggin', and looks like to me he mighta did it all the time. Hell, I don't hold it against his ass. My only quarrel with the sumbich is that he was a gotdam Yankee. Fuk a buncha habits.

Everybody's got *some*. Plus, I don't know who Cooter Brown ever was, but I judge he musta been a mighty drunk muthafukka to get as well known as he did.

Anyhow, it's the Yankees I'm most concerned with. For one fukkin thing, it was really all their show. The Confederates were mostly in the bushes, in the shadows, and in the hair on the back of the necks of those farm boys from up there in Wisconsin and Iowa and Illinois who made up the majority of the coksukkas that participated in that fantastic fukkin undertaking that took em way-ass into the Mississippi Delta, snakin' down them little rivers that was so overgrowed on the sides the tree limbs knocked the fukkin smoke stacks off the ships, and they just had to stay in them boats with their heads down, hemmed in by high water everywhere they looked, so much so, that when they finally got down there around Greenwood, most of em couldn even get out of their "transports" because there wuddn hardly no dry land to stand on—much less *to take a stand* on.

But it didn't bother them old Confederate boys. No sir-ree. They was knee deep in water in a place called Fort Pemberton, which wuddn much more'n a buncha cotton bales put up by niggas. But —and this is important—them Rebs had em a special gun.

It was a six-point-five-inch Whitworth rifle, which was a fukkin cannon, and it tore the livin' shit outta them Yankee ships. You see, that rifled barrel could th'ow out a cone-shaped shell with more muzzle velocity than you could say Oh Hell-o Bill to. It hit one nem r'nclads—*The Chillicothe*—so hard that it knocked the bolts holdin' the armor together back into the inside of the cabin, and them bolts acted just like bullets,* ricochetin' around in there, and

---

* Library of Congress: *Official Records of the Union and Confederate Navies in the War of the Rebellion*, Chapter XXXVI, Series I— Volume 24, Part I: "Naval Forces on Western Waters" (January 1–May 17, 1863), 270–273. The report is written by Jas. P. Foster.

kilt a whole gang of them Yankee sailors . . . and tore up some others pretty bad. I think it's safe to say that, apart from the Delta itse'f, it was mainly the Whitworth rifle and its fast-ass "conical shell" that turned the blue-suits back—well, that and the fact that the naval commander of the whole Yankee expedition went nuts.

Personally, that don't surprise me none. I've always thought there was something about this place that makes people go crazy. Anyway, according to Ottis, the sumbich did in fact do just that. His name was Watson Smith—Lieutenant-Commander Watson Smith. All this, mind you, was goin' on right in there on the map before where the Tallahatchie meets the Yalabooshee* and gets to be the Yazoo.

But them Yankees never got past our boys. Lieutenant Commander Watson Smith wouldn' go no farther and was all for turnin' around and goin' back to Moon Lake. Personally, under the circumstances it looks to me like he was the only one who *wuddn* crazy. Only, Ottis says he was, and I think the commander was beginnin' to see things that wuddn there.

The Yankee r'nclads had some big guns. They was called eleven-inch Dahlgrens, and they was protected by thick-ass armor—and I've got a z-rocks to prove it. But it didn't do no fukkin good. Them Yankees didn't never get no closer to the Confederates than eight hunnuhd yards, and the Yankee soldiers, lyin' around back up-river in their "transports," couldn' do nothin' but twiddle their thumbs, swat mosquitos, worry about snipers, play with their tallywhackers, and, as one famous-ass historian said, *shoot at alligators.*† I got all this from Ottis, and he told me *he* got some of it from that fellow in Meffis who become famous for knowin' all about the Civil War

---

* Yalobusha River, fr. Choctaw Yaloba/frog + Ushi/child = tadpole.

† Shelby Foote, *Civil War, a Narrative*, Vintage Books edition, 1986, p. 205: " . . . the men aboard the transports and gunboats slapped at mosquitoes and practiced their marksmanship on alligators . . . "

and was on TV. I can't 'member his name right off, but he was a good ol' Delta boy from down there around Green-ville. 'Course, like almost every other sumbich in the world, he does live in Mef-fis now. But hell, if you're a sho-nuff historian, you *got* to go to a lot bigger place than Green-ville. They don't even have the *airbase* there no more. Anyhow, Ottis said he liked him because he trusted his ass, and he wished there was more fukkin historians like him. Well, if that's the way Ottis feels, bygod I do, too!

CHAPTER 4

Love — Anguilla Benoit — Lt. Commander Watson Smith —
Lt. Colonel James Wilson — Peyote is Considered — Old Colonel
Duncan Benoit's Experience with a Drug — Smith's Disease
— Anguilla Boards the Chillicothe — A Hardwood Jungle —
Junior Ray's Hot'n'Tots

The fact is there was one more historian besides that feller in Meffis that Ottis could have put faith in. And it was Mr. Brainsong. He had done *retired* from bein' the school superintendent by the time Voyd and me met up with Ottis on the bridge over the Pass at Moon Lake, but he was still doin' just fine, dependin' on how you looked at it . . . considerin' one or two things . . . that had happened to him, then.

As you may remember, he was the one who confirmed to Miss Florence that me and Voyd had in fukkin fact done found a German submarine outchonda across the levee, near Hawk Lake. So, I always liked the hell out of him. First, because I just fukkin did; second, because I just fukkin did, and, third, because he seemed to like me and didn't hold it against me that I was a rough-ass redneck sumbich. He even liked Voyd, and that made him pretty gotdam exceptional, if you want to know the truth. He treated Voyd like he was a human being, which is an honor that little piss-ant *never* deserved.

One thing, though, about Mr. Brainsong I never understood was he was always talkin' about "waitin' for Guhdoh." He said there was two guys once that was supposed to meet up with a fellow named Guhdoh, but he never showed up. I said, hell, I'da just gone out after the sumbich, but Mr. Brainsong said it wouldna been no use because there wuddn no such coksukka in the first place, and then I was really confused because I couldn figure why anybody would want to wait around for him. But that's the kinda of stuff people with a lot of education think about. Personally, I can't see why they'd pay good money to go learn about some muthafukka that don't exist—much less wait around for his ass—unless of course they was some kind of a preacher.

Mr. Brainsong was gettin' way on up in years. So it was fortunate I got to talk to him about the stuff I had learned from Ottis about the Pass, but I don't know why he didn't just move out of town a long time ago. Looks to me like he coulda been happier, although I did talk with him before, well, before I couldn no more, and I have to say that, in the end, I think I mighta known him better than anybody else.

Anyway, fuk that. The point is Mr. Brainsong also knew all about the Yazoo Pass Expedition. I think he knew more about the real details of it than any coksukka, present company excepted. Hell, he was the first person I thought of after I had been listenin' to Ottis. Ottis said he wouldn have nothin' to do with Mr. Brainsong, but then Ottis was a narrow muthafukka who never cut nobody-who-didn't-go-to-his-church no slack a-tall. Him and that bunch was so strict they'da made Jesus wash up, cut his hair, and go to Ole Miss before they'da let him in. And if they'da found out he was a Jew, well, sir, it'da been all over! You know them Baptists, scared all their boys is gon' marry a Ko-rean and that ever' coksukkin lillo thing is gon' lead to dancin'.

And it does, too. Fukkum. Plus, you know they always turned up their noses at the *Holy* Rollers.

Other'n all that, Ottis is okay, and even though he didn't care for Mr. Brainsong, I was high on both of em, because Ottis's hard feelings toward Mr. Brainsong really didn't have nothing to do with what I had become so interested in, namely, history—and the Yazoo

Pass Expedition. It was like pussy: I could not stop thinkin' about it. But that's what it takes if you want to become a historian.

Now, apart from how un-gotdam-believable it all musta looked, the thing that caught my attention the most, concernin' the Yankees' Yazoo Pass Expedition, was what the fuk happened to Lieutenant-Commander Watson Smith, who was the head of the navy's end of the operation. Accordin' to Ottis, nobody seems real clear about what was actually wrong with him. It coulda been anything from syph'lus to the flu—and I tend to want to go with syph'lus—although Mr. Brainsong had what he called *an interesting theory*, which made sense to me, even if it didn't to the fukkin experts. Plus, I know Ottis didn't think much of it, even if he did like to listen to me tell about it.

Mr. Brainsong said it was just plain ol' *love*, in a manner of speakin', that fukked up the Commander and kilt him. He believed Smith was in love, but the girl he was in love with (if in fukkin fact he was), Anguilla Benoit,* who had close relatives in Mexico, was a spy.

She was the youngest daughter of old Colonel Benoit, whose sister was married to some kind of half-French Mexican millionaire back then, and so Anguilla had spent a good deal of time down in Mexico with her auntee in a place called Guanacevi. And she, accordin' to Mr. Brainsong, *mojoed* Watson Smith's ass in an unusual way. As you know, Mr. Brainsong was a student of unusual shit, so I expect there is a lot to it—even though later I come to realize Smith was too sick in another way to be in love with Anguilla or anybody else.

Anyhow, Lieutenant-Commander Watson Smith was sort of the darlin' of the Yankee admiral, Rear-ass Admiral Porter. And when Grant decided to put on this fukked up backdoor maneuver to get in behind Vicksburg, or to the side of it, anyway, Admiral

* Pronounced Angwilla B'noyt.

Porter selected Watson Smith, who he had a lot of respect for as a sailor, to be the head of the thirty-two-boat flotilla.*

This was a big fukkin mistake. And Smith did not want the job, but there wuddn nothin' he could say or do except shuffle his feet and say yassuh. Something was definitely wrong with the commander from the start, only it's difficult to pin down just what it was. Smith hissef wrote that he had took sick down on the lower end of the Yazoo, but even he never said what it was.

Anyhow, he did a lot of crazy stuff. For instance, after that prick army engineer, Lieutenant-Colonel James Wilson, who hated Smith, got the Pass cleared and the boats could *pass* the Pass, so to speak, that po' sumbich Smith had to stop the whole fukkin show from chuggin' along every day just to have lunch. It was behavior like *that* that really got under the skin of a dikhed like Wilson, who was in fact the chief engineer and one of the up-at-the-front honchos in the whole in-sane thing. *He's* the one who blew the levee and got the show on the road after Grant said do it. Plus, he, Wilson, said *he* now knew how the Egyptians built the fukkin pyramids, because when he and his men was clearin' the channel of them huge-ass sycamores and chestnut oaks—which the planters and the niggas had th'owed across the Pass to block it—after he'd done got em off to the side and out of the way, he said that was when he realized bygod that if you put enough men on a rope, you could do just about anything.

Anyway, this coksukka Wilson figured out something was not right with the naval commander even while they was hangin' around Moon Lake waitin' to go through the Pass once it got cleared. It was more like Smith just was not in touch with what was goin' on. And

---

* More like a twenty-three-boat flotilla. Junior Ray thinks there were twenty-two light transports for the soldiers instead of thirteen, plus the ten naval warships . . . and two coal barges. From a dramatic point of view, I'd like to think there were thirty-two because, in fact, there could have been.

Wilson said he saw "constantly, a far-away look" in the coksukka's eyes. That's a gotdam re-search fact. I got a z-rocks on it.

Accordin' to Mr. Brainsong, it was that very fukkin far-away look that nailed Smith's ass by bein' one of the reasons the hero in blue got involved with the daughter of a local planter. It was the lost stare that let her know he was, if not no spring chicken, definitely a pigeon. More important, she could tell right off the bat that his brain was gooberized.

For the sake of the game, Anguilla made a big to-do about not wantin' to be attracted to a Yankee, sayin' she would never have nothin' to do with a man who had not lost an arm or a leg for the South, but, in the fukkin end, so she advertised, love would win out, whatever the fuk that meant. It was just a crock of jibber-jabber. Anguilla wuddn studyin' no love.

She was a cold-hearted spy, and it was her—and a gun—that finally put the screws to the Yankees' Yazoo Pass Expedition. In the end didn none of it make no difference, cause Vicksburg fell in July just a few months after all this I'm talkin' about occurred. But . . . *it did make a difference*, if you look at it in a larger sense. Them Confederates wuddn gonna win the war, and they knew it, but they were determined, any time they could, to make monkeys outta the Yanks. And, with the help of General Use-less Ass Grant and the Yazoo Pass Expedition, bygod, they done just that.

Mr. Brainsong said that he knew he might be goin' out on a limb, but neverthe-fukkin-less he "felt he had ample reason to believe Anguilla did give Lieutenant-Commander Watson Smith some kind of a drug that really fukked him up. So Mr. Brainsong ast me one day, "Junior Ray, as a law enforcement professional, you've heard of LSD, haven't you?"

"Is it anything like LSU?" I said. I think I *had* heard something about LSfukkinD back then, but I wuddn too sure what it was.

Anyway, he said he wuddn *really* talkin' about LSD nohow;

what he truly believed she used on him was some kinda dope called *pay-otey*, which he said come from cactuses out West and down in Mexico, and that for centuries the muthafukkas of that region have used it in their religions. That may not be exactly his words, but it's close.

More important, he said she carried a funny lookin' sumbich around with her as a personal servant, named Chiwiddywee. He wuddn no nigga nor no greaser, nor no Choctaw neither, and he never said nothin'—plus, it was known he always toted a small satchel over his shoulder full of dried-up, woody-lookin' stuff, which Mr. Brainsong said had to be the pay-otey and that, apart from his own experience on a trip he took once to Arizona, he drew most of his conclusions from readin' the personal papers of old Colonel Benoit, which are in the Colonel Duncan Sherard Benoit Public Library down at Lushkachitto. Now, in those papers of his, the Colonel said two things about the woody-lookin' stuff. One was that he "... *understood from little Anguilla it was a bit of the soil of [Chiwiddywee's] mountain homeland, far above the great canyons of Mexico's mysterious Sierra Madre Occidental, whence this dark, ephemeral Aztec—with my beloved daughter Anguilla and her devoted African slave, Kitty Dean—plans to return once this terrible conflict is resolved.*"

I can't imagine nobody wantn to run off down there to Mexico in that day and time with no roads, no telephones, no TVs, nor nothin' else, just to live with a buncha fukkin Pepper Bellies. 'Course, I ain't never been there, and I guess it was somewhat different with her uncle bein' a Mexican millionaire and all, but a hot-tamale is just a dogmeat sandwich as far as I'm concerned, unless of course it's made from a dog in the Delta.

Well, she never did go back there, cause the Mexicans was busy with their own squabblin' durin' that time. And her uncle got shot with a Frenchman who had been runnin' the country.

Anyway, things sort of fell apart for her, for a while at least, and then she married a man from Meffis, a real prominent sumbich at the time, very successful in the cotton business, called by his nickname, "Snake" Frontstreet—but I think his real name was Baley Banks Frontstreet. They lived down in the Delta back then on a big-ass plantation, called Goree,* and had a buncha chillun, and her descendants—and, of course, his, mostly anyway—are scattered all over and up and down the Delta to this very day, so that it's hard to find any sumbich between Hard Cash and Walls, whose family's been around for a long time, that don't claim kin to her, and to him, too, one way or another.

Chiwiddywee disappeared. Accidentally or on purpose. "It is thought," Mr. Brainsong said, "that he returned to his native land." And he added, "With, I believe, the blessings of the Benoits." More-fukkin-over, Mr. Brainsong claimed they was some of them Indians in Mexico that could run fifty miles a day, and ol' Chiwiddywee mighta been one of em. If that was true, the sumbich woulda got outta here and all the way across Texas faster'n a fukkin Ohzee-Moh, which is what, way back yonder when I first started workin' as a deputy for Sheriff Holston, that worthless nigga Ezell, who lived in his own special cell at the jail and went in and out whenever the fuk he wanted to, used to call a Ohzmobile. Truth is, that situation with Ezell wuddn all that unusual back in nem days. The Delta was full of things like that. Later, though, when the gotdam Civil Rights fell on our ass, the sheriff and nem made Ezell go free. Hell, they kicked his no'count se'f outta jail. Then the triflin' sumbich carried on sumpn awful and wouldn speak to nobody for a fukkin month, but finally he got used to bein' out, and now I think he likes it. He's damn-near old as I am. But, you know, ways are hard to change. Which is why I ain't never changed none of mine.

The second thing old Colonel Benoit wrote about the dried

* Pronounced Go-ray.

up, barky-like bitter stuff was long, so here it is, straight off my z-rocks:

On one occasion I saw upon a small table a few fragments of a substance which I took to be the same that little Anguilla's manservant seemed always to keep in a sack of some sort on his person. Without thinking I reached and picked up several pieces of the unknown matter and put them into my mouth. I chewed them and swallowed them. Shortly thereafter I became nauseated and vomited in the rose garden. I seemed to be quite well until about half an hour or three-quarters thereof later when I noticed an unaccustomed acuteness in my hearing. Some of the slaves were singing, and I could hear the very origin—and the precise and minutely detailed formation—of every note, whereupon I perceived a multitude of harmonies I had never before encountered. The sensation was fascinating; yet, I failed to connect the phenomenon in any way with the bitter bark I had ingested earlier.

Shortly before the end of supper I was forced to quietly excuse myself from the table. I did not offer an explanation for my departure as, indeed, I would not have known how to phrase it, but the reason was this: as I attempted to serve myself a helping of butter beans, those delectable flat leguminous seeds seemed to be moving as though they were alive, swarming like blind, mindless grubs. I said nothing, fearing I should be thought to have gone mad, and, certainly, I felt that I might in fact be just that. In any case, I went to my room, the door of which widened and yawned, audibly, as I approached it. After entering, I lay upon my bed and was suddenly frightened by the appearance of my chamber pot, which, as I looked at it, was actually where it always was, there beside my bed. But that was the peculiarity of the incident. I found that, all during the night, as I huddled on my unturned counterpane, ordinary objects assailed me and terrified me with their sudden imposition on my senses. I knew not the nature of my illness, but I was determined to hold onto my sanity as best I could until dawn.

I survived the night, and, when morning came, I went outside. Ordinary objects no longer flew at me and made me afraid. Instead, there was a quietness and a singularity of moment I thought was exceedingly odd, and what seemed best to define this part of the experience was that the crocuses, just beginning to emerge and to bloom, appeared to be more animal than plant. The branches and the leaves of trees and those of shrubs seemed warm and, in some fashion, what I might describe as personable—much as an affectionate dog might seem to a kind master.

In addition, the azaleas were also beginning to bloom, and their colors were so luminous as to be almost iridescent in their brilliance. It was as though the flowers were infused with a radiance more *super*natural than natural. And I felt that all the plant-world and I were in close, personal correspondence.

There might be some who'd believe that all that stuff about Anguilla and the Yankee naval officer was a beautiful fukkin love story symbolizin' how our great-but-torn nation needed to "heal" itssef and get back together, but it ain't true. There wuddn no symbolism in it. And I have tried my best to go along with Mr. Brainsong's LSD theory, although I'm just about certain syph'lus is gon' win out. Plus, there is no doubt about the fact that Anguilla was a coksukkin spy. Furthermore, from my own *re*-search, as I have said, I don't believe that after, maybe, the first day, Watson Smith was no more in love than a fukkin toad frog. He was too overwhelmed with the jungle he was floatin' around in, or I should say *with the jungle that was bobbin' around in him.*

I don't know why I sound like I'm so down on Anguilla. She woudna had nothin' to do with me, but I'da been fightin' them

Yankees, too; yet, I guess I just feel sorry for old Watson Smith because I really hate to see any po' sumbich get fukked-over by a woman. However, I have decided the whole deal played out the way I'm gon' give it to you. Bear in mind I don't *know* if this is the way it was, and I would like to say I don't give a shit, but of course I really do. I guess it's just natural for a person to want to have some say-so in what the fuk actually happened. And I believe the way I am goin' to lay it out for you *is* what happened on that Yazoo Pass Expedition, that this is it, that *this* is gon' be *my say-so* about what really happened back then.

It wuddn just Mr. Brainsong but Ottis, too, who said a lot of stock could be put in old Colonel Benoit's personal papers. And Ottis also admitted Mr. Brainsong had a good point, or, as he put it: "Mr. Brainsong could very fukkin well be right, Junior Ray, could very, *very* fukkin well be right even though he is a queer and damned to hell."

AFTER THAT, I SEEN it all pretty clearly. There they was, all them Yankee soldiers and sailors anchored in the middle of Moon Lake, waitin' for the go-ahead to chug it on into the Pass.

And there was the army engineer guy I told you about, who blowed the levee across from Helena way back on the third of February, Lieutenant-Colonel James H. Wilson, with his work crew, puttin' them five hunnuhd swingin' dicks on a big-ass rope to drag the tree trunks outta the Pass to clear a channel so they can all start snakin' them thirty-two steamboats through the swamps of the Delta. Somebody said it reminded them a little bit of a movie called *The African Queen,* but this ain't got nothin' to do with no niggas.

And settin' out in the lake on what little deck there was of *The Chillicothe,* which was one nem r'nclads, in other words a fukkin battleship, havin' hissef a "leisurely lunch" is that snakebit little squid, ol' Watson Smith, who was the commander of the navy's end of the deal but who actually was in charge of the whole show. Even though he mostly rode on the U.S.S. *Rattler*, which was what was called a tinclad, yet that muthafukka was two hunnuhd fukkin feet long and, I believe, on the whole, a lot more comfortable than the *Chillicothe*, which is probably why he also slept on the *Rattler*.

Anyway, the story was that he had done already took sick with something down on the lower Yazoo, which was separated by the Rebs from the upper part, which was the part they got on by goin' through the Pass, and he really didn't want to be leadin' no expedition up the ass of the Yazoo Pass just to get back down to where he had been in the first fukkin place; however, he didn't have no say-so in the matter, because Admiral Porter wanted him to take charge of the expedition, and Smith, as somebody said, had to do it because, even though he was somewhat older than Porter, Smith was kind of like the Admiral's "pet."

'Course that didn't keep the Commander from finally havin' to th'ow up his hands and say, "Take me out, Coach" and holler calf-rope about the time him and the two r'nclads was finished bein' shot to bits and pieces by the Rebs at Fort Pemberton around March 17. And then, right then, of course he was shipped back up the Tallahatchie, into the Coldwater, out the Pass, and across Moon lake back over to Helena, Arkansas, on the other side of the Mississippi and, from there, was carried up North all the way to Trenton, New Jersey, where the po' sumbich died a little over a year later.

After the whole mess was over, Admiral Porter said po' Smith suffered from "softening of the brain," and that's what let me know Smith probably had the big syph, instead of what Ottis and Mr. Brainsong thought—and, even though, as I've said, I always liked Mr. Brainsong's theory the best, I'd say back then it would have been a helluva lot easier of get syph'lus than it would have to get

LSD or some kind of happy dust from a Mexican Indian at Moon Lake, Mississippi. I still hold out the possibility that Smith coulda had sumpn else wrong with him, like a brain tumor or somethin' maybe they didn't even know about back in nem days, but I think syph'lus is the winner.

The difference is that the LSD, unlike the love pox, wouldn have taken ten or twenty years to squeeze the juice out of his brain. 'Course that's just the way I like to think about things. I can't seem to never leave it at just a mosquito bite and a sneeze. Plus, I know if it had been the Smilin' Mighty Jesus,* he'da been dead a lot sooner.

Hell, he coulda got hold of anything, typhoid, you name it. Only he would have had to have caught the syph'lus quite some time before and somewhere else for it to start goin' up into his brain and all. But, now, in that part of the world, in the deep South, a lot of people had it. Shoot, even in the 1950s, the federal doctors come into Mhoon County and give everybody a Wasserman, and one fourth of the population showed up positive. I hear it was that way all over the Delta, with some counties havin' as many as one third of the population carryin' it around. The niggas was the main ones with it, so, natchaly, the planters had it, too. Hell, if you ask me, they're the ones probably had it in the first place.

Leland Shaw's uncle by marriage had it, Judge DeBevoise's nephew had it, and the story was old Dick McComercy† had it, but he always claimed he caught it in Cuba. People said he went to Cuba with a long nose and come back with a short one, whatever the fuk that meant. All I can figure is that it musta had something to do with him havin' the syph'lus, and I don't know if a Cuban

---

* Spinal meningitis, from a Walker Percy article or an interview with same in which Percy mentioned some of the misconstruances of medical terms appropriated by Southern blacks.

† Pronounced Muh'Commerce-y.

doctor cut off part of his nose to make it shorter or if it was et off by the germs. Plus, he was so fat he used to have to carry a little nigga boy around with him in his buggy to unbutton his britches and fetch his weenie out when he wanted to pee; and, one time, the story was that the little fella was tryin' his best to help the old sumbich take a leak, and Uncle Dick, as they called him, said, "Hurry up, boy! What's the matter?" and the little nigga said, "I can't find it, Mr. Dick," and old Dick McComercy said, "Can't find it? Can't *find* it? Boy, whatchu mean you can't find it? You the las' one that had it!"

They don't make em like that no more.

Another thing, too, is people say Uncle Dick, when he was younger and not so fat, had sex with near bout ever' black woman livin' on the place, and there was at least a hunnuhd of em, which I've always thought is one of the reasons people around here all look alike, black *and* white. I say one of the reasons because of course it was too big a job for just one man.

ANYHOW, ONE DAY DURIN' one nem long lunches he was famous for, Watson Smith looks up from his pork chop and sees a rowboat, out on the lake, comin' toward the *Chillicothe*. Settin' in the back of the boat is, as he probably put it, "the most beautiful fukkin creature I ever beheld." Rowin' the boat was that some-kind-of-Mexican-Indian-coksukka, Chiwiddywee. And of course the girl in the back, twirlin' her umbrella, was none other than sweet little ol' Anguilla Benoit.

Smith hollered, "Bo'sun,* assist these good travellers!" And the bo'sun leaned over the side and tied the muthafukkas up to the *Chillicothe*. Then, Chiwiddywee hopped out of the rowboat and

---

* Junior Ray insisted on pronouncing boatswain as "boat-swayne." I could not bear it, so I changed the spelling in the text to reflect the proper rendering of the word.

up on the deck of the battleship and helped Anguilla get on board, too, which was risky because she had on one nem hoop skirts, and, in tryin' to step from a flimsy-ass rowboat onto an r'nclad, almost anything could have gone wrong, which is what Smith was prayin' for so he could get a shot at what was under all that dress. By that time his dick was big as his spyglass.

"Commander Smith," she said. "I am Miss Anguilla Benoit, and I and my weird-ass manservant desperately seek your help."

"Fret no more, ma'am," he said. "I, myse'f, and the en-tire fukkin navy are at your complete disposal. Indeed," he added, "whatever your sweet cunt commands shall be done in a blue-suit flash, or my name's not Lieutenant-Commander Watson dumb-butt Smith."

"Oh, kind sir," said Anguilla, "somehow I knew I could find the gallantry in you that I so admire in our *own* courageous boys."

"Do be assured, Miss Benoit," said Watson Smith, "that we men of the North also honor womanhood in just the same fashion as the brave lads of whom you speak, with the very marrow of our cockbones—won't you join me for lunch?"

"You are too generous, sir," said Anguilla; "Yet, seein' as how I am hungry as shit and am absolutely certain I have your ass by the balls, I accept your kind offer with great pleasure. But, sir," she added, "can the nutritional needs of my manservant be attended to as well? He eats but little, and that mostly grits."

Though wouldn you know it, them Yankees didn't have one datgum bowl of grits in the whole flotilla. But that didn't stop Watson Smith. "Of course," he said. "Bo'sun, take this wild-lookin' sumbich below, and feed his ass."

"And," he continued, "tell them other coksukkas down there not to fuk with him."

I am tryin' to give this all to you as it might have sounded back then. People spoke somewhat different in those days, as you have probably noticed if you're like me and watch a lot of TV.

Once on deck, Anguilla intended to stay on that boat. "Sir," she said, to Watson Smith, "may I impose upon you and your whole fukkin navy to give me and my manservant a ride?"

"My dear lady!" exclaimed the top squid, "we are an armed flotilla on our way into battle. I would fear for your safety."

"Oh, be not concerned with trifles, my good sir. Fuk all that, for I know that I shall be perfectly secure while I am in your care. Indeed, I shall be yours to command . . . *Cuh-ma-in-duh*."

"Wooee, kiss my ass!" he hollered, not out loud but inwardly and *spiritually* of course. "I am in love!" And all that was helped along a lot by the fact that Anguilla—and I seen a pitch'r of her—was truly good-lookin' enough to make a man's tongue hang out like a red necktie. Plus, she knew it, too, which was one of the things that made her an effective spy and out to put a rock in the commander's peas. More sooner than later, though, any kind of love feelings he might have had for Anguilla was goin' to become a non-issue. He was goin' to have too much on his mind, which was really doin' all it could, at the time, just to deal with lunch.

Anyway, he went on: "We have reason to believe we shall be challenged at Greenwood," he told her.

"Then all is well," said Anguilla, "for my *autochthonous**-ass manservant and I intend to disembark at Big Mound, on the east bank, where of course the road from Ca'lton† meets the Tallahatchie, and that is well above . . .," and she near-about come right out and said "Fort Pemberton," which would have th'owed up a flag right then and there, but she caught herse'f in time and said, ". . . above, above . . . above that particular village you speak of—although I do have friends in Ca'lton who own land in the Delta, near Greenwood, which, as you know, is extremely inhospitable in climate much of

---

* I mentioned this word to Junior Ray during a discussion of this portion of the book.

† Carrolton.

the year. Now, dear sir, do put your mind at ease; we wish only to travel as far as Big Mound; and, as you Northerners have broken our levees, travel by water is the only means available to us, plus, my generous commander, we must get there. My poor mother will be waiting!"

Watson Smith, without wonderin' about how Anguilla's mama was gonna know when they was gon' get there, sort of mumbled offhand that he thought the road to Carrolton was probably goin' to be underwater like everything else in the Delta, but he checked his map and seen that Big Mound was way up river from Greenwood—and from where Fort Pemberton was goin' to turn out to be—so he said, "I shall be honored to do all that you require of me if you will get naked this very instant and show me what your legs look like."

"Well," she said, liftin' her hoop skirt up just a hair, "try to imagine."

"Big Mound it is!" said the commander.

"You bet," said Anguilla.

"Fukkin 'A,'" said the Bo'sun and saw to it that she and her *shadow* was settled in, not below in the uncomfortable *Chillicothe*, but right next to Acting Commodore Watson Smith's room in the more accommodatin' two-hunnuhd-foot-long tinclad *Rattler*. Well, they give Chiwiddywee a couple of blankets and a couple of cotton bales up under a roof cause he was a servant, plus they wuddn sure what he was, black or white or Chinese, so, bein' Yankees and all, they treated him partly like a white man and partly like a "negro," even though it didn't seem like he necessarily was crazy about bein' with em nor wanted to run off nowhere, neither. And, I guess, because they was Yankees, they didn't know what the fuk to make of him, havin' seen nobody much in their whole lives except other people that looked like themse'vs. Which I believe was how it was up North back in nem days.

Keep bearin' in mind it is my job, as a historian, to provide the best view possible of the way things looked and sounded—or could have—durin' those old-timey times. Mr. Brainsong and Ottis, both, was always sayin' they wanted to find out the truth about everything. Well, I admit I ain't so much interested in the truth as I am in how I best understand things, and I guess you might say, with their help, the rest was up to me. Plus, I find that when I have it my way, history really does seem like an interesting subject and not like that doodywah they teach in school, although I didn't learn much of it nohow and don't remember half'a what I did hear of it. I do recall that the old country sumbich who taught us history had a hard time pronouncin' the words in the fukkin textbook. Even I could tell that. And I couldn pronounce em neither.

But back then they didn't let us in on the stuff about thousands of soldiers on gunboats floatin' around Moon Lake and beautiful girls with pay-otey nor that there was generals all over the fukkin place. Chr*EYE*st! There was General Grant to begin with, then there was General Ross, General McPherson, General Quinby, General Gorman, General Prentiss, and General Washburn—not to mention Rear-Admiral David Porter, who at first thought the whole thing was goin' to be his ballgame and, I can tell you, he also had an unbelievable unrealistic idea of what he was gettin' into. He thought Smith and them was goin' to just speed right through the Pass, down the Coldwater, hop into the Tallahatchie and whiz up to Batesville, which was then called Panola, to cut the railroad bridge, then zing back down the Tallahatchie where, later, they'd blast-ass up the Yalobusha to Grenada and cut the railroad bridge there, too; and, after that, swoosh on back down to the Yazoo, capture Yazoo City—that dumb sumbich was goin' to give em twenty minutes to surrender and hand over everything, what an ass'ole—and scuttle all the Confederate gunboats that was supposed to be hid up in the Big Sunflower River, then finally go on to Haynes Bluff and bring a quick end to the stand-off at Vicksburg. Well, the army got into the picture, and Porter had to come down off the fukkin ceiling, but the truth is even almost all them generals except General Gorman thought, in the beginning, this whole scheme they was all callin' the Yazoo Pass Expedition was goin' to be easy as a goldfish soup. You never saw so many generals, so much gotdam manpower, and so many big guns in one little old bitty fuk-up in all your life. And our guys stopped em with one special cannon, some tree trunks, a good-lookin' girl, and a cactus.

THAT'S TRUE BUT NOT TRUE. What stopped em was two things: *place* and *time*. Place got em because, when you come into the Delta, you're in another fukkin world. Them Yankee boys from Indiana, Wisconsin, and all up in there thought they was still in America, but, even today, the Delta's probably more like Africa or the fukkin Philippines. And time got em because they didn't move fast enough.

That's why Anguilla was there. The Confederates needed time to get their Whitworth in place, and they couldn get it set up until the first of March. Later, that's what Lieutenant James Wilson figured out and realized it had been the delays that was causin' the failure of the operation, and he of course blamed it all on Watson Smith, which, if you want to know the straight of it, was not partic'ly fair.

For instance, it was Admiral Porter who told Smith to go slow so as to save coal. And Smith did so, though later he tried to step it up, at least accordin' to him he did. I *don't* know if the admiral told him to have all em leisurely lunches, but I do know that a lot of times when things look real bad one way, it's just because you don't know what the other way *is* to look at em. If you've ever known anybody that was divorced, you know what I mean. Plus, you have to realize I have a lot of z-rockses, and I have copies of the actual dis-patches all these diklickers sent back and forth to one another. Hell, anybody can get em. Ottis got em at the liberry in Meffis and give some to me, which he said he had two of and was so glad that I was takin' an interest in this thing.

Or he may have give em to me so I would stop botherin' his ass all the time. I could sort of tell, finally, because whenever I'd catch up with him to ast him a question, he'd sorta look up real quick like a train was comin' at him; then he'd straighten his face out and answer my question, but I could tell I was gettin' on his nerves, so I think he did the smart thing. Plus, I prefer bein' on my own.

Anguilla was there to slow down the Yankees once they got the tree trunks out of the way. She made Watson Smith to fall for her, and she chopped his log, so to speak. The fact is all the officers and any other man who saw her bout fainted, including old cob-up-his-ass Army Engineer Lieutenant-Colonel James Wilson, which may be another reason he had it in so bad for Smith. I don't know. It was Mr. Foster, Smith's second-in-command, though, that—as they say in the duck store—had his hand in the teal. Anyway, the whole war was fukked up if you ast me. But, Lord, I wisht I'da been there. I'da lot rather ride a gunboat on Moon Lake than flop around on a gotdam pair of water skis.

Lieutenant-Colonel James Wilson and his labor gangs of Yankee farm boys had the Pass finally cleared of tree trunks and other crap by the 21st of February, but Watson Smith and the gunboats didn't start to move through it until the 24th, and then it took em till the 28th to go the fifteen miles to where the Pass flows into the Coldwater. The Pass was deep enough, thirty feet in some places, and eighty feet wide, but it was very, very crooked, so it took some real doin' to get them long-ass vessels around all the narrow little twists and turns.

Remember, the Confederates, with the help of some planters and their trusty-ass slaves, had th'owed log jams across the Pass in a couple of spots. One nem jams was a mile long, and the other was two miles. Plus, these trees, cut down by the slaves, was eighty to ninety to over a hunnuhd feet tall and four feet thick, and some of those sumbiches weighed close to thirty-five fukkin tons. So that's why it took from the 7th of February to the 21st for the army to make the Pass passable.

Personally, from what Ottis and Mr. Brainsong has said, I believe General Washburn and Watson Smith, too, would just as soon have called the whole thing off when they seen what the difficulty was. And, there again, them Yankees could not keep a fukkin secret, and the Rebs had found out what they was up to, even before they was up to it, and that's why the blue-suits was goin' to get the shit shot out of them when they finally did get to Greenwood, only they didn't know it and thought they was just gonna breeze right past. But the drums had done spoke, and them Yankees was performin' heroic feats for nothin' in the middle of what was—even at that time—probably one of the biggest, thickest, wettest, wildest-ass stands of hardwood timber in the world. For them ol' boys, back then, from up there in Wis-fukkin-consin, it woulda been like them bein' in Vietnam today, snakin' down a river and not knowin' what was on either side of you, above you, in front of you, behind your ass, or under you. Watson Smith said it about as well as it could have been said: "All is swamp." And that sums it up. There was hardly any shoreline a-tall, just water everywhere, and the Pass and the two rivers . . . just channels through the trees.

Gotdam, all this talkin' has made me hungry. Here's another one of my recipes:

✿ JUNIOR RAY'S HOT'N'TOTS ✿

Step 1. Get a carload of frozen Tater Tots.

Step 2. Thaw the muthafukkas out, then . . .

Step 3. Mash the sumbiches up real good, with a little bit of sour cream, and . . .

Step 4. Set em aside.

Step 5. Chop up some garlic and spring onions and fresh, hot-ass, green chili peppers.

Step 6. Chop the sumbiches up again, and th'ow em in an iron skillet, and stir em around with just a teeny-ass bit of olive oil —cause too much butter will give you a heart attack. (I know, but don't fuk with me about the sour cream.)

Step 7. And don't stop saw-tayin' till you can see through the onions, then . . .

Step 8. Dump the mashed-up Tater Tots in on top of all the stuff in the skillet, and . . .

Step 9. Moosh everything together till it's all one big-ass blob.

Step 10. Cover the skillet, and set it in the oven on the middle rack for thirty-five minutes at three hunnuhd degrees.

Step 11. Then you can start fixin' your catfish almondine.

Step 12. If you want to, you can leave out the sour cream.

CHAPTER 5

The R'nclads Enter the Pass — Chiwiddywee — Tea & the
Commodore's Quivering Lips — "All is Swamp!" — The Rebs
Drop In — A Severed Head on The Beaudollar —
The Gold Goes Overboard — The Road to Hell
— Mr. Foster Gets a Blow Job

So they enter the Pass, and Anguilla goes to work. She and Chiwiddywee is ridin' along on the *Rattler* with Watson Smith—I say *riding* along, Lord, as you know, it took em four days to go just fifteen fukkin miles, so pokin' along is more like it. And that was Anguilla's cuppa tea, if you know what I mean: the slower the better.

After they had done got up in the Pass a little way, Anguilla rubbed up against the commodore and said, "Is that one nem thirty pounders, or are you just glad to see my ass?" No, she didn't! That's a joke. What she probably said was this: "I should be honored, kind sir, if you and your second-in-command, Mr. Foster, would join me for tea during our voyage—say about half after three on a daily basis?"

And Smith, bein' sick to begin with and possibly a little bit in love, said, "I shall look forward to it, and I shall so inform my first officer, Mr. James Foster." And he was just a little bit th'own there for a moment, because he didn't realize why Anguilla had done asked for Mr. Foster to be present.

But Anguilla had a good reason for the extra company. It was to keep Watson Smith from makin' any kind of connection between what was goin' to happen to his ass and her feedin' him tea every day. The sumbich was about to start seein' giant coon dogs in the middle of the road.

Old Chiwiddywee just appeared, and then he'd disappear, somewhere off in the corner of your eye, as if he wuddn no more'n a gotdam dream. It was like he was a fukkin afterthought made out of flesh and bones, and he never made no sound when he moved, not none at all; plus, he never said nothing neither, and when he and Anguilla talked with one another, they just faced each other and looked down at the ground. One would look thissa way while the other looked in the opposite direction; their lips wouldn even move, and they'd sometimes touch the tip-ends of their fingers together ever so lightly, but then it was over, and you'da knew something had been said but not spoke, or maybe it *had* been spoke and you hadn't been able to tell it, but in any case, every time one of those meetns took place, you would have known something had either already happened or was sure as shit about to.

See, she was dosin' Smith's ass every afternoon with a certain amount of that pay-otey, the woody stuff that Chiwiddywee carried around with him in that little bag of his. Anguilla had what she needed all powdered up, and Smith couldn taste the bitterness of it in his tea because Anguilla packed his fukkin cup up with honey, which she once, for just a second, led the commodore to believe he might get to lick off her finger, but it was just one of those here-it-is and there-it-ain't kind of things, and after it was over, he wuddn even sure he had read it right. But he had, and she *had* teased him, and it was her who licked the honey off her own finger, very close to the commodore's quiverin' lips.

She slipped the pay-otey into Smith's fra-gile, hand-painted tea cup, in very tee-niney amounts at first, and kept it *out* of Mr. Foster's cup, which he held with his little finger stuck up in the air, and of course she made sure not to put none in her own. I believe Chiwiddywee had done had so much of that stuff that he was really just a walkin' hallucination. I don't know. But I've heard that it can fuk you up—not that he was, in the sense that you or I might be, because he'da been used to it where he come from. For that wild sumbich, a little pay-otey probably wuddn no more'n a cup of chicory-fied, Lu'ziana coffee would be to a coonass, but for Watson Smith, who hadn't wanted to go on the expedition in the first place, it was the beginnin' of a trip a whole lot different from the one he thought he was on.

And so, durin' the four days it took em to go from Moon Lake to the Coldwater River, Anguilla was busy as a little beaverette every afternoon feedin' dope to Watson Smith and makin' a fool out of Mr. Foster.

"Do have some more tea, my dear Commodore," she would say, in her best *pre*-Ole-Miss-Campus-Cutie's voice. Then, as Mr. Brainsong once told me:

"Watson Smith would take sip after sip, and when he'd look into Anguilla's eyes, he saw not the eyes of a beautiful Southern girl but the seashores of paradise where the sands of time opened and closed, beggin' for his footprints."

That business about the sand mighta meant more to me if I had known at the time what I know now about the GuffaMexico, but when Mr. Brainsong said all that, I hadn't never been much further than Jackson and that was a long time ago when I was a deputy. I didn't think a whole lot of it, to tell you the truth.

Anyway, back to history. Mr. Foster let his mouth fall open like a drunk about to drool as she swished and glided in amongst em pourin' the tea . . . "into their *sweetened* teacups."

The boats sat still at night and moved only in the daytime, and the only thing Watson Smith could say was, "All is swamp. All is swamp, Mr. Foster."

"Aye, aye, sir," Foster would say back to him. "It sure as shit is."

And it *was*, too, but that wuddn what bothered Mr. Foster. It was the *way* Watson Smith said it that was not right. Any fool could see that all *was* swamp, but a normal person would have commented on it without makin' it sound like it was the end of the fukkin world, although, I have to admit, it probably did seem like it might be. Even today, with most of the trees gone and paved roads runnin' off everywhere, outsiders visitin' the Delta still have a hard time understanding that they're in the United States.

BUT OF COURSE THERE was more to it—more'n any of them Yankee boys common-sensically could have begun to imagine—like the night of the 28th in the Pass, just after the first few gunboats had done got through into the Coldwater.

The whole flotilla stopped for the night—which I just can't understand, even though I know the reason they done it—and the *Chillicothe* and some of the other "battleships" was tied up with their noses downstream, in the Coldwater, while the rest of the boats was all strung out and jammed up back in the Pass. And settin' right there north of present-day Birdie at the mouth of the Pass where it hits the Coldwater, but maybe just a hair back up in the Pass itse'f, was the army paymaster's boat, the *Beaudollar*.

Remember, one of the problems they was dealin' with right from the jump was that of the overhangin' limbs. All was swamp, like the commodore said, and overhead there was so many tree limbs that, even durin' the daytime, the boats was in kind of a tunnel of tall trees with low, overhangin' branches, comin' from both sides, like a ceiling over the channel. By the time they did finally get to Greenwood, a lot of the ships didn't have no smokestacks; and, on some, parts of their upper decks was really tore up, or, as one of my z-rockses said, they was "swept away."

So there they was, stone-still in the water, with no shoreline to speak of, and the night dark as a bat's ass. Then, long about two in the morning, *thunk, thunk, thunkity thunk*, something or some*things* was hittin' the upper deck of the *Beaudollar*. *Whump, whump*, and when the watch, who in this case happened to be, for whatever reason, the paymaster hissef, when he come out and shined his lantern around, he looked straight into the faces of some of the roughest old Reb boys he ever seen, and they was all grinnin' like a sumbich, each one with his hand still on a rope that hung down from the blackness above em.

"Hand over your fukkin money," said the biggest of them pekkawoods. "Hand over the money, muthafukka, or sleep late in the morning!"

"Fuk yew," said the paymaster, and he went to draw his piece, but before he could get it out, one nem good ol' boys swang a sword and cut his neck off at the collar, so that the only sound was something like "snick-plop."

Later, after the fighting was all over and the Rebs was gone, it was discovered that when the paymaster's head had fell off his shoulders onto the wooden deck, it broke his nose.

And then it started. The Rebs piled inside the cabin and tried to roust the rest of the Yanks out onto the deck, but the blue boys put up a helluva fight, started shootin' at close quarters, and drilled holes in some of their own.

Didn't none of the Confederates get shot—or, if they did, they never let on and just kept a'fightin'. Some of them boys was so mean they didn't pay no attention to life *or* death, and Mr. Brainsong said that was because they was just about as "unconscious" either way. I never did know exactly what he meant by that.

The paymaster's boat, the *Beaudollar*, was not as long or as wide as most of the others. In fact it was about half the size, just a little over a hunnuhd feet, around thirty feet across, and carried twenty-five or thirty soldiers to guard the money—only they never thought, really, that anybody was ever goin' to drop in on em durin' the middle of the night out of the fukkin trees.

Anyway, the commotion woke up Watson Smith, Mr. Foster, and all the rest of the Yanks right in there; but, apart from shinin' a buncha lanterns around, there wuddn a whole lot they could do, as there was no shoreline to speak of, and they couldn really go skippin' and hoppin' from boat to boat, besides which, they didn't truly know the location of all the hoohaw. It was a mess.

Anguilla heard it, and she just smiled and rolled over, but of course all them Yankees in the boats that was near enough to what was goin' on was up in their underwear, jumpin' around, and bumpin' into one another, mostly in the dark; yet there wuddn nowhere they could go—nowhere! And they could not shoot into the night over toward where the shots and the cussin' and the scufflin' was goin' on and where they seen a few lights boppin' this way and that, because they couldn tell what they'd be shootin' at—plus, bein' Yankees, they were somewhat overly concerned with safety.

Also, the lights they had really didn't do em no good, and in some respects made it even harder to make out what was happenin' than without em. One thing the Delta had a lot of back then and has a considerable amount of to this very day is darkness. There was a sumbich come down here from Seattle one time, and he told me he never had seen *night* till he got to the Mississippi Delta. I told him that was just one of many things we was pretty fukkin proud of.

But this kind of confusion in the dark is what the Rebs had planned. They just used what you might call some of the Deep South's natural resources, darkness and confusion, if you know what I mean. And, in fact, none of the Rebels was killed or shot up in any way whatsoever. They was too smart and too quick for that; plus they had the drop on the Yanks from the jump, and they had gone to a lot of trouble to make their raid foolproof. Of course, they could not take all the credit, because it really was *circumstances* that put the blue boys at a disadvantage. It was the Delta that did em in.

Anyhow, before the Yankees could even begin to get their act together, several was shot and stabbed and hacked up and kilt in various fashions, and those that weren't threw up their hands and said, "Take me out, coach," except for two of em who just hollered, "Adios, muthafukka!," and jumped-ass overboard into the Pass and stayed there till the Rebs was gone and their own men was all over the paymaster's boat. There may or may not have been a few ten-foot alligators awake there in the water, but, even though it was the last part of February, the weather here, as you know, can still get warm enough for the snakes to come out, and it was one of those times; so I reckon the alligators, if they was any there, could have done as good as the moccasins. But, remember this, even with the moon out, underneath all them trees, it was darker'n a sumbich. And full of mosquitos.

However, while the fight was goin' on, the Rebs was lookin' for what they come for. And, in no time at all, one of em yelled out, "I got it!" He knew pretty much where it was supposed to be anyhow, and they didn't have to blow no safe because what they was after was the gold pieces, and the paymaster kept them in a special box, which, of itself, in a way, was a safe, and it was heavy as a muthafukka. Anyhow, two Rebs grabbed hold of the coksukka and muscled it up onto the upper deck. They worked fast so the Yankees on the other boats wouldn have no time to figure out a way to get to em—they could hear the blue-suits off in the darkness on the other boats, raisin' hell and fallin' all over each other, run-nin' around like a flock'a chickens with their necks wrung, wavin' lanterns that was too bright in a dark that was too dark.

One of the Rebs reached up into that darkness and pulled down a chain; then him and another'n fastened it round the paymaster's box of gold pieces—only they done it a little too quick, and when one of em give the signal, somebody somewhere way up above em there in the dark, probably with a block and tackle, gave a hard pull to haul it off the boat and up into the trees. The box was lifted off the deck, and it swung over to the north side, near the front—Mr. Brainsong called it the port bow—where it hung stock still for about a second, then took one jerky jump straight upwards and come loose from the chain . . . and it fell into the Pass. And that was the end of it, with them Rebs standin' there, each one with his hand on a rope and his mouth open, not believin' how bad they had just fukked up.

They knew the gold money was gone beneath thirty or more feet of black water, but, more'n that, and worse, they knew it was goin' to be under damn near thirty feet of mud too, because that's the way the bottoms of a lot of them bye-ohs and small lakes is down there. Shoot, even little chirrun play in quicksand—when it's only a foot and a few inches deep. That stuff's so common down here in the Delta that when a sumbich says another muthafukka has his "feet on the ground," he ain't really sayin' much.

One of them Yankees with his hands in the air just looked at the Rebs and said, "Serves your ass right." And a Reb looked at him, pointed his pistol straight between that Yankee's eyes—put it right *on* that sumbich—then he let his hand fall. He stuck his pistol back into his waistband, grabbed a rope with both hands, looked again at that Indiana farm boy, and said, "I believe you are correct."

Then all them Rebs slung their weapons, took ahold of their ropes, and in no more'n a split second, they and the ropes, too, was gone. And, except for some soft rustlin' high above the boats, there wuddn nothing left but a fair amount of blood, some dead Yanks, and a headless paymaster with a busted nose. Everything was back to normal.

The Yanks on the *Beaudollar* stopped holdin' their hands in the air, found their guns, and shot up into the blackness and the branches above them, but didn't nothin' nor nobody fall down. And, when the first of their buddies from the other boats come up on deck, a young private from Iowa who had been in the fight said, "They've kilt the paymaster and dropped the gold in the drink."

The sergeant who led the rescuers wanted to know the rest of it, and the boy said, "We're six dead and two overboard, and there's the paymaster's head layin' yonder, over by the rail."

"Gotdam!" the sergeant said. "What'd they do that for?"

"They didn't want to make no noise," the private said.

"That's a helluva note," the sergeant said. "I expect all this was heard clear back to Helena."

"Spec so," the boy replied, "but I b'lieve I can tolerate it loud better'n the other way. Quietness is the work of the Devil."

"This *land* is the work of the Devil," said the sergeant. "And the Yazoo Pass is the road to Hell."

"Well, I don't like that quiet," the boy said, and the sergeant set about gettin' the soldiers to clean up the mess and to make sure the paymaster's head was put with the paymaster's body. Plus, he wanted to make damn sure that everyone understood that the paymaster's nose had been broken when his head had hit the deck after it was lopped off by the Reb and not busted later by none of his clean-up crew. He said he wanted the officers to understand what had happened, and he made it plain to the soldiers who had been in the fracas that they might be called on to verify the nature of the circumstances.

"We'll send all these poor dead fellows back to Helena at daylight," he said. "Damn," he continued, thinkin' about the paymaster's head, "damn, that's a helluva thing to do."

THE PAYMASTER'S HEAD NEVER made it back to Helena. And nobody knew what had happened to it, because the sergeant had made real sure that it had been wrapped up and set alongside the rest of the paymaster inside the cabin of the little cutter they used to take the bodies back to Helena. However, when the bodies arrived, the head wuddn there, but there wuddn no big to-do made about it because the sergeant and the soldiers was way-ass down the Coldwater, and the sailors that brung the bodies back to Helena hadn't had nothing a-tall to do with puttin' the bodies in the boat in the first place. So the whole thing was overlooked, and they went on with the war.

Later, though, some questions was asked about the head, but by that time too much had happened; too many people who'd been there wuddn around no more, and so the whole thing just sank into the background and disappeared, the way things that need to be tended to have a habit of doin'.

Watson Smith did not come to the paymaster's boat until eight o'clock that morning. General Ross was already investigatin' and in serious conversation with several of the enlisted men who had survived the attack. He and the other officers wanted to know how the Rebs had got on board, where they come from, and where they went to after it was over. Or, as Mr. Brainsong told it:

"A corporal stood among his superiors, pointing up into the early budding, wickered thickness of the mostly bare-limbed trees above them. The Yankees, of course, knowing only that the Southerners had come down upon them on ropes and had gotten away on ropes, could not figure out the rest of it—where did they come from 'up there' and where did they go 'up there'?"

Then, about eight-thirty, one of the blue suits spied it. He seen something high up through the limbs that didn't look quite natural, and then he seen another something, and another, and then they all seen what he seen, which by then was shapin' up into a definite man-made construction. At first glance, the average sumbich wouldna seen it at all or, if he had, wouldna paid it no attention. But you know how it is when one little thing catches your eye, and then the longer you look, the more you see. It's that way a lot of times with water and blood. But this was different.

Way, way-ass up near the top of them giant cottonwoods and white oaks and cypresses, eighty or ninety or a hunnuhd feet high, the Rebs had built a catwalk that run for a good quarter of a mile back up the Pass. But at the mouth of the Pass it made a right-angle and run for nearly three-quarters of a mile down the Coldwater, zig-zaggin' back and forth across it; however, you couldn have noticed it, slight as it was and up high like that amongst all them branches. The thing was rickety in some places and well-built in others. And there was pulleys and ropes all up and down it. It's important to remember that the environment here in them days was what Mr. Brainsong called a "deciduous jungle," and the Confederates was up in the "canopy," which of course means the wove-together tops of the fukkin trees.

The Reb raiders that night—or morning, whichever you want to call it—had half climbed up and half been *pulled* up off the deck of the paymaster's boat. And once they was way up there, they simply ran down the Coldwater River through the fukkin treetops, three-quarters of a mile in the blackness, climbed their butts down, got on their horses and rode off in the shallows or, if they was on foot, pushed off in a duckboat and disappeared into the dark-ass branches of history.

The Rebels had built the thing back in the previous summer, thinkin' the Yankees was goin' to blow the levee in the early winter when there's still a few leaves left on the trees, but they did take the possibility of their bein' wrong about that into account and constructed the catwalk with lots of irregular joints and ups and downs to blend in as much as it could with the uneven, jaggety shapes of nature.

Plus, they figured the Yanks, in just tryin' to get to the Cold-water, was goin' to be so preoccupied clearin' the logs th'own in it by the planters and the slaves that they, the Yanks, wouldn be lookin' upwards hardly at all except to keep the limbs from knockin' their smoke stacks off while, with them big-ass ropes and their gangs of five-hunnuhd men, they fidgeted their boats around im-fukkin-possible twists and turns until they finally got through the Pass and onto the Coldwater which, though a little bit wider, was about the same as the Pass as far as difficulty of movement was concerned—well, it wuddn *quite* the same, but it wuddn a whole lot better neither.

And the Rebs was right about what the Yanks would be focusin' on and about what they would and would not notice. The leaves had all fell off the trees by the first of February, but by the last of February, some of em was just beginnin' to bud out again and even get a little fuzzy lookin' at a distance, which, far back as I can remember, is not uncommon here in the Delta.

So hell yes, the Yanks *could have seen* the catwalk if they'da been lookin' up, had *known* to look for it, and had looked twice. But they wuddn, and they didn't. They was lookin' down, at the godawful endless-ass flooded wilderness around them.

Plus it was just another case of the Yankees not movin' fast enough. Watson Smith had got his two r'nclads and some of his six tinclads out of the Pass and into the Coldwater on the evening of the twenty-eighth of February, but instead of steamin' on to-ward Greenwood, he ordered his men to ease downstream just a little way, tie up, and wait for a bunch of the other boats to make it on through the Pass and get into the Coldwater too, because he believed they all needed to stay together, which they really didn't. On the other hand, he was followin' Admiral Porter's orders to a "T" not to travel at night.

I never understood that. I don't know that Admiral Porter did either. I did see in one of Ottis's z-rockses that it had not been pos-sible at all for the gunboats to travel at night while they was in the Pass. I can sure see that. But I *don't* see why they couldn have run the Coldwater and the Tallahatchie at night, at least a little bit.

I don't know. Apart from the risk of tearin' the bottoms out of their boats, Admiral Porter could have thought night travel made the Yanks more vulnerable to snipers, but, in that time and place, things weren't any easier for the snipers than they were for the snipees. Navigatin' would have been somewhat more difficult at night because of the snags and all, but there again any movin' would have been better than no movin'. Plus, the Yanks had blown concealment long before they blew the levee.

Even today, if something happens forty miles away, somehow it must send a ripple through the mud—you whisper something in Clarksdale, and people in St. Leo hear it, just like whales on TV . . . especially if they're havin' coffee and just generally fukkin off at the Boll & Bloom.

Smith's judgment was not the best, and it got worse and worse every afternoon at 3:30, because that is when Anguilla had her tea parties.

Anyway, the point is, had the paymaster's boat gotten out of the Pass and been in the Coldwater three-fourths of a mile downstream, the Rebs could not have raided it at all; plus, the paymaster's head wouldna been whacked off, and he would not of broke his nose. All that just goes to prove the road to Hell is paved mostly with just sorry-ass luck.

It was another story the next morning when Smith was there on the *Beaudollar* with General Ross, Lieutenant-Colonel James S. Wilson, and Smith's own second-in-command, Mr. Foster.

Smith couldn take his eyes off the paymaster's head until one of the soldiers carried it off to place it with the body. And Smith didn't have much to say about anything—at least not anything that anybody could make out. His lips was flappin' all the time, and it was like he was sayin' something way back down inside hissef. But, put it this way, couldn nobody have quoted his ass.

And after both parts of the paymaster was tucked away to be sent back the next day to Helena, Smith could not stop gazin' up into the trees at the catwalk. Mr. Foster felt he had to actually take the commodore by the hand to lead him off the boat and into the skiff to get him back up to the head of the flotilla, but, after about four seconds in the rowboat, Smith jerked his hand away from Mr. Foster and commenced to holler: "Onward! Onward, lads!" And then he pointed up at the catwalk and looked like he was goin' to say something about it, but, instead, he just looked, pointed his finger, looked back at the men on the deck of the *Beaudollar*, looked up again at the catwalk, still pointin' at it, and began to laugh one of them ho-ho-ha-ha kind of belly laughs, and he did that all the way out of the mouth of the Pass into the Coldwater and on south, past the tinclads and around the bend, out of sight, so that the soldiers on the paymaster's boat couldn hardly hear it no more till right at sundown that day, when everything in the flotilla was settlin' in for the next night.

That sumbich was wild. But he stopped laughin' and hollerin' "Onward" durin' the afternoon long enough to have the usual tea party with the beautiful Anguilla Benoit, and then, about an hour after that, he started it again but kept it up for only a short time.

MR. FOSTER HAD BEGUN to look forward to these occasions. And, the fact is, Anguilla did, too, and not just on account of she was workin' for the cause.

Anyway, after the tea party, and after the commander had done excused hissef and gone to his own quarters, where he had commenced again to carry on, Mr. Foster was left alone with Anguilla and Chiwiddywee, who Anguilla told to clean and straighten up the room while she would see if Mr. Foster would escort her out on the top of the *Rattler* to get some fresh "Delta air." Even though it had been stuffy and hot as a big-dog inside the cabin, Mr. Foster didn't give a fuk for air or nothing else; he would have shoved a two-by-four up his ass if she'da ast him to. As far as he was concerned he didn't have but two organs in his whole body: one was his heart and the other was his dick, and both of em was poundin' like hammers and near bout ready to bust out of his uniform and run around the fukkin room. It was like tryin' to hold back a brace of blueticks once they've smelt the coon.

"Mr. Foster," she said, in that little "Miss Hospitality-*Made-of-Fukkin-Cotton*"* voice of hers, "Would you be so kind as to accompany me onto the *upper dick of our vesicle?* I would so enjoy the air and, shall I say, the music of my native slough, even though it is technically still winter."

Now, Mr. Foster, who had, ever since the first day he met her, done fell head over heels in love with her and who, every time he came to one nem lillo tea parties she put on for the commodore, Lieutenant-Commander Watson Smith, durin' which he, Mr. Foster, had to hold his hat over the front of his britches and really coulda just hung it there, said, "Fuk yeah, follow me," and then climbed up to the top of the boat—which, of course, since they was under orders from Admiral Porter, hissef, to run only in the day time—was settin' stock still in the water.

It *was* cooler *and* a whole lot darker up on what, Mr. Foster explained to Anguilla, was called the hurricane deck than it was down below where there was lanterns; plus, they had to watch their heads on account of the limbs, which, even though the boat wasn't movin', was nonetheless everywhere all around them and somewhat dangerous if only in a minor way, unless of course you was to walk up on one of em and put your fukkin eye out.

In fact, there wuddn no lanterns at all up where they were, which is why Anguilla wanted to go there in the first place. She

---

* Paranomasia with "Maid of Cotton," a title won by smart and/or beautiful young women who were sent around the country promoting cotton.

was one of them women that always known exactly what she was doin' and don't mind doin' it.

Bear in mind that Mr. Foster's dick is so hard at this point that the whole six thousand soldiers and sailors coulda stood on it and walked all the way to Greenwood. Plus, Anguilla had purposely not worn her hoops, not so she could demonstrate how patriotic she was, like so many of them Southern belles did at the time, but so that, when she worked out how she could bump into him, she would know when she had got herself, so to speak, a situation on the handle. Mr. Foster's mouth was dry, and his heart was pumpin' like two con-victs on a handcar tryin' to outrun the long arm of the Panamaw Limited.

"Oh, Mr. Foster," said Anguilla, "I may have to stand a little closer to you for warmth—I'm afraid I didn't realize how chilly it was."

"Yes'm," he croaked, and he felt the folds of her dress, like a big silk pussy, closin' in around his whang the way one of them jungle flowers does on the TV when a frog hops into it. And then his "thang"—which, itself, was strainin' and probin' into them skirtfolds like it was some kind of little *creature* that had done got loose and didn't have no connection at all with him and, like in them space movies, had in just a short amount of time growed to the size of a fukkin catfish—come to a dead halt somewhere on the lower (or was it the upper) part of her invisible body which, then (because he also, without thinkin', had done put his right arm around her back so that the heat of her small shape burnt his ass clean through his uniform as though she was standin' there nek-kid), fit perfectly in the palm of his hand which had come to rest on top of her right hip bone, which I'm bettin' was just one more in a sudden-ass series of female-firsts for him. The way she felt to his hands was like nothing his fingers had ever come across before, because, bein' a well-brought-up Yankee boy, he had never had the opportunity to do none of this, and it made him want to pass out. You know how it was in them days.

They didn't have cars back then, so a man could be pretty old before he ever knew what touchin' a woman *felt* like. And he sure as hell never woulda saw one in shorts or been able to dive under water at the Clarksdale swimmin' pool and look up their bathin' suits like we done back when I was just gettin' a little bit too old to do it and get away with it.

"Oh, dear Mr. Foster," she said, "you seem so, so *tense.*" And here Anguilla let her left hand fall to where the head of Mr. Foster's whacker, held back only by his sailor britches, and blowin' up tighter'n a fish bladder, was pressed against the left lower part of her stomach inside the soft silky puffs of her big-ass skirt, where she was movin' her hips ever so gently—but ever so unmistakably—from side to side, with, you know, that little hard hump thing flippity flippin' back and forth over the end of his norkus.

Then, soft as a quail fart but very deliberately, she took ahold of his you-know-what and said, "Mr. Foster, dear friend, you *are* terribly tense. Why, I can sense the stress that I know is so even with a brave man-at-arms such as your-say-ulf."

"Gurrgle," said Mr. Foster.

"Dear *suh,*" said Anguilla, "I have studied medicine in Mexico, and I can assure you that, when the effects of spiritual stress make themselves manifest physically, as they have here in you," and she gave his hooter a little squeeze, "extreme, and I might add, *emergency* measures are required to alleviate your suffering," And she caught his thing between her thumb on the top and her index finger on the bottom and started runnin' them back and forth, lengthwise, but, because his britches was so tight—and kind of thick, too—her little fingers hunted for his buttons, found them, and undid em; then she reached in and fished around till she got a choke-hold on his prick. "Now, sir," she said, "is this better?"

"Thrimmm," said Mr. Foster.

"You're so very brave," she said.

"Furrrbb," he replied.

"Does this feel good?" she asked.

"Yag," he said.

"Allow me to continue," she whispered, and slowly, slowly, she just seemed to sink down outta sight, and the lips of her even-softer wet mouth opened and closed, and tightened over the head of his love rocket, and he felt her lips and her tongue, too, goober-gobblin' their way down his dick like a hungry little perch tryin' to swallow a corndog, right on toward the place where, balls and all, his en-tire cock was about to achieve liftoff from the end of his stomach. By this time and even though this was the first part of March and at night, Mr. Foster was sweatin' up a storm and hot as two fat people fukkin on a four-wheeler.

"Moomff," he said, lookin' down at her head bobbin' around in the dark.

"Urml," she replied.

CHAPTER 6

Rebel Horsemen Ride on Top of the Water and Fly across the
Tallahatchie — There Is No Shoreline — Smith's Condition Is
Debated — Mr. Brainsong & The Band Sissy — Irish Travellers

History is an amazing thing. Once I got started, it just more or less begun to write itself. But that's not too surprising. I have always been a student of human nature, and don't nobody need no professor to fill em in on that. I call it the natural flow of truth unfukked-up by facts.

Even though the Coldwater River was wider and deeper than the Pass, there was just as many limbs that knocked off the Yankees' smokestacks and tore up their upper decks. Some of the bends in the Coldwater was as bad as in the Pass, too. But on the whole, things was a lot easier and got even more so when, by the sixth of March, the flotilla was pretty much steamin' out of the Coldwater and into the Tallahatchie.

As you may or may not know, that would be, in these times, right over there between Lambert and Crowder. They's a bridge just a few yards south of where the two rivers come together, and you can go stand on it and see exactly where the flotilla come chuggin' out of one river into the other.*

For days—well, actually, ever since the whole fukked-up thing started—one sumbich or another had been comin' up to po' old Watson Smith tellin' him about the Confederate cavalry. Nobody had actually seen em, but everybody knowed somebody that had.

---

* The Yazoo River is really the Yazoo "system," a group, if you will, of rivers that join together to create the Yazoo, which empties into the Mississippi River right at Vicksburg.

The big question was where was the Rebs gonna ride their horses? There wuddn nothing but water anywhere you looked.

Remember, most of the time them Yankee sailors couldn see no shoreline, just channel and trees and water—no matter what direction they looked, it was just water and more water, and swamp, swamp, swamp, with an occasional open space which generally indicated there might be a cotton field at the bottom of that stretch of water. And it would still be like that every fukkin year if we didn't have the gotdam levee that runs for two hunnuhd miles from Walls to Vicksburg.

Mr. Brainsong said that just about the time the r'nclads and the tinclads and the "rams" and the transports had all cleared the Coldwater and slid into the Tallahatchie, Smith and nem calculated they had traveled over fifty miles and hadn't seen but about eight plantations.

Anyhow, as I told you, after the raid on the *Beaudollar*, Commodore Smith hooped and hollered sumpn awful for a good while, and then he shut up and said even less than he had when he done like that before. He was piddiful. But there *was* one thing he would say ever' now and then, and that was: "All is swamp! All is swamp!" At night he bunked on the *Rattler*, but durin' the day he spent most of his time with Mr. Foster on the *Chillicothe*, up in front of the whole wet-ass convoy.

So then in a day or two on about, I guess, the eighth of March and steady but slowly puffin' along down the Tallahatchie, Watson Smith begun to get more agitated and nervous and started actin' nuttier than usual, which is sayin' a helluva lot. He commenced to jumpin' around from one side of the pilot house on the *Chillicothe* to the other, back and forth, then out of nowhere and all of a sudden he started to jabber about seein' some Confederates, off to the right side on horseback.

Do bear in mind, this is in the middle of a coksukkin world-wide flood across the the whole Yazoo and Mississippi Delta. Yet there that po sumbich was, blabberin' out: "Cavalry! Cavalry, Mr. Foster! Do you see the cavalry?" And he said it over and over.

Meanwhile, Mr. Foster was lookin' hard as he could, but he didn't see no fukkin cavalry.

"Cavalry! Cavalry, Mr. Foster! See them there?" He pointed to where he was lookin' and repeated what he was sayin'—"Cavalry! Cavalry, Mr. Foster, cavalry!" And all this time he was still runnin' from one side of the *Chillicothe*'s pilot house to the other and stoppin' in between to look up ahead. But when he'd point his finger, he'd point it over to the west.

Mr. Foster was upset. He didn't have no idea what to do with the po' sumbich, who had gone one day from screamin' "Onward!" to not sayin' much of anything, and, now, to lookin' wild-eyed and babblin' like a muthafukka about Confederate cavalry bein' in a place even the ducks and the gotdam mudpuppies was havin' a hard time gettin' around in.

Anyway, there Mr. Foster was with a couple of sailors, all of em standin' with their fukkin mouths hangin' open while the incredible-ass *flotilla* and the army transports paddle-wheeled on toward Fort Pemberton to what—in fukkin fact—was goin' to be an even bigger surprise than just that of their watchin' the commodore see shit couldn no other sumbich see. I get a creepy feelin' ever' time I think about it.

However, and not too much later, in fact just after the commodore had remarked to Mr. Foster about em passin' only eight plantations in fifty miles, Smith cocked his eye out in front of the *Chillicothe*. He looked straight-ass ahead, and he looked thissaway, and he looked thattaway. Then, squintin' his beady eyeballs so he could focus farther out—and scannin' way over to the right across what appeared to be a big lake—but which, as I have already mentioned, would most likely have been a large flooded cotton field—*Smith seen em.* He *seen* them sumbiches!

There was about a hunnuhd of em altogether, comin' from the west towards the *Chillicothe* lickety-split with their horses at a dead run across the *top* of the water in that big open space, at a right angle to the channel and smack-dab into the path of the *Chillicothe*. Those wild-ass boys was gallopin' straight for the shore line—only of course there wuddn no shore at all, just a place, more or less marked by the feathery tops of oaks and willows and hickory-nuts—that separated the openness of the channel from the openness of the flooded field, or the lake or whatever the fuk it was; what shore and bank there mighta been was, like everything else at that Mississippi moment, in the whole fukkin Yazoo Delta, definitely under thousands of square miles of dark and muddy water in the spring of 1863.

Yet that didn't matter none to the Rebs. They spurred them ripplin' horses *right across the ripples of the water*, and them old boys, with clouds of gotdam seagulls* flappin' above their hats, was standin' up in their stirrups, leanin' forward, swingin' nem long-ass swords, and hollerin' like drunks at a homecomin', but not makin' a single splash as they raced theyse'ves and their animals across the muddy swirl of that floody Delta sea, just like ol' Jesus on the Lake of fukkin Galilee! Only of course they weren't doin' it to impress no apostles in a sail boat. Their horses' eyes was burnin', and there was fire, too, in the eyes of the Rebs; and both the horses and their howlin' gray riders was aimin' those flames directly at po' Watson Smith, who was lookin' back at them, from the pilot house of the r'nclad *Chillicothe*.

On and gotdam on them wild muthafukkas came. And Smith called to Mr. Foster to blow em down with the big-ass guns: "Fire!" He said. "Fire, Mr. Foster! Fire! Shoot them fukkin guns!"

---

* Gulls are quite common over the flooded fields of the Delta in times of high water.

Mr. Foster looked at that crazy sumbich, then looked over at them other yo-bobs standin' around and seen all their mouths was hangin' open even wider than before, including his own.

"Shoot, Mr. Foster! Aim and shoot, Sir! They are almost upon us!"

"Shoot at what, Commander?" said Mr. Foster. "Shoot at what, sir?" And he looked as hard as he could on both sides of the boat and to the front, but he couldn see nothin' except the Tallahatchie River.

"The cavalry, Mr. Foster! Cavalry, sir! Off the starboard bow!"

"But, sir—"

"Shoot! Gotdam your ass! Fire! Those coksukkas is almost to the trees!"

"But—" said Mr. Foster.

Then Watson Smith turned to him. The commodore's face was lookin' like it coulda belonged to somebody else, and he stared Mr. Foster dead in the eye; then, calm and cool as a coot, he said, "Shoot, Mr. Foster . . . or *I* shall have to shoot *you*."

"You got it, muthafukka," said Foster, and him and the yo-bob squids* let loose with all of the guns they had up at that end of the boat.

Watson Smith, though, watched them Reb-cava'ry sumbiches lash those strainin' horses till they reached the treetops stickin' out of the water at the edge of the river, but he couldn do no more'n stand there pop-eyed, as every snort'n horse and whoopin' red-eyed rider rose, *rose*—I mean *rose-ass up off the water* and into the fukkin *air itse'f!*—where they galloped in a' arc up over the channel of the Tallahatchie River, smack across the path of the r'nclad *Chillicothe*.

---

* Junior Ray was never in the "service," but he picked up the term "squid" from his trips to Memphis, which for a long time was the place of recreation for the young sailors who trained at the Millington Naval Air Base, the world's largest inland naval base, about forty clicks northwest of Memphis. The locals called the trainees "squids."

And as them yippin' sumbiches flew over the river and above the flood, every one of em, hellish horse and grizzly-ass rider alike, turned their devilish heads to the left and grinned straight into the eyes of Lieutenant-Commander Commodore Watson Smith.

Then, down they come on the other side of the river where they run off—*again across a stretch of open water*—with all of em yellin' and wavin' their pistols and blades; till, quick as a wink and quiet as a fart at the Rotary Club, they disappeared in the Scatters* like a fog in the trees.

"Cease fire, Mr. Foster! Cease fire!" said Watson Smith. But Mr. Foster didn't hear him and kept on shootin' his cannons, bustin' up the daylight and layin' waste to blue sky and turtles.

So the commander put his hand on Mr. Foster's shoulder to get his attention. "Cease, fire, sir," said Smith again, this time in just a plain old calm tone of voice, and Mr. Foster, with a blank-ass look on his face, ordered the yo-bobs to stop shootin'.

Smith resumed not sayin' nothin' and went back to the *Rattler* and locked hissef in his cabin. General Ross and Lieutenant-Colonel James H. Wilson, plus everybody else, was busy bookin' on down to the *Chillicothe* to find out what the fuk was goin' on, and, when they ast Mr. Foster about the shootin', all *he* could say was, "Orders, sir. The commodore's orders," because he wuddn ready right then to flat out declare he thought Watson Smith had gone nuttier than a Goo-Goo Cluster.† But he didn't have to. General Ross and Lieutenant-Colonel Wilson had been thinkin' it for a long time and had been sayin' it, too, in so many words, ever since they met up with Watson Smith. Plus, they was army

---

* "The Cypress Scatters," an area on the Tallahatchie not far from present-day Greenwood, where good ol' boys, planters, and Memphis professionals hunt ducks among the cypresses. Furthermore, though Junior Ray says he has a "z-rocks" of the "cavalry" episode, he has not produced it.

† A popular Southern candy bar that has, among other things, a lot of peanuts in it.

guys and they didn't like takin' orders from a sailor. As a historian, I have to give the Devil his due because I could see from readin' my z-rockses that there was a definite pissin' contest right at the jump between the Army sumbiches and the Navy. All the expert plannin' was of course all fukked up. The Army was blamin' the Navy and the Navy was blamin' the Army. Both of em was pissin' and inscribin' their names in the local mud, but it was in General Grant's handwritin'. I'm certain Wilson was an ass'hole, and Smith was very, very fukkin sick and nuts at the same time. Wilson was smart and a hard worker. Smith paid attention to de-tails and was smart also, but he and Wilson was as different as two muthafukkas could be and still be members of the same species.

I'll admit I like readin' them official reports—once. But it drives my ass crazy to go back over em. The same thing happens to me as when I try to look at things in alpha-fukkin-betical order. I can't do it. It hurts. I'm not shittin' you. That's why I could never stand to work in an office. Anyway, I could put all them reports in here, in the book. But you wouldn't want to read em neither. Plus, if you just had to, you could go to the Meffis liberry, like I did.

Ottis and Mr. Brainsong, and me, finally all come to the same conclusion that Smith was out of his mind. Maybe that's because he had fever with malaria or the walkin' pneumonia or somethin' a whole lot worse, but personally I like Mr. Brainsong's theory about the *pay-otey*, and that's the one I'm goin' with. I mean, you can investigate a thing to death and ruin it by findin' out too many fukkin out-to-the-side, off-the-road facts.

I think history ought to be a matter of preference. That's how I got to likin' it. Hell, if I thought for a gotdam second I had to spend all day with a bunch of fukkin *facts*, I'd be as crazy as that po'-ass sumbich Watson Smith.

MR. BRAINSONG DONE HISSEF in. At first I thought something

historical had fukked him up; although, later, I remembered a conversation I had with him, and I knew I had the real answer. And it wuddn all about the scandal—which happened a fairly long time ago, you know; although it seems like anything that ever made any difference to me is always something that was a long fukkin time ago. Except for TV, I ain't never cared much for modern times.

Anyway, the reason he kilt hissef was more complicated than what everybody had settled on—yet, on the other hand, it was maybe too simple for them to be inter-rested in, and so they just stuck to what you might call the standard stuff cause it was easier for them to get their notions around . . . like the scandal, itself, of him bein' caught up in Overton Park with that little band sissy, Bud Vayce.

That little shithead was a local boy that lived right in the middle of St. Leo. It was durin' the Cotton Carnival, and the Mhoon County High School band had been invited by the City of Meffis to come up and play for the niggas at the Meffis Zoo, cause it was on a Thursday, and, in Meffis, in those days, Thursday was the niggas' day to get to go to the fukkin zoo. It was all about good will and shit like that, but mostly it was about tryin' to keep the niggas happy so they wouldn run off and go up to live in Chicago and leave the gotdam planters stranded in the middle of all that cotton without nobody to pick it for em. In nem days, a planter couldn be a planter without the niggas. Back then niggas was the key to everything, includin' the bank.

En-tire busloads of em from Meffis would go down in the Delta on Saturdays and whenever else they could durin' both the pickin' season, which was in the fall, and the choppin' season, which was in the summer, and the only way to keep the Johnson grass and all the other weeds from takin' over the fields was to chop em out with a fukkin hoe. And you had to have a lot of hand labor for both times of the year. You couldn do it that way now. There ain't no more hoe-hands nor no more cotton pickers neither, and it's all done with chemicals and big-ass machinery.

In some respects the whole business was just a case of Mr. Brainsong bein' born too early because, now, times has changed all the way around and up the ass of what times used to be, so that today, I mean right fukkin *now,* besides tweety birds and bugs, there ain't nothin' else in Overton Park but gotdam queers. And the niggas can go to the zoo whenever they take a notion.

Personally, back in the old days, I could look at all the animals I wanted to right here in Mhoon County, and as far as goin' to a coksukkin park in a city was concerned, I couldn see no sense in that. But, hell, later on, them planters cut down all the trees for twelve-dollar beans, and made the whole place look like Texas—which might be just fine if you're a fukkin cowboy, but I'm not.

I just can't believe them sumbiches cut their woods down for a fukkin bean. Yet, knowin' them planters the way I do, nothing surprises my ass. Them sumbiches would disc up the sky if they thought they could get another acre or two. I mean, look at the place now. Those coksukkas have done chopped up the trees, run off the animals, and kilt the fukkin fish—and made the water so nasty you can walk on it. And now—oh fuk, now—the gotdam government is offerin' them money to put it all back the way it was! Chr*EYE*st! If you or me tore something up the way they did, wouldn nobody, much less the U.S. government, be offerin' us money to fix it. They'd have my ass in jail.

But you can't get over on them fukkin planters. They've got it, they've had it, and they're gon' keep it, and there ain't a fukkin prayer for the rest of us. The only people that ever had the upper hand on those coksukkas was the niggas. And, even though the planter tried out the Chinese, the Indians, and the gotdam Mexicans, he never could get hissef loose from the niggas. Them black muthafukkas had his ass where they wanted him, and there wuddn nothin' he could do about it, till of course the machinery come in.

It's all changed now. Ain't nothing even in the least like it was. The older ones of us don't recognize the place, and the younger ones might as well be from O-gotdam-hio. The past was only possible because we was down there all to oursefs, and nobody really knew what we was up to. If you ast me, that was the real secret of the old South. Hell, the War Between the States didn't change nothin'. Endin' slavery never changed one single gotdam thing for more'n about the ten minutes it took the planters and the bankers to hop-ass out of their gray officer coats and then get the bit back between their teeth after the Federals cleared out. But, finally, the two world wars and the radios and the roads blew the whole thing wide open, and the rest of the country looked at the TV and said, "Wait a fukkin minute here, coksukka. You can't be what it looks like you've been." And that was the beginnin' of the end of it. The change began durin' the First World War, mainly by gettin' people— white *and* black—out . . . which I guess all of a fukkin sudden gave em something to compare the place to. That's what really kicked off the slide into these here so-called modern times.

ANYWAY, HERE I AM, more or less a law enforcement professional, workin' security in the parkin' lot of a fukkin casino settin' in the middle of what used to be a coksukkin cotton and bean field between the levee and the river. Plus, now that the dirt has done started sproutin' slot machines and we're rockin' along on roulette wheels, the planter don't never have to worry about nothing, includin' the rain, again—unless of course it brings the river up into the lobby, and he don't care about that, neither, unless he's rentin' to em; otherwise he's done got his money and run. Actually, these casinos, though they look like regular buildings, is all built on barges and are settin' in a pool of water, which you don't really notice cause you don't really see it, so that if the river rose, the gambling halls would rise with it, but, I believe, in doin' so, they'd tear up all the buildings they're attached to, like the hotels and the restaurants, cause they didn't have to be on water like the gambling halls.* So, apart from havin' a rip or two in their super-structures, the hotels and the restaurants would all be full of water, because the Mississippi don't need no reservation to get a room.

Plus it's all put up on the wet side of the levee, which, if you ast me, is just an invitation to a swimmin' party. If you ever saw the Mississ'ppi at flood stage, it would scare your ass off. Hell, it'll scare you when it's not, unless you're in one of them states nearer the actual headwaters; down here, that fukkin river looks like pictures you see on TV of the gotdam Amazon—or the Ori-fukkin-noco.

Anyhow, Mr. Brainsong, the school, some of the other teachers, and the band was there at the zoo, which was and is to this day right there in the park, and this thing happened. Mr. Brainsong tried to say he was just tuckin' his shirt-tail in, but that little faggot, Bud Vayce, claimed otherwise and seemed to enjoy bein' the center of attention, like he was receivin' some coksukkin award—or visa-fukkin-versa. The little sumbich was smart—the vale-*dick*-torian—so I ain't ever understood why he had to do what he did to Mr. Brainsong. I mean it wuddn like the little sumbich wuddn a gotdam notorius-ass diklikker, and the whole fukkin town knew it as well as they knew their own gotdam phone numbers. But ever'body'd always just say crappioca like: Oh, Bud is so ar*tis*tic . . . he is so GOOD to his muuhhthuuuh . . . and play the piano, whoo*eee*! The usual gobbagooty people always say about a sumbich when they don't want to come out and face the fact that the little ass'ole is goin' around suckin' dicks. Not that I give a fuk or think

---

* With the exception of "casinos" on Indian land, any facility in the state of Mississippi that offers "gambling" must be on a navigable stream, a condition which has been more narrowly defined to include only the Gulf of Mexico and the Mississippi River and any land that lies between its channel and the levee.

Jesus does, either. And see, I don't want to get into the suck*ees*! Oh, hell no, and of course neither did the fukkin town. It was easier just to hang Mr. Brainsong. And quite frankly, even though they all called it "his retirement," I ain't never forgave their ass for it. Fukkum.

I guess Mr. Brainsong thought he was safer up there in Meffis near the zoo than he woulda been down here. And if it hadn't been for that mounted policeman just that one day, he woulda been. But as you might imagine it was a major hoohaw, and even though there wuddn no arrest made, and there wuddn no goin' to court or nothin' like that—cause word was that the mounted policeman was a Mason, and Mr. Brainsong was a Mason, and somebody said Mr. Brainsong said something and that after he said it, the police-man said he was just tryin' to make sure everything was all right, and then he got back up on his horse and rode on off. But, by then, it was too late because a couple of the other teachers, one of whom was a big-time dikhed and the other the head of the Baptist Youth Group, they got back down to St. Leo, told the story, and de-fukkin-manded that Mr. Brainsong be let go.

He was, and, as I said, they called it "retirement." Mutha-fukkas.

Anyhow, you can tell that even though I can't stand a gotdam queer, I really liked Mr. Brainsong a whole lot, and I was sorry about what happened to him. I mean, when you come right down to it, there ain't a great deal of difference between an ass'ole and a pussy. Still, why a sumbich would want to fiddle around with a dick if he already had one of his own is beyond me. People are funny.

Of course, nowadays, it's the niggas and the queers—and even the datgum *girl* queers—that's runnin' everything. It's like, "Don't fuk with me, sumbich; I'm a nigga and a queer—oh, yeah, and a girl, too, muthafukka!" I suppose I'll never know why we was so worried about the gotdam Russians when the *big three* was right here under our noses the whole time. And look what we was doin': We *was too good to* the muthafukkin niggas, we *ignored* the coksukkin queers, and we treated the women like they was *ladies!*

And *all three* of them ungrateful sumbiches has turned on our ass. I tell you, it ain't like it was in the old days. Back then, if you run up on a queer, you could just cornhole the sumbich and show him what a real man was all about, but not now, muthafukka, not now. And if you try to open a door for a woman, seven times out of ten she'll just look at you like you was lower than an odor-eater.

Sure, I guess you could say Mr. Brainsong was a queer, too. There probably ain't no way around it. But I liked him.

I never did get rough with Ottis about it—although there was times I shoulda piped up and said something in Mr. Brainsong's favor, and I'm sorry now that I didn't. For one thing, I could have shut Ottis's big-ass mouth in a fukkin hurry if I'da reminded him of all them afternoons down at the Mule Barn—I know they's still several of them Irish Gypsies who owned it, now back livin' with the rest of the tribe up there in Meffis, that remembers. Plus, I know they'd get a big laugh out of it, too, although at the time if their granddaddy had knowed what all was goin' on, he'da kicked the gotdam Irish stew out of em.

Now, though, there ain't no more demand for mules, nor maybe for real one-of-a-kind, exceptional people neither, so, to succeed in life and live they way they want to, all them smart sumbiches—the men, anyway—travels out across the country, mostly in the summers, and paints stuff. They'll paint just about anything that'll hold still, but the tribe itsef is still right up there in Meffis—and has been for over a hunnuhd and fifty years—and all their mobile homes has statues of important saints, even, here and there, old Jesus hissef, right smack in the front yard. However, except for His ass, I don't know nothin' about none of them other super-natural historical Cath'lics, although I guess I could invent some if I wanted to. Yet, if good luck is one reason them statues is standin' there, then I have to say there's something about plaster of Paris the Gypsies know and we don't.

Bear in mind, they don't like to be called Gypsies. Cause they ain't. They're Irish, and they calls theysefs the "Travellers." And I bydamn wish there was a lot more of em. Hell, I wish I, me personally, was one! But my folks wuddn nothing but plain old poker-faced pekkawoods who didn't have near the kinda bang out of life that them Travellers do.

Plus, I'll tell you what, everybody in the Delta—planters, niggas, bankers, and pekkawoods alike—all of us—ever' fukkin one of us liked the Travellers, and above all else we respected them, because, for one thing, it was them who owned and operated the mule barns, and they was the ones who supplied the planters with the mules that pulled the planters' plows, so the long and the short of it is that we was all better off on account of them. And nobody better ever say anything bad about em in front of *my* ass, bygod! They was my friends. So don't fuk with em.

But, to get back to what I was sayin' about the sumbiches I come from, even when my kinda folks get to singin', they stand up there next to each other like a buncha dead bodies tryin' to act like tree stumps. They don't never move, and their faces don't never change. And I never understood how come. Maybe I do have something else in me besides pekkawood, only I don't know what other kind of pekkawood it could be.

Hell, that thing with Mr. Brainsong and the *band sissy*, it ain't no different, when you think about it, in what he done and more or less in what happens to some other older sumbich when he gets mixed up with a gal that ever'body else thinks is too young for him. Take Bobo Lyon, after his divorce, and all that doo-wah-diddy he got into with that little spinner, Thalula Bridge, down in the south part of the county. Everybody said that, because of her age, they felt she was "extremely vulnerable." Maybe so, but Bobo was, too. That po' sumbich was a drunk fifty-year-old man, and I doubt there's anything on this gotdam earth more vulnerable than that!

Plus, if you ast me, I always thought Thalula was about thirty-fukkin-five cause you could find her just about any Saturday night drinkin' with her aunt and nem, and her no-count cousins, out on the side of Moon Lake—most of the time at that Eye-talian's joint about a mile south of Twitty's.*

Anyway, po' old Bobo was drunk and fallin' out his chair one night too many, and Thalula offered to drive his sloppy ass home. That was the worst good deed he ever run into.

I don't care who a sumbich is or what he comes from: Under the right—or maybe I should say the *wrong*—circumstances, anybody after twelve o'clock midnight is goin' to be at a helluva risk. If he's a he, all any woman's got to do is rub up against him, and that sumbich is gone. And if you're a woman, and I ain't, the same thing is true. If your ass has had too much likker, you're gon' wind up fukkin some sumbich in a car, rollin' around in a motel room, or you gon' go with him to *his place* and wake up the next day with your life in more of a mess than it normally is and wishin' you hadn't done what you done, until, after about four days, when it goes away and you don't give a shit no more, then you will probably go out, get drunk, and do the same thing all over again.

A sumbich—or a sumbichette—under those circumstances I just mentioned, drunk after midnight, ain't gon' have no more steerin' ability than a three-wheeled Volkswagen with a busted tie rod. Especially if you ain't where you're s'posed to be in the first gotdam place.

But oh hell people *love* to hear about some piddiful muthafukka who gets his ass fixiated by pussy gas. The human American pussy is the deadliest and most uncontrolled substance in the whole gotdam

* Conway Twitty owned a popular nightclub at Moon Lake in the 1960s.

world. Chr*EYE*st, talk about a concealed weapon! Sumbich, you ain't got a chance against a woman carryin' one of them things. I don't give a shit if you're Billy Graham and the fukkin Pope all rolled up into one big pig-in-a-blanket, the *thighs* have it, and your hand is no longer on the wheel.

Even the Lord Godalmighty ain't gon' save your ass, cause He's the one that invented pussy in the first place and made it the powerful, death-dealin' weapon of mass-ass destruction it is today. It's in the gotdam Bible. So chalk it off, muthafukka; unless you cut your own balls off and put em in a place where you can't never get to em, you, just like the rest of mankind, are a potential victim of your own dick and the relentless American pussy.

Myse'f, I ain't never had any first-hand experience, mainly cause I don't never take a drink, so I don't do nothin' by accident. If I knock the shit outta somebody, it's because I've thought it out carefully and fully intend to fukkin do it. But, as I explained up at the front of the book, by me bein' a law-enforcement professional I have seen a helluva lot, and the line between a good man and a bad one is mighty thin. Sometimes, on a Saturday night, you can't hardly tell the difference.

Mr. Brainsong lived right there in St. Leo for a long time after his "retirement," but maybe a year and a half before he apparently felt he had to end it all, Mr. Brainsong said, "Junior Ray, I always wished that I were an expert in something, but I never was. I was always just sort of pleasant fellow who read a lot of books and knew a few peculiar things."

"Like what kind of submarine it was me and Voyd found that time way back yonder up in the woods cross the levee," I said.

"Yes," he said, "like that, and what Alexander the Great usually ate for breakfast." I didn't ask him what it was. Plus, that was the first time I ever knew he watched wrestling.

I couldn figure out exactly what had him so down. He said it

wuddn the thing that had happened in Meffis with that little ass'ole
Bud Vayce. "Junior Ray," he said—and that although he was sorry
about him havin' had to *retire* and everything and that the *disgrace*
of it had been a hard thing for him to bear—"I came to terms with
the way I am many, many years ago. I really don't feel bad about it
anymore, even though I have often wished I were heterosexual."

Hell, I thought, bein' a queer is bad enough without bein' that,
too. But I didn't say nothin'. I don't like queers no more'n the next
sumbich, but, as you already know, I did like Mr. Brainsong and I
hated for him to be feelin' bad about himself or anything else for
that fukkin matter. Let me tell you something: Mr. Brainsong used
to talk to me as if I had been to college like anybody else, and when
I'd say something to him, he listened in a way that made you feel
he thought it was the most important gotdam thing he had heard
all day. That's why I liked the man. Except for wantin' to suck
dicks or whatever, he was the kind of fellow every sumbich ought
to be. The real truth is, it don't matter what a sumbich does with
parts of his body, or with somebody else's, as long as he's a decent
muthafukka, which, if we put the fukkin cards on the table, is the
way things ought to be.

Myself, I never even ever wanted to make it a point to be decent.
Too much of it can lead to some major ass'ole-ism. But of course
bein' decent don't ruin some people, and Mr. Brainsong was one
of those—decent in a bigger way than what you normally think
of as bein' decent. With him it didn't seem like a bad thing at all.
And that's the sort of decent-ness I admire.

THEM ARCHIVES IS WONDERFUL things. But they don't have the
whole story. You have to either be from here or to have lived here
in order to fill in the gaps. You might say that the de-tails are not so
much in history as they are in the historians—which is why I liked
listenin' to Ottis and talkin' to Mr. Brainsong before he done hissef

in of course—and the truth is, as far as *this* subject is concerned, I wouldn know which to put my money on.

As I said earlier, and as Watson Smith knew, too, right from the beginnin', there wuddn gon' be no *element of surprise* by the time all them Yanks got to Fort Pemberton. Smith even wrote to Admiral Porter about all the fuk-ups and the delays.

If you've ever been in the army or the navy or the national guard—and I ain't—you know what I'm talkin' about. How so much organization can be so disorganized is something I never could figure out. But them organizers never do seem to get a grip on whatever it is that fuks em up.

I say if you're gonna hit somebody, knock the pee-wine stew out of em. Get to the fukkin point, and don't be dancin' around. You gotta be direct. And I'da been direct if I'da been with the Rebs fightin' the Yanks on the Pass, and up and down the Coldwater and the Tallahatchie. I'da greased up and me and a bunch of other sumbiches woulda got in the water at night and cut holes in the bottoms of their boats. We'da been historical frogmen. And what we done would have clogged up the Pass and both them two rivers till now—with one-hunnuhd-and-eighty to two-hunnuhd-foot boats all sunk into the mud between Moon Lake and what remains of Fort Pemberton, which is mainly just a few humps in the ground.

I don't know why them Rebs didn't think of that, but I guess they was too busy tryin' to ride horses and chop down trees to have time to think of something more exciting. You know it is possible to be too fukkin industrious; plus, they was probably just so close to the situation they really wuddn able to see all the possibilities the way a historian can.

Anyhow, so there it was again, tea time on the Tallahatchie, and the threesome was settin' in Anguilla's room on the *Rattler*.

"Why, Commodore," said Anguilla, "you're mighty fukkin pensive, suh—whatever could be the matter?" Naturally, Anguilla knew damn well what was the matter. At least, excusin' his original disease, whatever that was, she knew a large part of what was the matter.

Watson Smith looked up at her and seen her face balloon out to the width of the room; he stared at her mouth that was openin' and shuttin' and not makin' no sound, and he began to try to see back inside her throat, thinkin' how interesting it would be to go in there and slide all the way down her gullet, then crawl through her intestines and pop out her butt so as to get up under her skirts, but he knew that goin' into her mouth that way, even if it were big enough now for the boat itself to steam through, was something no fukkin gentleman would ever do.

Then he thought: what if there was no bottom, no exit, and, well, if her mouth was this big, how big would her butt be once he got there, and where would he go after that, and . . . ? These were important considerations, especially for a systematic sumbich like hissef who never wanted to go off half-cocked.

"Mo' tea, Commodore? Mo' tea?" said Anguilla, now back to her regular size.

Watson Smith stretched out his hand, and Anguilla took his cup; she turned and went to the little table where the teapot was, fiddled and foodled for a moment, then rustled back and handed the commodore his tea cup—with honey and hot milk and you-know-what . . . *the pay-otey.*

"Sir," Foster piped up, "you look as though you do not feel well. I might say, sir, you appear to have a fever."

"I have not been well, Mr. Foster, since before I left the Yazoo to command this expedition. And I must say to you, sir, we have lost all hope of surprising the enemy. They are watching us, sir; they are watching us and . . . " He was gettin' louder and louder and bouncin' up and down in his chair.

CHAPTER 7

More on the Commodore's Sickness — More about Pay-Otey
— "Big Mound it is!" — "Them po' sumbiches from up North"
— Colonel Benoit's Bicycle Blimp — A Word About Niggas —
Sherman's Memwar — Taterbug Café — Hippies

Watson Smith had gone into a gullet all right. And it seemed like he got more and more lost the farther he floated down inside the innerds of the Delta. Mr. Foster caught himself not givin' a shit because he, hissef, was gettin' so caught up in bein' in *LUV* with Anguilla who was just Miss fukkin *Vi*-gotdam-*vacious*, pourin' tea and feedin' pay-otey to the commodore, who was, day by day and hour by hour, turnin' into nothing more'n a hat rack.

And he was really sick, too, not just in the head, and every afternoon he would have a fever, usually comin' on around 3:30 or four o'clock, just at the time he'd be havin' tea with Anguilla. But I'll have to say this for the poor sumbich: he kept goin' and goin' like a fukkin Timex. Somewhere inside himself he was sayin', "Hold it in the road, Watson. Something's wrong, but don't let go!" And he didn't, until the 17th of March. But that was after they'd come around the bend above Fort Pemberton at Greenwood, on the eleventh, and had gotten shot to shit by the Rebs and had been stopped there for six days. It was also after he and Mr. Foster had said goodbye to Anguilla and Chiwiddywee at Big Mound.

By then he'd had so much of that pay-otey that, when he rounded the bend on the eleventh, he could see the rebels' conical shell comin' out of the muzzle of the 6.5-inch gun toward the *Chillicothe*. He seen the thing. He could see it leave the muzzle of the Whitworth. He saw it rotatin' as it floated toward the r'nclad, and when it hit, he could see each piece of metal, every splinter of wood, and even each individual tongue of fire that flew all over the place when the Whitworth's pointed shell hit the armor plate, tore up all the pine wood beams behind the metal, and knocked the bolts holdin' the armor to the wood all over the inside of the boat killin' and woundin' several of the yo-bobs.*

The whole thing was all in slow motion, and I know this because, unless I got the Orlon pulled over my eyes, Ottis claimed he found it wrote up in Smith's diary in the archives at the Naval Department in Warshin'ton. Well—Watson Smith wrote it all down after they shipped him back up North and before he died, of course, which wuddn too much later after he got there. He wrote two things: the official report he sent to Admiral Porter, sorta recappin' the expedition, and this thing I'm talkin' about in his "diary." Man, I love the shit out of re-search.

WATSON SMITH *WAS* IN love with Anguilla, I *guess*. Hell, this may be the only time I ever didn't go along one-hunnuhd percent with whatever Mr. Brainsong thought! The truth is I just don't know if Smith really was or not. Personally, I think it was probably Mr. Foster that fell for her the most. Anyway, the more Anguilla stoked Smith up on pay-otey and the sicker he got with his original disease, the less in love it seems to me he became till finally, it weren't even an issue no more. I mean, just because a sumbich has an introductory hard-on for a woman does not mean that it has any lastin' value. And, in my semi-fairly-well-informed view, just from what I have learned about the situation, the only one of them muthafukkas actively involved in romantic thoughts about Anguilla was definitely Mr. Foster—who was the one she should probably have been givin'

---

* The truth is that Smith may or may not have been on the *Chillicothe* when the incident occurred.

the pay-otey to instead of whangin' his dang. But, hell, she was somewhat human, too, and you know how women are.

You have to understand that Mr. Foster could spend more time thinkin' about Anguilla because the little muthafukka knew that the success of the expedition, or the lack of it, was ALL on po' ol' Watson Smith's shoulders, so Foster knew it wouldn be him, as second-in-command, that got the chewin' if things didn't go right.

I think Foster had a few weasely qualities that he tried to hide, and personally I don't think that little Yankee chicken-choker had a hair on his ass.

As YOU KNOW, BIG Mound is on the west side of the Tallahatchie about two *hewmongus*-ass meanders before you get to the bend and the straight stretch of river above Fort Pemberton, which is the same thing, really, as sayin' Greenwood. And, when that day come, Anguilla was packed and standin' on the *Rattler* by where the gangplank was goin' to be laid out for her and Chiwiddywee to get off the boat. It was around eight o'clock in the morning on March the eleventh, 1863.

Up ahead was the *Baron DeKalb* and then the *Chillicothe* beyond that, up front. The rams was behind the *Rattler*, and they was followed by the five other tinclads and the twenty-two light transports. And half the poor sumbiches on the transports had the fukkin flu.

Mr. Foster came off the *Chillicothe* onto the *Rattler* just so he could say goodbye to Anguilla. The commodore, Lieutenant-Commander Watson Smith, was in the pilot house of the *Chillicothe* dealin' with one hallucination after another, and he didn't give no thought to Anguilla. Pussy was the last thing on his mind. He had bigger fish to fuk.

Gotdammit! I *know* Mr. Brainsong could *not* be right about Smith and the love thing. Because anything like Smith bein' in love or thinkin' about pussy—the way a normal man would be doin', was by then completely out of the question . . . the *pay-otey*, his own sickness, and the Mississippi Delta had done took it all clean out of him. All that regular kind of stuff belonged to another world to which he had done lost the map.

When the gangplank was put out, nearly straight over to the muddy bank, which was one of the few pieces of ground stickin' out of the water, Anguilla and Chiwiddywee skipped off the *Rattler* like they was in a helluva hurry. Mr. Foster was standin' there, again with his mouth open, and all Anguilla did was throw up her arm without even lookin' back at him and say, "Bye y'all." And she and that wierd-ass Mexican Indian went on up the bank to meet some men and a woman who was all standin' in the middle of a bunch of white folks' tombstones up on top of the Indian mound, and then they went on off a little way and got in a huddle. There was three big skiffs pulled up on the bank, and it was obvious that, later, they—the men, the woman, Anguilla and Chiwiddywee—was all goin' to get in them and row over to wherever there might be a piece of dry land on the other side so Anguilla could go on toward the hills to get to Carrolton.

And that was that. The *Rattler* pulled in its gangplank, and the flotilla continued on down the Tallahatchie, where, about eleven o'clock that same morning it was goin' to run into the Confederate guns at Fort Pemberton.

Neither Mr. Foster nor Watson Smith had any idea at the time that Anguilla and that wild-eyed Mexican Indian of hers had been playin' them all for fools, and they sure didn't know nothin' about pay-otey. If they had, I am convinced they couldna got enough of it, when you think about the sorry situation they was in.

Plus, I doubt Mr. Foster, and I know Watson Smith, never ever heard of, or from, Anguilla Benoit again. For one thing, Watson Smith didn't live long enough after he pulled out of the expedition on the seventeenth of March, and she didn't really see nothin' special in Foster to begin with. Plus, you know, there weren't no phones back then.

Them muthafukkas just thought the place, the war, the politics, and just the plain old inability to do things right was what screwed em over. And, remember, Watson Smith was the only one who had been dosed up with the pay-otey. He didn't know which end was up. But he knew when the game was.

Now-days when I think about those Yankee boys floatin' around in the Delta, back up in them little rivers and bye-ohs, I think about the movies and newsreels showin' the American GI's floatin' around in Vietnam. It was the same thing, in a way, except in the Delta we do have seasons. All them Vietnamers has is a wet and a dry kind of thing, from what I've seen on the TV.

And over there the Americans was shot at by a lot of tee-niney little slant-eyed coksukkas hidin' off in the bushes along the shore, and there was tigers, too; whereas, here in the Delta, back in 1863, it was exactly the same except they was shot at by regular-lookin' humans like you and me, who were also, of course, hidin' off in the bushes, so to speak. And I'm fairly certain there might have been a painter* or two.

Hell, there still is. But even then them big cats was probably more inter-rested in deer and turkeys. Shoot, I'll always believe they was a painter runnin' around Mhoon County in 1959, when I was chasin' Leland Shaw.

But there's something worse than a datgum painter, and that's people. There ain't a tiger in the whole fukkin world that's as bad as a man. I ought to know. Plus, what makes it even worser is a man's supposed to show more sense that a cat. Fuk a bunch of instincts. A man's got that, too, if he knows how to use em.

You take all the tigers and painters you can think of, and they

---

* panther: Felis concolor.

ain't done no killin' that could even begin to compare with the killin' men has did. You just have to put things in perspective. And I always do. Maybe I ought to say that things is always *already* in perspective: you just have to learn how to see it.

Anyhow there they were, six thousand Yankee soldiers and sailors, swallowed up in the Mississippi Delta, trapped by water on all sides, and confined like a chain gang on a string of thirty-two boats—or shall I say, ships; a gotdam one-hunnuhd-and-eighty-foot boat in a bye-oh *is a fukkin ship*, especially if the sumbich is carryin' a buncha cannons.

Them Yankee sumbiches musta thought they was never gonna get home again. Some weren't—well, for all I know, every single one of them may have bit the dust later on, but only a few got killed outright on the Yazoo Pass expedition.

For one thing it was mostly the sailors in the two r'nclads that did any real fightin'; however, there was a one or two times a number of the soldiers got out on a little dab of dry land and captured several of the Rebs. I don't really know how that could have happened, because there wuddn many places to stand, but, though not much, it did take place; plus, the Yankee soldiers were able to set up a little bit of their artillery in a semi-dry field to help out the *Chillicothe* and the *Baron DeKalb* once they got down to Fort Pemberton, though it was about as useless as a hiccup. But, for the most part, the soldiers just twiddled their thumbs or pulled their Yankee doodle-dandies while they set out the war in their twelve—or their twenty-two—light transports stacked back up the river. Plus, as I told you, some of em took pot shots at alligators, and of course others went fishin' off the side of the boats.

They was carp in the water big as my leg—they come in out of the Mississippi with the flood and swum around all over the place . . . in the woods, across roads, in the fields. It don't matter none to them scaley little scownboogas. There was buffalo,* too, and those muthafukkas gets a lot bigger than a carp. The bones can kill your ass, and the meat is tough and coarse, and so it, along with gar, was et mostly by the niggas, and, natchaly, by a few of us pekkawoods as well. Still, buffalo looks good when it's cooked and layin' up on the table. But, even though buffalo can be tender and nice, if it ain't cooked right and it sets around, it's likely to chew like a fishy-smellin' two-by-four.

And, like I said, a lot of them old Yankee boys in the transports was fishin' to pass the time, keepin' their heads down, although, for the most part, it was fear and not actual snipers they had to deal with.

Gar were rollin' alongside the transports, too. In fact one was netted out of Moon Lake that was twenty-three feet long, and they laid it across some saw horses and took a pitch'r of it. I don't know if a huge-ass alligator gar like that would eat a man or not, but it's big enough to bite a gotdam rowboat in two. Plus, as they got closer to Greenwood, the real alligators was more and more numerous, so didn't nobody want to fall off the boat on a warm day.

I DON'T SEE HOW they did it, but they did, and, even though the whole thing was a fukked-up mess, I do have to hand it to them Yankees, because what they did, whether there was any use in it or not, was a gotdam accomplishment. That counts for a whole lot in my book, even if the sumbiches were Yankees.

A sumbich can't help what he is. If he's born a Yankee, it's not like he *chose* to be one. So I'm not faultin' a muthafukka for what he didn't have nothing to do with. And, hell, his parents couldn't help bein' Yankees neither, so, in a way, none of em had any choice about why they was where they was and who they was. It was all just the luck of the draw.

---

* a fish.

There was one guy, Acting Master Brown of the *Forest Rose*, who appeared in a skiff at the side of the *Rattler* shortly after the flotilla had stopped for the night. He was in bad shape—the dumb sumbich had been experimentin' with explosives, tryin' to develop a han'grenade which he believed would be useful if him and his men had to board a Rebel vessel. But one of his "ideas" had blowed up right when he th'owed it—kablam, and he was singed all over. However, he wuddn dead, and he seemed to be able to keep on managin' the *Forest Rose*—which, by the way, had been the first boat to run through the Army engineers' cut in the levee that February. Brown had to wait till the water on both sides of the cut had equalized, and that took about four days. Then he ran the *Forest Rose* up the short, small west portion of the Pass, which went from the Mississippi on into Moon Lake where he kept goin' for about five miles till he reached the place where the Pass exits the lake and slithers around for another twelve or fourteen miles to its connection with the Coldwater River, and it was in that slitherin' part that all the heavy work of clearin' I've told you about had to be done.

Anyway, there was something fishy about the sumbich—and had been from the very beginnin'. You didn't never know whether he was lyin' or tellin' the truth, but you mostly concluded he was lyin'. He had a habit of blinkin' his eyes real fast when he was tellin' you something. And his eyes was way too close together.

It may be that what he was really interested in was not fightin' the Rebs or even ever gettin' past Greenwood but pickin' up cotton cheap and makin' a big profit. In fact, later, he was caught-but-not-caught at some of that, workin' what looked bygod like hand-in-hand with one of the Yankee generals.

Commander Smith got the doctors to tend to Acting Master Brown, and they did all the wrong-ass things to heal him and make him feel better, but he survived anyway. And everybody was relieved to know he had blowed hissef up and had not been blowed up by the Rebs.

There was Confederates out there, but they couldn't do a whole lot of damage on a daily basis because of all the high water. You know, it's a funny thing about the Delta that there are some common denominators rollin' around in the minds of the people who live here. One of the denominators is, of course, "craziness." Another is "shooting" things—especially people—and the third common denominator is "high water."

If you remember anything about the notebooks of Leland Shaw, that crazy sumbich who I never did get to shoot was hipped on the subject of high water, thinkin' it was the way he was goin' to "get home," where he already the fuk was, if you recall, but didn't believe it.

I don't know why it's that way, but it just is. And I like it. I wouldn't want to live around here for a minute if I didn't think half the sumbiches here wuddn nuts, and I wouldn't truly fit in nowhere that the people didn't want to shoot each other once in a while—although, from what the CNN says, I guess now that's just about everywhere.

But the high water is something else. Except for an occasional major flood—which has not occurred since right before my people moved here from Clay City, in the hills, to the Delta. That was in 1937, ten years after the big one, and even though the levee did not break in '37, it was a flood all the same because everything—the ditches and the bye-ohs and the sloughs and the rivers, like the Coldwater, the Tallahatchie, and the Yazoo—all swol' up on account of none of the water couldn't run out into the Mississippi at the mouth of the Yazoo just above Vicksburg.

Now, in 1927 the fukkin levee broke, down around Greenville somewhere—up at Scott, I think—and that was when old Wendel Littlewoods had gone there to see a girl or buy a shotgun or somethin'; but, he said, when he arrived in Greenville and got downtown, he looked up at the end of the main street where the levee was and seen a *steamboat in the sky*, so he turnt his ass around and come back to St. Leo. Good thing, too. Cause he was livin' to tell the tale. Otherwise his bloated corpse woulda been racin' by New Or'lins on the way to the GuffaMexico.

Anyway, most of the high water we've enjoyed has just been that: *high water*, and nothing more. Plus, at those times, most of the roads are passable, because they're built up high, a little above the level of the cotton fields, so we get to go on with our lives, farmin' and, then, when the fields flood, we like to look at the water, too, which is, I think, pretty fukkin fascinatin' because the fields all turn into little oceans—and I'm talkin' about big waves with the white tops on em and everything. Hell, I've seen gotdam whitecaps on the waves in ordinary rice fields when some of them pitch-black killer clouds come up across *the* river, out of Arkansas.

Them clouds is something. I 'member in 1955 we picked up bodies out of the fields for two weeks up at Robinsonville after one nem things with a big-ass tornado attached cut a swath right through where all them fukkin casinos is now. That sumbich killed fourteen little black chillum in a one-room schoolhouse settin' up next to the levee. It was plum awful and sadder'n you could imagine. Then it went and twisted up a gin so bad it looked like a piece of tinfoil.

BUT, BACK TO THEM po' sumbiches from up North . . . It's funny in a way because they was perfectly safe except for catchin' a germ and occasionally gettin' popped by a Reb sharpshooter—and I can't help thinkin' how different it would have been if the Rebs had had airplanes. Then of course, if there'da been airplanes, the Yankees wouldn have had to try something as godawful stupid as what they were doin' in the first place.

Anyway, I'm hedging. I didn't want to sound like I had put the wrong brains in the eggs for breakfast. I am tryin' to avoid gettin' into the thing about old Colonel Benoit's *bicycle blimp*. He says in his papers he had nothing to do with it, but Ottis claims he did and that for unknown reasons the old colonel felt like he had to deny it.

Bear in mind nothing is wrote about it in the official dispatches, but it did exist, and it did fly over the flotilla and drop some bombs off in the swamp, and it performed all of that on the 17th of March . . . 1863.

Years and years later Joe D. McGhee found the thing underneath his aunt's house which, by the way, had belonged to McGhee's great-great-aunt . . . Anguilla Benoit, who did in fact *not* finish out her life in Carrolton, over in the hills just east of Greenwood, but spent her old ladyhood up in Meffis, so, as they say she said, she could "have a gotdam good time where there was sumpn goin' on." And I don't think it's right that Anguilla was more known as the wife of old "Snake" Frontstreet instead of as herself and for the way she lived her life, for a while anyhow, and for what she done to the Yankees.

But, you know, people don't give a woman the kind of credit she ought to have, unlessen she's some tweety-tweet pillar of the fukkin church or a good coksukkin cook and has eleven-hunnuhd little punk-ass grandchillun. Then, when she dies, they write her up for all that tweety-tweet shit and show a picture of her dressed in a purple dress, with blue hair, and all of it misses the whole point of whatever it was she was, unless of course she wuddn nothin' in the first place—which was not the case with Anguilla.

Plus, "Snake" Frontstreet was an ass'ole. From what I heard, he used to cheat on her; however, they do say one time he was goin' out the door to see one of his girlfriends and that the sumbich smiled one nem "confident-ass" smiles ass'oles all seem to have and said to

Anguilla: "See you later, mother of six," and she said back to him, but under her breath, "See your ass later, father of three."

So I reckon it's safe to say Anguilla did what she wanted to do, and that slick dikhed she was married to never knew the difference. He was the kind of man that always seems to be grinnin' there just behind his eyes, because he always thinks he's on top. But in every room he goes into, there's gon' be at least one sumbich that knows he ain't. You can count on it.

It was a contraption all right. The balloon part was made of double-ply silk, and below it was slung a light but strong canvas-covered wood frame, like a boat, that had two big-ass fans attached to it and a seat on which a couple of sumbiches could sit. The fans was attached to belts which was attached to pedals, and the two men in the cloth-covered wood frame—which Ottis called the gon-DO-la—would set there and just pedal away.

If they wanted to turn right, the man on the right would stop pedalin', and the man on the left would pedal like a muthafukka, and the *bicycle blimp,* which the Colonel, even in denyin' there was such a thing, referred to as the "pedaloon," would turn to the right— even if it didn't actually *go* thatta way because of the wind.

They could even back it up—well, there again, only if the wind permitted. Navigation, gettin' where you wanted to go and bein' where you wanted to be, was the main drawback. It was the same with them guys below, settin' on the Tallahatchie, but it was a different wind that was blowin' them around. Theirs was the wind of what I call uncontrollable crap. And a sumbich don't have to be no philosopher to know what the fuk that is. And he sure don't have to go to Ole Miss to find it out. I'm livin' proof of that.

Anyway, in case you didn't know it, just about any historian can tell you that all the fightin', except in a couple of cases, was done in the South, and those blue-suit sumbiches from up North burnt down almost ever'thin', includin' the fukkin schoolhouses. But Mr.

Brainsong said *that* was a whole other story by itself. According to him, the South didn't have the best educational situation before the war; and after, it didn't hardly have none at all, like now.

Things was in a mess, and, at the end of the war, a good many of the planters was broke, and some lost their land to the carpetbaggers and other rasty-ass scownboogers like that.

Course, old Colonel Duncan Sherard Benoit wuddn broke. That sumbich had some Northern kin, and between them and his own foxy sef, he put his money in stocks and commodities up there and had a bank account in Philadelphia full of U.S. dollars while, just for show, down here he flashed a wad of Confederate money. But he knew what time it was, and he knew the Confederates didn't have a Chinaman's chance. Unlike a lot of them rah-rah ass'oles, he kept a cool head and stayed in touch with reality whenever possible.

Now, A WORD ABOUT the niggas: the slaves didn't know *what* was goin' on. They was less in touch than the rest of the coksukkas. After the war, a lot of the slaves who had got wind of emancipation and all that shit thought it meant they wouldn never have to do no work no more, so they trotted off hither and yon and mostly got took advantage of. Most of em didn't know the difference between Africa and Alabama, and at the time there probably wuddn none.

But a lot just stayed exactly where they was and kept on farmin'. They and the planters picked up the pieces and made a crop of it. Even today there's white people and niggas that's been right here since those times. They ain't necessarily farmin' still, and things has changed a good bit. But they're the same sumbiches, and livin' together ain't nothing new to em. It's the cities that have fukked everything up. But then, a lot of the coksukkas that live in em are the very ones that left the land in the first place. So I guess it comes down to whether it's the place or the people. I say it's the place. I say the place makes the people, not vice versa.

Hell, I ain't no *ologist* or nothin', so I *could* be wrong.

On the other hand, if you want to know the truth, a good number of them planters was sick to death of the coksukkin war and wished it would get the hell over with soon, so they could go back to livin' the way they more or less used to before they was ruined beyond all gotdam repair. The rich ones probably did want the South to win, but not all of em would have come right out and said what they really thought one way or the other. Then there was the younger ones who didn't really know nothin' about responsibility and all that shit, and they of course was all for the fukkin war, and they was hell to deal with. Anyway, here's what Mr. Brainsong and Ottis, both, said that sumbich General Sherman said about it in his memwars—well, it was in a letter he wrote to another another high-up Yankee muthafukka, a general named Halleck, up in Warshin'ton, and, as with all the other stuff, Ottis give me a z-rocks:

September 17, 1863— . . . and now they begin to realize that war is a two-edged sword, and it may be that many of the inhabitants cry for peace. I know them well and the very impulses of their nature; and to deal with the inhabitants of that part of the South which borders on the great river, we much recognize the classes into which they have divided themselves:

First. The large planters, owning lands, slaves, and all kinds of personal property. These are, on the whole, the ruling class. They are educated, wealthy, and easily approached. In some districts they are bitter as gall, and have given up slaves, plantations, and all, serving in the armies of the Confederacy; whereas, in others, they are conservative. None dare admit a friendship for us, though they say freely that they were at the outset opposed to war and disunion . . . Still, their friendship and assistance to reconstruct order out of the present ruin cannot be depended on. They watch the operations of our armies, and hope still for a Southern Confederacy that will restore to them the slaves and priviledges which they feel are otherwise lost forever.

Second. The smaller farmers, mechanics, merchants, and laborers. This class will probably number three-quarters of the whole; have, in fact, no real interest in the establishment of a Southern Confederacy, and have been led or driven into war on the false theory that they were to be benefited somehow—they knew not how. They are essentially tired of the war, and would slink back home if they could. These are the real tiers etat of the South, and are hardly worth a thought; for they swerve to and fro according to events which they do not comprehend or attempt to shape. When the time for reconstruction comes, they will want the old political system of caucuses, Legislatures, etc., to amuse them and make them believe they are real sovereigns; but in all things they will follow blindly the lead of the planters . . .

Third. The Union men of the South. I must confess I have little respect for this class. They allowed a clamorous set of demagogues to muzzle and drive them as a pack of curs. Afraid of shadows, they submit tamely to squads of dragoons, and permit them, without a murmur, to burn their cotton, take their horses, and every thing; and, when we reach them, they are full of complaints at the smallest excesses of our soldiers. Their sons, horses, arms, and every thing useful, are in the army against us, and they stay at home, claiming all the exemptions of peaceful citizens. I account them as nothing in this great game of war.

Fourth. The young bloods of the South: sons of planters, lawyers about towns, good billiard-players and sportsmen, men who never did work and never will. War suits them, and the rascals are brave, fine riders, bold to rashness, and dangerous subjects in every sense. They care not a sou for niggers, land, or any thing. They hate Yankees per se, and don't bother their brains about the past, present, or future. As long as they have good horses, plenty of forage, and an open country, they are happy. This is a larger class than most men suppose, and they are the most dangerous set of men that this war has turned loose upon the world. They are splendid riders, first-rate shots, and utterly reckless: Stewart, John Morgan, Forrest, and Jackson, are the types and leaders of this class. These men must all be killed or employed by us before we can hope for peace . . .*

That Sherman was a tough sonavabich. And I kinda like him. Except that he was better educated than me, I believe we woulda hit it off just fine. Plus, except that he's somewhat thinner, he even looks like me, and he didn't like them fukkin planters no better'n I do. Of course, unlike me, he didn't just come right out and call em a bunch of ass'oles, and, too, I realize, from readin' the letter, that he didn't much care for *my* ancestors, neither, or really fukkin much at all, but I can forgive him for that because I happen to agree with him and know that he was right about em. Truth is fukkin truth, and I sure as hell ain't one to dodge it, unless of course I just have to.

The fact is, if I'da been livin' back then and been fightin' for the South, with no shoes on and nothin' to eat, takin' orders from some silly sumbich ridin' a horse while I'da been rollin' in the gotdam dirt, I'da actually been fightin' for a buncha coksukkas that hated everything about me and who I come from. Fukkum. I might not have gone over to the Yankees—I wouldna wanted none of them foreign muthafukkas tellin' me what to do neither—but I'da somehow figured out a way to split the difference. I guaran-fukkintee you.

Anyway, me and Voyd done a lot of ridin' around down at the

_____

* This "z-rocks" is from *Memoirs of General William T. Sherman*, Vol 1, Appleton, 1875, pp. 336–7.

Pass and along the Coldwater and ever'thin'. Hell, we'd get in Voyd's big old fart-soaked Ohzmobile—which, as you recall, that worthless nigga Ezell—as well as my friend Run-Low, who was a nigga too and not worthless a bit, up at the City Barber Shop, which ain't there no more—used to call a *Ohzee-Moh*. I'll tell you a little bit about Run-Low at another time. He fell asleep one Sad'dy night with his legs partially over one rail of the train tracks, and that's how he got his name, cause from then on he had to walk around on his shins with a pair of special Goodyear knee pads. He made his livin' shinin' shoes, but he's dead now. Anyway, one thing I will say about a nigga is that if you give him a fukkin word, that sumbich will improve it.

I have often thought that, in a way, down here, they really had a separate language. Way back, when out of twenty thousand people in the town and county combined, only two thousand was more or less white, a buncha Scotchmen came through St. Leo on a visit, and Sheriff Holston had me show em around. It was a Saturday, and I took em downtown, if you could call it that, and them Scotchmen was busy takin' notes and whippin' out recording devices, sayin' they was fascinated with what appeared to them to be an entirely different language from any they had ever come across. And I said, "Shoot, it's just plain ol' English," and them sumbiches looked at me like I was outta my fukkin mind. Well, afterwards I thought about it, and I finally realized that, to an outsider, the way a nigga talks, at least down here in the Delta, *would* seem like a foreign language, and, to tell the truth, I sorta got a kick outta that . . . because, if that was the case, then I was bygod bi-ass-lingual.

Anyhow, there was a place me and Voyd always liked to stop and eat at in Lula. It ain't there no more, either. Hell, everybody's got a car, and don't nobody do nothing around here on a local level no more. Plus, what hadn't already disappeared through natural causes, finally was wiped away by the coming of the casinos. Let me just say this, what the fukkin Union army couldn do, the casinos have.

It was a great place, the Taterbug Cafe. I liked it because Miz Lewis always had lots of veg'bles. Voyd didn't eat nothin' but meat and potatoes, and gravy. He had to have gravy on his meat, gravy on his potatoes, and gravy on the side so he could dip his light bread in it. Whenever Miz Lewis told him he could have three veg'bles besides his potatoes, Voyd always picked macaroni and cheese, Wonder Bread, and cobbler.

Now, that little prick would jump all over my ass for what I ate. I used to get Miz Lewis to bring me a bowl of brown rice with every garden-type veg'ble she had, dumped on the top of it. Then, I'd hit it a few good licks with the Crystal pepper sauce, and lay into all that good stuff. It was like eatin' the front yard, and I loved it, but Voyd always piped up and said, "Junior Ray, you eat like them gotdam hippies at that place in Clarksdale."

And I said, "Fuk yew, Voyd, you popgut sunavabitch. You're the kinda muthafukka who eats shit and wonders why maggots is crawlin' outta your butt."

Anyway, what I was talkin' about was this: Right after the civil rights thing got settled, some of the white students who had been livin' down there with the niggas opened up a vegetarian restaurant, which didn't last too long, but long enough for everybody up and down Highway 61 to see what it was they ate—and, to be truthful, some of the white people plus some of the niggas ate there on a regular basis. I went in once, myse'f, and, though I don't have no time for no hippies, I did like the food.*

One nem hairy sumbiches was a Seventh Day Adventist, and that sucka could cook up spaghetti better'n anything the Presby-

___

* Junior Ray did eat with the hippies in Clarksdale and at the Taterbug Café in Lula, and when he did, he in fact ate what he said he ate. But, as far as there being any sort of healthy, counter-culture diet that is now part of his regimen, such is far, far from the case. And he really shouldn't be so hard on Voyd.

terian Church ever fukkin thought about. And it had a meat sauce that didn't have no meat in it. It was soy beans. The funny thing about that was, a lot of them bean farmers turned up their noses at it. Now that really got away with me. Here they is knockin' down every fukkin tree in sight and changin' the shape of the entire planet just to plant soy beans, and when they seen something amazing done with the very thing they done hung all their hopes and dreams on cooked up in a hippie restaurant, they wouldn have nothing to do with it.

That beat ever'thin' I ever saw. I'm tellin' you, them sumbiches are ass'oles. I mean, I ain't got no time for hippies, neither, but, as I say, I do like their food. And if they grew soybeans, they wouldn turn up their noses at em at the dinner table.

Personally, I think them planters could take a lesson or two from the hippies. Just cause a sumbich dresses funny, looks funny, and eats funny don't mean there ain't nothing to him. Likewise, just cause a muthafukka graduates from Vander-fukkin-bilt or W-and-gotdam-L and farms thousands of acres of beans and cotton don't mean he knows his dick from a Mexican meat stick. 'Course fair is fair and the straight of it is that, even if they didn't get to go to Mississippi State, some nem sumbiches do know what they're doin' and are pretty good at it. And I have to admit it's the fukkin truth. Gotdammit.

Anyway, after a while, up in the eighties I reckon, after the good ol' boys got through wantn to shave the hippies' heads and all, hell, they and every other fukkin pekkawood in the state started wearin' long hair, and some of em even grew beards and wore them splotchy T-shirts and—get this—*still* managed to keep on hatin' hippies! That's what makes good ol' boys so fukkin dangerous. They can see everything but themsevs.

Anyway, the hippies did get me to thinkin' about bein' a better eater. That's why I have come up with a number of quick and—if you fix em the way I tell you to—easy-ass things to cook up. If you're like me, you won't want to fuk around too much and read a bunch of fine print loaded up with a lot of gotdam fractions just to get the sumbich ready, on the table, and in your mouth. So here's one* that's faster than a preacher's daughter:

❀ CHICKEN CHILI CON CORNY ❀

Go to the hippie store and get you some canned vegetarian chili, low-fat. While you're there, get one nem already-cooked chickens in the hot case.

Buy some corn—in a can, but look on the label at what's in it to be sure they didn't include no sugar. If you decide to use fresh or frozen corn, you'll have to parboil it a little bit before you add it to the chili.

Get out a fairly big pot, with a top, and put it on the stove. Open the can—or cans—of chili, dump all of it in the pot, and begin to heat it up. Then, quick as you can, pull the meat off the chicken, and th'ow it into the chili. Be sure there ain't no bones. Add the corn.

When it all gets good and hot, let it simmer some, then eat it.

You coulda added some cayenne if you'da wanted to. But that depends on what you can stand and who you got for company.

Plus, it's a good idea to get some oranges, so you can peel em and stick the sections *around* the bowl you're gon' eat your Chicken Chili con Corny in. It looks real good, gives you some color, and keeps your mouth from gettin' tired of

---

* As far as I know there is no other recipe like this, though nothing in it is that original.

the chili. You'll be glad you did it—put those orange slices on the plate your bowl is settin' on. Or, just th'ow the sumbiches in the bowl and don't worry about it.

Grapes are good, too. Make sure they're real sweet and don't have no seeds. Green ones are the best to use because, like the orange slices, they give you some color to offset the brown-ness of the chili.

CHAPTER 8

The Paymaster's Gunboat — Nostalgie de la Boue —
Mad Owens — Diving for Gold — Voyd's Big Ass Idea
—Things Work Out — The Magic Pussy Cabaret & Club —
Mad's Poems — More Love — The Illusion Is Shattered —
Another Blow on the Job — Break Up — "Sireen"

B ut, back to what I wanted to talk about—we used to ride
out east of Rich toward Birdie to where the Pass comes
into the Coldwater. We was interested in the paymaster's
gunboat. All them sumbiches that had growed up in that area will
tell you the paymaster's boat is sank right in there about where the
Pass goes into the Coldwater. Ever'one of them coksukkas'll swear
to it, and they *all* know somebody who seen it . . . stickin' up . . .
out of the fukkin mud.

But ain't none of em ever found none of the coins or the box
they was in. They was supposed to be mostly gold coins. That
meant, if the story was true, the water wouldna ruint it. And it'd
all be down there in the mud in mint-ass condition. You'd just have
to be willin' to go down inside the mud to get to it, as most people
are when it comes to makin' a quick lick.

Personally, I thought it was a crock of googah. But as time went
by and I learned more and more about the Yazoo Pass Expedition,
like anything that seems as though it might do you some good, I
couldn't help believin' it. Somehow the idea of gettin' rich *now* has
always been more appealin' than goin' to heaven *later*, even though
I can see a similarity between the Yankees and Jesus—we'd try to
run both of em outta town. Hell, the Yankees was the enemy, and,
if his photograph is anything to go by, Jesus woulda looked like a

137

fukkin A-rab, and the Baptists wouldn have no time for him.

Anyhow, the more I thought about it, the more I wanted to do something. The question was whether to do it in the winter when the water was high and there wuddn no snakes or to do it in the middle of the fukkin summer when there wouldn be hardly any water at all but a helluva lot of snakes. Plus, it wuddn gon' be the water that would be the problem. It was gon' be the mud. And I thought: How the fuk am I goin' to dive down into the mud?

Mr. Brainsong used to talk about a thing called *notes algee duller boot*,* which he said meant "longing for the mud," and I had thought that's where the "boot" came in. But he said it was poetic mud, not actual mud, and that it meant "the extent to which a nice person would lower himself in order to feel better about himself." Plus, he said it did not affect people like me. And I was damn glad to hear it.

I knew one thing and that was, I did not have no longin' to jump down into that deep gook at the mouth of the Pass—unless of course I could come up with a buncha gold coins.

We was gon' have to hire somebody. And Mad Owens was the most logical choice. His real name was James Madison Owens, and he was part of that planter bunch and a nephew of old Miss Helena Ferry, but all that's not neither here nor there. He was an okay sumbich—and I got a whole lot to tell you about Mad later on in the book—but the main thing, at the time, was he had a divin' suit, and all the equipment to go with it, and had even done underwater salvage work at the bottom of the gotdam Mississippi, if you can believe that. He was an unusual sumbich to say the fukkin least. Mad was one of these men that people said had been places, and had worked at lots of jobs the average sumbich ain't ever even heard about and wouldn't know how to do.

Anyway Voyd and me called him up and told him what we

---

* *nostalgie de la boue*

wanted to do and told him we was willin' to pay him, but he said he'd do it for free just cause he was interested but that if we was to come up with any treasure, he would like twenty-five percent of it, and that would suit him fine.

It didn't set so well with me an Voyd, but we said it did, and planned to meet down on the roadside by the Coldwater right across from where the Pass comes into it, which is down at Birdie.

WE MET THERE, AND since it was in the fall, we decided to go ahead and split the difference between the summer snakes and the winter water and get into the thing. That was on a Friday. A week later the weather was fine and Mad met us at the river again. He had a rubber raft and some scuba gear—which he said would be better than usin' his divin' suit because that would have required too much other stuff to go along with it, and besides, he said, if he got down there in the mud with it, he'd never get back up. That made sense.

By nine o'clock Mad was in the water and divin' down to see what was underneath it. Plus, by about nine-fifteen a fair little crowd of planters and managers had come up and was standin' by their pickups lookin' down at what was goin' on—which was mostly Mad divin' down and comin' up sayin' he had seen nothing. So after about three and a half hours, we decided to give it up. But Mad said he had a pump that could suck up some of the mud—the only thing we'd have to do was to find something to put the mud in once it was sucked up.

We thought about it, and Voyd said he had the answer. The next day Voyd went over to his brother-in-law's to borrow the pontoon party boat—without tellin' him what it was for; well, he couldn because they was all, his brother-in-law and Sunflower's sister and, I'll have to say, three really right manful little boys, out of town. They, and sometimes Voyd and Sunflower and their girl and her girls, used the party boat when they went out to the Cut-Off near St. Leo.

Anyway, Voyd's idea was that Mad could suck up the mud onto the deck of the pontoon boat; then we—me and Voyd or all three of us—could wash it, glob by glob, through some big-ass yellow plastic colanders he got at the One-Dollar Mart.

Well, we was tryin' to keep it as simple as we could. So, we hitched up the trailer with the pontoon boat on it to Voyd's Ohz-mobile and took off to the Coldwater at the mouth of the Pass. The problem was goin' to be how to get the pontoon boat down into the Coldwater River. We couldn cross John Corners's field to put the pontoon into the Pass, because we'da had to cut him in on the deal, so we stuck to the public road, which is gravel to this day. Anyhow, the bank was steep and covered by all kinds of brush, which we had managed to negotiate all right when Mad took his little ol' raft and scuba gear down, but the pontoon party boat was another story.

I said, "Fuk." But Voyd had the answer to that, too. We hauled the pontoon boat on its trailer back to his brother-in-law's house where he hot-wired that unfortunate sumbich's huge-ass six-wheeled, extended cab, four-wheel-drive pickup with a winch on the front.

Without as much trouble as we had thought it was goin' to be, we got the thing down into the river and Mad went to work suckin' up the mud—onto the deck of the party boat where Voyd and me was busy as a dog lickin' his balls puttin' the mud from the deck into them big-ass yellow plastic colanders and washin' em out to see was there any gold coins in the goop. The mud was somewhat runny and collectin' pretty fast and, actually, would have all more or less run back into the river if it hadna been for the sides of the party boat, which was about hip high and which had a tight little gate so that it formed a sort of perfect-ass trough to hold all the mud. Really, it was like a barge with a nice-lookin' green-and-white-striped canvas top. And Voyd and me was up under it, right in the middle of that huge, runny-ass mound of sludge.

It bothered me somewhat that the mud was gettin' all over everything and into the steerin' gear, but Voyd didn't pay it no attention, so I just said fuk it; it was between him and his brother-in-law. Anyway, just as we had hoped, the pontoon party boat was holdin' the mud as it was pumped up from the bottom of the Coldwater and the mouth of the Pass by Mad Owens.

But that was good news and bad news. The sides held the mud in, but it musta been too much weight, because the coksukkin deck of the boat just bent damn near in two right down the center; it just folded up, so to speak, with us pinched up in it, like two little fukkas in a taco. And then it sank. I guess Voyd and me did not know enough about the laws of mud. Hell, it's no wonder the Delta is so fukkin flat—the mud is holdin' it down. And there's so much of it. A hill couldn rise here if Jesus told it to. Like I'm sure that sumbich would ever want to get caught dead in Mhoon County.

Course all this time, Mad Owens was down on the bottom of the river steady suckin' mud up, at that point, to nowhere—cause Voyd and me was swimmin' to the shore, and the pontoon party boat was near bout all under water except for the green and white striped canvas top. And all I could think about was six thousand Yankees all putt-puttin' with little electric motors down the Coldwater in pontoon party boats. It was a helluva thought at a time like that.

Plus, when we clumb up the bank to the road where a bunch of them planters and managers and, by then, a fair number of niggas was, we looked up at the belt buckle and then into the eyes of the most pissed-off muthafukka I ever hope to see, and it was Voyd's brother-in-law who had done come home early and left his family up at Hardy, Arkansas.

Hell, I just crawled off to the left and into a thick stand of khaki pants, outta Harlan's (that's Voyd's brother-in-law's) line of sight. All I could hear was: "You little sonavabich, what the gotdam muthafukkin hell are you doin' with my boat, you weasely-ass little coksukka!?"

Voyd *is* small for his size. And he is weasely. So Harlan was pretty much on target. I guess I just didn't realize Voyd didn't have as much privilege with the use of Harlan's stuff as I had more or less hoped he had. Well, fukkit. I was plannin' on layin' everything off on Voyd anyway. Right from the beginnin', if we'da gotten in trouble, I was goin' to say, "Dang, Harlan! I never dreamed that little coksukka didn't have your permission to use your truck and the pontoon party boat! In fact, I reckon I thought you was in on the whole deal!" And, then, if he'da said "What deal?" I'da told him about the possibility of the paymaster's gold coins and woulda hoped he'da said, "Junior Ray, you dumb sumbich, ain't you got nothin' better to do than jerk off with that wormy-ass brother-in-law of mine on silly shit like that?"

But, if he had said that, I was plannin' to come back with: "Well, Harlan you know me, I know how silly that Voyd is but I was really just tryin' to be he'pful only I reckon I just got *too* soft a heart for my own fukkin good. I shoulda thought it out more. *Next time* I'll know when that no-count little poot-bird is tryin' to pull the extra-virgin orlon over my eyes but I swear Harlan I never in this fukkin world *dreamed* he didn't have your permission!"

If that didn't work, Harlan would just say, "Fuk yew, Junior Ray, you lyin' muthafukka," and then he'd turn around and walk off. But it wouldn't last long. In six months he'd be tellin' the story all over the Delta and lovin' the hell out of it, which is exactly what happened. Voyd loves to hear him tell about it, and him and Voyd is friends again. The fact is, Voyd thought he had done gone and shit in the well when he lost that party boat, and, I have to say, he was about as worried as I've ever seen him be. But, I told him: "Voyd, there's worse things you coulda done and worse trouble you coulda got into."

"Like what? Like fukkin my dog at the preacher's pot-luck supper?"

"No," I said, "like fukkin the *preacher's* dog . . . and not showin' up at the supper."

"Fuk yew, Junior Ray," he said.

"Kiss my ass, Voyd," I told him.

Anyway, when Harlan decided it was the funniest story in the Delta, that's when Voyd got back to his old self again. Any time you know somebody thinks something awful you done is funny, you're in good shape. Then it's like everybody has you to thank for the laugh of their life, and everybody's high on you and is really glad you're such a gotdam fool. Things have a way of workin' out.

As it turned out, I never did have to say nothing to Harlan, cause he laid it all on Voyd and never paid no 'tention to me. Thank the fukkin Lord.

And he never even seemed to notice Mad Owens was in on it a-tall. Mad's like one nem fukkin ninjas. Don't nobody ever notice his ass, yet he is potentially one of the most noticeable sumbiches in the world.

AT THIS POINT, I have to say some things about Mad and what happened later, after I got to know him somewhat better and he seemed to consider me a friend. Anyhow, the fact is, when it comes to the blues, them Yankee boys couldna never had it no worse than Mad Owens did.

I guess Mad is about the smartest sumbich I ever knew, and I used to say, "If Mad says it, it's so." And I'll believe that till my dyin' fukkin day.

See, he went to all them colleges and shit and studied all that stuff nobody gives a crap about except other smart muthafukkas, but there's a good reason for that. First of all, at least half the important stuff in the world is that kind of stuff, only it don't just jump out at us. Take all these fukkin churches for example, and all the money that's poured into em. And what's it all about? It's all about a bunch of googah that ain't got nothin' to do with a gotdam thing that's any use at all—all that wooodly-wooodly about men in robes and beards and risin' from the fukkin dead and virgins havin' babies and goin' to Hell just cause you don't believe that mess, and I'm here to tell you it's big business. That's what it is: big-ass fukkin business, sellin' mostly imagination and stuff you can't put in a sack and go home with.

Well, *but*, and here's the big-ass difference: history and philosophy and litter-ture is *not* built on imagination—not even a buncha imagined stories because you know from the jump they're all imaginized, *unlike* them churches, where all the imaginated bullshit is supposed to be swallowed like it was the whole fukkin truth, which it ain't. If God and Jesus and them other sumbiches is goin' to send my ass to Hell for sayin' that, then there ain't much use in dealin' with em nohow, if you ast me.

Whereas history *is* because it *was*. And philosophy is mostly about "thinkin'" and not just "believin'." There's too much of that, bygod. And it's gonna be the death of us.

Now, as you know, I'm already a fukkin historian, and, I might add, a fukkin *ar*ther, too. So that, just in itse'f, more or less, hooks me up with litter-ture. But, hell, I'm a born philosopher—a sumbich can't live down here in the Mississippi Delta and not be. And that's all I've got to say about that, for the time bein' anyway.

But back to Mad. I am goin' to give you some of that info I said I would about Mad Owens. And I guess you could say there is more'n one kind of Yazoo blues than just those po' bastards-from-up-North-Yankee-boys that had to endure pure Hell when they was sent down here to be on the Yazoo Pass Expedition, in eighteen-sixty-fukkin-three.

Bear in mind, now, that geo-fukkin-logically the Delta, the one I'm concerned with here, called the Mississippi Delta, is really the Yazoo Delta. It ain't got nothin' to do with that muck-mire down below New Or'lins. I know, to a foreigner, it's pretty fukkin confusin'.

Anyway, to talk about Mad, I have to say some things about love, and about how he fell into stump-hole full of it with a Meffis nekkid dancer named Money Scatters.

Now you remember I told you McKinney was goin' to stash around a few of Mad's poems in the book, so here's one of em—and no, sumbich, I did not see this page because wuddn nothing wrote down. I was just settin' there talkin', and McKinney told me to hold up and say this so the poem could be "intro-fukkin-duced."

BEAUTY
Beauty may not be
Inside the eye at all
But beheld in one
Small moment
Of my surprise
To see it flash and fall
Upon me, quick,
And strike like falcons
After light.*

---

* All poetry in this book was written by James Madison "Mad" Owens IV. "Beauty," above, and "Passion" were published in *Honeydü*, a literary quarterly, Vol. 1, No. 2, and also in *Message for Miss Tchula-Ofogoula Co-Ed Christian Academy*, Mad's slim privately printed volume of verse. All other selections were included in *Message*. A word, though, about Tchula and Ofogoula, Mississippi: they are a couple of towns in the Delta, and they have suffered the fate of so many like themselves that were founded upon a plantation economy that no longer exists.

First of all, you could take what I know about love and stick it up a bug's ass. Yet, there are some things that don't take a helluva lot of knowin'; you just have to not be blind as a muthafukka, and that's how I know about that whole situation between Mad Owens and Money Scatters. Plus the only reason I'm even talkin' about it is that over the years I got to know Mad pretty well, and even though some people might think he shouldna never even had nothing to do with me, that ain't the kind of man he is, and I like the hell out of him for it, but mainly I like him because he likes me.

Plus, I liked him because you couldn never predict how he was goin' to look at something. Mad had what you might call *a sense of different emphasis*. For instance, one time he had done gone over in the Hills to the Chickasaw Fair at Ludlow and drank his ass silly with so much of that home-made whiskey that he come home without his car, wearin' only one of his shoes, and woke up in the back yard underneath a gotdam canoe, but what bothered him the most was not knowin' what happened to his necktie. He chewed on that for a week.

And, I don't know, there's just something special about a muthafukka that's crazy in a certain way, and I suppose that certain way could best be described as him actually bein' a whole lot saner than most of these other ass'oles down here who, when they

---

The little town of Tchula and the even littler one of Ofogoula, because of their proximity, often combined activities. And so it was that their meager resources were joined when it was thought necessary to provide a solid, fundamental Christian education, for white boys and girls. I should add here that the hamlet of Ofogoula, now reduced to perhaps a single store and a few houses still standing is much like its namesake, the Ofogoula tribe of the lower Yazoo River, that was first mentioned in, or shortly after, 1699 by Iberville, who in fact did not actually see them. But in 1739 it was reported that the Ofogoula—or Ofo—had only "fourteen or fifteen warriors." Their language is not Muskogean, like the Choctaw and Chickasaw, but Siouxan. I am not a scholar like young Mr. Brainsong; the reader can know everything I know about the Ofogoula simply by reading about them in *Bulletin* #47 of the Bureau of American Ethnology..

ain't just wild as a peanut popsicle runnin' through a suburb in a seersucker suit, are plain-ass dumber than a gotdam bumper—and that's another story entirely.

But Mad is what a sumbich ought to be. In other words, he didn't have to have a dick to be a man, and you knew two seconds after you met him he wouldn never go back on his word and that there wuddn nothin' about him that wuddn what it seemed to be, unlike with a lot of them ass'ole big shots whose families come in here more'n a hunnuhd years ago with a buncha niggas and money already in their pockets, from North-ass-Carolina or some such shit as that. Fukkum. Especially their tweety-tweety gotdam sugar-mouthed, flitty-ass little Ole-Miss-Campus-Cutie-cunts they're married to. Lord God, don't get me started on these muthafukkettes; it'll make my blood pressure get all out of whack. But, mainly them coksukkas, the men as well as the women, is really nothing more'n a buncha gotdam mannerisms handed to em by their mamas and re-arranged by their papas, for business purposes.

GOALS AND OBJECTIVES
Lovers choose
To rise incandescent
Out of gravel,
To become as travelers
Bending space
Through desperation
And desire for time.
Their destination,
Created only by the journey,
Obeys no compass,
Holds no promise
Beyond that bright, uncharted spot
Upon a map of fire.

Anyway, I knew from the first that Mad was in for a pisspot of trouble when he took up with Money Scatters. A sumbich cannot keep hissef right side up bein' "in love" with a woman who spends all day playin' with other men's dicks. I don't care if it *is* just a "job"; it ain't gon' work. And that's the long and the short of it, no fukkin pun intended. Whatever that is.

Money was a nekkid dancer at the Magic Pussy Cabaret & Club up in Meffis, which is where Mad met her and lost his coksukkin mind. Well, he didn't lose it at first as much as he did later.

Money had been just a lillo girl from down around Tchula, south of Greenwood, who was good lookin' and smart as a cat o'nine-tails, and decided she'd come to Meffis to make her way in life as, at first she thought, a Meffis policewoman. She did what she had to do and got hersef into the po-leece academy, graduated at the top of her class, and became a law enforcement professional same as me. But not too long later, she changed course and adopted another, somewhat more comfortable, uniform.

They had put her on undercover duty at one of the big Meffis nekkid dancin' clubs, cause they thought she could blend in—she was just supposed to go inside with another cop, who was supposed to be her boyfriend, and she was just to sit there with him and drink soft drinks while the two of em observed the violations perpetratin' all around them—like the girls bein' buck nekkid and such and givin' lap dances on the couches in the so-called VIP Lounge, with nothing on in those instances more'n a G-string, which didn't really amount to much as far as actual clothes is concerned. Anyway, one day she come in to work at the precinct and handed over her badge and her gun, and though she didn't say why to none of her supervisors, she had done made up her mind she could do more for mankind in a G-string than she could with a pistol on her hip.

And that was how Money Scatters come to be one of *the top* nekkid attractions at the Magic Pussy Cabaret & Club.

HERE'S A DANCE FOR YOU, LORD BYRON
When the naked dancer
Steps upon the stage
And bathes herself in light,
She moves the way
The snake has taught her—
"She walks in Beauty,
Like the Night,"
Though
It's only four in the afternoon
In this throbbing,
Strobed and darkened,
Garden of Delight
Where
Midlife clerks, and other men
Of forty and beyond,
Follow her with eyes transfixed,
Like hopeful Magi,
Upon a hidden star
That, in the evening of their minds,
Burns hot
Just a hand or two below her navel
And leads them to believe
They will see the Gates of God
Which, in fact,
Her beauty holds enfolded,
In the shadows of her hips;
And, when she shows them
What they've come for,
They hear their names in whispers
In the softness of her fingers,
In the moisture of her lips.

They see more than they have dreamed
In their fluorescent halls of light,
Those offices and factories
Where life is out of sight;
Then,
Just when they are boys again,
That's when the music stops, and
Eden slips away.
The starlight's on the ceiling,
But, in the parking lot,
It's day.

At first I thought it was a good thing, and so did he—a lot of sumbiches down here has their favorite dancer they go see in the afternoons to get a quick hand job in the VIP Lounge or, for a few dollars more, upstairs in The Upper Room of the MPCC, in one nem big, half-eggshell-lookin' tiltawhirl love seats they got up there, where you can just about do anything you and the girl want to do, plus there's a bouncer watchin' the door of The Upper Room so if the cops come, as they do once in a while to give ever'body a ticket for *lewd*-ass behavior or some other bullshit, the bouncer can warn you to put your clothes on and hide your hooter and sit there like you was just passin' the time talkin'. 'Course the girl is there in nothin', at that point, but a G-string that just barely covers her little whoomadoodle, if that much, as I mentioned earlier.

All that's not unusual a bit, and it's quick and probably semi-safe and all that shit. Anyway, lots of muthafukkas are "regulars" for one nekkid dancer or another up there at the club. And you can bet don't nobody ever tell who they saw there, if you get my drift, cause just about all of em is married to somebody in the fukkin choir or the DAR or some such horse-shit as that. But some of course is single and divorced and everything, but bein' potbellied and ugly as a '39 Ford, the MP is all they got, dependin' on how you look at it.

So when Mad run up on Money one Tuesday afternoon, I didn't pay much attention to it. He got to goin' up there three or four times a week, and he seemed to be a lot happier overall than he normally had ever appeared to be.

And that began it. Mad liked to talk about love the way most men like to talk about huntin'. In other words, *all the fukkin time.* Which reminds me that whenever I see a photograph of Jesus and Moses and nem, and of course the Wise Men, I say to myse'f: "Must be duck season, cause the sumbiches all got beards."

That's because down here in Mhoon County, all these silly muthafukkas' wives will let em grow beards—but only durin' duck season! Then, after that, it's zippity clip, and off they comes, unless of course the po' bastuhd wants to live in a stump-hole, eat duck soup, and stay in the swamp the rest of his life, which, if you ast me, don't sound too fukkin ducky. That's a joke, gotdammit.

On the other hand, I know some of em it might suit just fine, but they ain't gon' do it, and that's because, when it comes to huntin', their wifes is the ones that calls the shots.

Sometimes it seems like a wife here in St. Leo might actually, somehow, be employed by a special secret corporation, one that has to be owned and operated by the state of Tennessee. And their job description—as official Delta wifes—wouldn't require but one thing: namely that they'd just have to drive back and forth to Meffis every single day of their lives. I'm tellin' you, just ast one-neez sumbiches, "Hey, muthafukka, where's your wife?" He won't bat an eye, but quick as a wink he'll answer you with: "She's in Meffis!"

I don't know. Maybe it has something to do with the notion that people want to be *from* the Delta but don't necessarily want to be *in* it. Hell, there ain't gon' be nothin' but niggas here no way. But then, of course, the niggas'll all finally move to the city, and then the white folks'll all move back to the fukkin country.

The thing I can't help but notice is that the white folks never minded livin' with the niggas as long as the niggas was useful to em and couldn't vote, but once that changed, seemed like everything in the whole fukkin world changed right along with it.

> PASSION
> An involuntary dash
> Into the darkness of beauty
> And the heart's old hunger
> For panthers in the morning,
> Why else would one
> Choose to be devoured?
> Love is not an ordinary feast
> But one that consumes the diner,
> A mixed metaphor at the captain's table.
> For there is sailing, too,
> Unseen upon a sea of edges
> Where the course is always
> Just between a depth and falling.
> Love is not a voyage for sensible explorers
> Or for temperate connoisseurs; and
> Passion is not a rational land.

Anyway, he, Mad, said one time he used to think of love as bein' something invisible floatin' around all over the fukkin place and that once in a while you'd run into it, like you would a jellyfish down on the Coast, and it'd get all over you and sting the shit out of you while you was floppin' around in the waves of passion and desire.

I knew then, if he was onto something, that I had done the right fukkin thing in stayin' away from it most of my life—well, actually, maybe all of it. The truth is I don't think I ever loved nobody no more'n a cat does when you pet it.

Mad had the idea that because the subject of "love" seemed so important in books and songs and movies and shit of that nature that "love," then, was somehow a major ingredient in the "recipe" of what he called the Existential Soup, whatever the fuk that is. I sure as shit ain't never ate none of it. Anyhow, I decided that even if I didn't understand something he said, whatever he said was o-fukkin-kay with me because he said it. I wouldn know "Existential Soup" from a gotdam extension cord, but of course that ain't the point. *The point is what you think of the muthafukka who said it.*

The first time Mad wanted to talk about love, I thought, oh, shit, here it comes: he's one of *them.* But that turned out not to be the case at all. Only I did feel funny about it, and it took me a while to get used to it.

Without beatin' around the bush—that's a joke—as far as I'm concerned, love is a pile of crap—I mean all the country songs is about love. Chr*EYE*st! It's always the same thing till it's comin' out your ass: Life ain't worth a shit, you're all-a-fukkin-lone, but don't worry, ass'ole, love is goin' to find your sorry self, and you'll be happy forever.

Everybody wants it. Everybody's lookin' for it. Except me of course, and I'da lot rather have me one nem flat-ass TVs and a semi-new Chevy Biloxi. Or even a 2000 Ford Mandingo with all-wheel-drive, a rhino guard, and some fog lights. That sumbich looks good in town, and it'll move like a muthafukka through mud.

I mean, what can a sumbich do with love? Not a gotdam thing except set around and googlewoogle at it, and worry about losin' it. So I say, fuk love—especially if a sumbich is tryin' to love the impossible, and that, basically, is what Mad's great-ass love affair with Money Scatters was goin' to be.

To Mad, love is both a science and a fukkin religion. He believes there *is* such a *thing* as love. I don't, as I have indicated many times. Far as I'm concerned, love is just like religion: plain old pure-dee *imagi-fukkin-nation.*

Money wuddn no trailer gal, nor no crackhead neither—nor no kinda low-life of no type whatsoever, the way most people might want to think of any of them girls that take their clothes off for a livin'. The fact is she come from some fairly well-off people. Her daddy owned a highly fukkin successful little factory that made nylon stockings. He made just one kinda stocking, but he had *two* boxes to put it in. One box was labeled Gorse & Hargrove, which was a fancy-ass department store up in Meffis, and the other box was labeled Dimes & Dingles that did a mail-order business all over the country. The stocking that went into the Gorse & Hargrove box sold for ten more dollars than the very same stocking in the box that went to the mail-order store. Same fukkin stockin'! Two boxes. He was a smart sumbich. From what I hear, all them Scatterses was.

Money sho was, like I said before, and probably the best-lookin' woman I have ever seen in my *en*-tire life. There wuddn really nothin' bad you could have said about her, unless of course you're one of them straight-laced religious sumbiches that think everything "nekkid" is a gotdam sin, which I don't, and neither did Mad.

But your head is one thing and your gizzard is another, and although Mad tried his best to believe her bein' in the sex business didn't bother him none, he was dead-ass wrong, cause it did—but what bothered him the most was that it bothered him in the first place. And he couldn't seem to get around it.

First of all when him and her finally told each other they loved each other, he said he'd done made up his mind to accept her way of life. And I said, "You mean like givin' blow jobs to salesmen in the afternoon?"

He had to think for a minute about that, before he come back with, "She doesn't actually do real sex; what she provides her customers is an illusion of sex. She's an artist."

And then Mad really got goin' and said "Junior Ray, love is composed of molecules formed from the atoms of un-named elements. Yet, for all of love's quantity of matter and energy, illusion is there also, as a blazing, but light, elastic barrier between reality and truth, and I am convinced that illusion is the very fabric of our existence. She's an artist."

THE ILLUSION
We go down into the lounge
Sit and chat a moment;
Then she rises to her feet
And stands in front of me.
Money takes her dress off
And lays it on the side
Of the comfort of the couch.
She removes her top. And
I am smiling at the beauty
Of her mouth.
From the silence of a second
Money comes to me; her hair
Falls forward to my face;
It has the lightness of an angel's
Sensuality of grace.
She is small and floats
Upon me like a wish;
I hold her in the sky of
My desire
While passion roves around me
Like a tiger made of fire.
I kiss her cheek

And tell her that I love her.
I caress her breasts; I smell her skin
And drink her breath
While room and sound and smoke
All fall down and away;
And she and I, there by love suspended,
Embrace upon the darkness,
Kiss among the silent stars and speeding dust,
Where forever is just a touch
And love is the end of time.

And I thought, "Uhn-huhn. I'm an *artist*, too, muthafukka." And I knew right then and there that sumbich was in trouble because he was missin' the most essential point. She *did* do real sex all over the VIP Lounge and especially upstairs in The Upper Room, and there wuddn no illusion to it.

But I guess illusions are pretty *major*-ly elastic or just don't have no limits at all because Mad and Money kept on bein' "a couple" for a good three years. And even durin' that time when one afternoon Mad come up to the Club just to say "Hi" to Money, he set there in the dark and still didn't see the light—he thought he could make her out, laid back on one nem couches in a section of the VIP Lounge, called the "Casual Corner," pettin' the manager's lillo yap dog, but what she was really doin' was lettin' a high roller that had come up from the casinos get between her legs . . . so he could lick her *you know what*.

There's something I need to bring up. I know you've been wonderin', but, yes, I do have a helluva memory, and if I hear something unusual, I can repeat it back to your ass fifteen years later, word for gotdam word. I don't always understand the words, but that ain't ever stopped me from knowin' what was said.

Mad really could see the whole thing through the dimness without actually knowin' what he was lookin' at, but I knew, because I was there, too, and he and I had been shootin' the shit right after he come in on up to the time he stood up and waved to her back in the back. Then he told me good-bye and went on into Midtown, there in Meffis, where he stopped by the grocery store to get some chocolate chip cookies for Money later, and then he went on to the little apartment him and her had over on Barksdale between Peabody and Union.

It took a lot to finally break em up. He could tolerate the phone calls from Money's "reg'lars" who wanted to know if she was goin' to be at work on such and such a day, and he could handle the sex acts on the main stage with her and another girl. And the dancin' nekkid in the little side cages with her swingin' her legs open and havin' the golfers stuff dollar bills between em didn appear to cause him what I would call undue concern, but one day . . . one night, actually . . . he couldn stand it no more.

> DANGER
> The plains of love
> Are filled with hunters in the grass.
> They clearly see the teeth and claws
> That wait within the softness of the green.
> But they are warriors
> Fed upon desire and do not shrink
> From serpents or from mythic risk.
> They are tarsiers in the garden,
> Ancestral lemurs armed
> With sharp and shining hearts
> Bulging in their genes.

SOME TIME AFTER HE finally saw the truth, in action, so to speak, he give me a phone call:

"Junior Ray," he said.

"What," I said.

"Junior Ray, I was wrong: Money does do real sex," he said.

I felt like sayin', "Duh-ruh, muthafukka, what the hell did you not understand about lap dancin' at the Magic Pussy Cabaret & Club?" But I didn't. I just flat didn't, and instead I said to him, "Mad, I didn't want to tell you way back yonder when you was thinkin' all these girls was doin' was just givin' out coksukkin illusions. A lot of em does just do that, but a lot of em don't and they provides the real thing but talks up the illusion that they don't."

What had happened was Money didn't show up at the apartment when she was supposed to, so he got worried and went out to the MP where he looked and looked and couldn't find her even though the manager and one or two of the other girls said she was still there. Anyway, he looked all around, and then, on the far side of the VIP Lounge, in the Casual Corner, he spied what looked to be a man slouched back on one of the couches with what Mad thought, there again, was that manager's dog up in his lap till he seen it wuddn no little dog at all but Money's head of hair that sumbich was pettin', bobbin' up and down on his thingamabob.

Mad told me he walked up and stood behind Money as she continued givin' the dude, who by that time was just lyin' there like a sack of meal with his eyes closed, a blow job, and that she kinda raised up, looked back over her shoulder at Mad, and said, "Hi, hon', I was just about to call you." Then, he further told me, she pointed to the man she was servicin' with her "illusion" and said, "This is Lambert. He's from Moorhead."

"That's right," said Lambert, out of one eye. "Moorhead, Mississippi. Where 'the Southern cross the Dog.'"*

---

* See earlier footnote in Chapter Two. See also: Memphis artist Carroll Cloar's painting entitled almost the same, i.e., "Where the Southern Cross the Yellow Dog."

That was it. Mad was already walkin' toward the door by the time he heard Lambert, who, I guess, was just about fully recovered, holler out after him: "Son, this lillo gal is the bes' in Meffis . . . I'm sho glad to meet you . . . You ought to be proud of her!"

> Ow!
> The moments of love
> Can burn the skin
> In fractions of a glance,
> A mere trajectory of
> Asymptotic touch,
> And in the act of parting.
> I cannot slide through the motions
> And must hide the panic in the rush
> Of all my falling blood.
> I am wild as sudden water;
> A bird that cannot light
> And has no feet for branches or for earth.
> I am in love;
> There is no joy,
> No help for me
> Or for
> The widow's boy.

Mad went back to the apartment and th'owed ever'thin' he owned in his car. And that included two lamps, a chair, and a small table. Then he doubled his stocky self into a small "c," got in the car and drove thirty-eight miles to St. Leo where he checked into the E..LUSIVE MOTEL there on the side of Highway 61, about three blocks—if you want to call em that—south of the Boll & Bloom Café, till, as he said to me later on, "I could decide what I was goin' to do and where I was goin' to go!"

The motel really wuddn named the E..LUSIVE Motel. Originally, when Mr. and Mrs. Wasserbaum—they was Jews of course and, naturally, had a store as well, downtown in St. Leo—anyway, when they opened up the little motel way back in the late fifties, it was called the Exclusive Motel, and the letters was up on a nice-lookin', lit-up sign. They was red on a blue background. And the bulbs didn't blink or nothin' like that. I used to think it was pretty fukkin tasteful. Later on, though, after a whole lifetime had done come and gone, some foreigners with a name longer than a gotdam Cath'lic funeral took it over. Then, one night, a car full of drunk pekkawoods from over in the Hills shot out the X and the C, and the foreigners never did have it fixed. So, since that time, I've just always called it what it says: the E..LUSIVE Motel.

Anyway, it was there at the E-fukkin-Lusive that Mad decided he was gon' go all the way down to Biloxi, on the fukkin GuffaMexico, to a place he said was at the "end of the earth," called Horn Island, where I, bygod—and I know you won't believe it—went to visit his ass. But I'll tell you all about that in a minute.

Mad called up the apartment the next morning, and Money answered the phone. He told her he couldn no longer love her no more and that he was leavin' and travelin' south. But, before he took off, she was down to St. Leo quick as a cat bite.

It didn't do no good. Mad had done made up his mind. He told her he never meant for her to ever not be true to herse'f but that, because of some kind of inner blindess on his part, *he* had failed at love, and there wuddn gon' be no goin' back.

But when he got inside his used green 1994 Lincoln Mark Seven and cranked up the engine, Money th'owed herse'f up on the hood and grabbed aholt of the windshield wipers, with one in each hand, and Mad eased on out of the parking lot with her splayed like that on top of the hood. He did not gun his motor or scratch off. Instead, Mad drove real slow, out of consideration for her situation—plus he didn't want neither one of em to be hurt no more'n they already were. And that's the way the two of em went down Highway 61, as far as the last turn-off to Jonestown, where Mad pulled off to the side of the road and set there without gettin' out or sayin' nothin'. Money Scatters got off the hood of the vehicle and, without never lookin' back, walked toward the office there at the Clarksdale Airport to find a phone, so she could get back to Meffis and, I guess, go on to work that evening at the Magic Pussy. Mad got back on Highway 61 and kept goin' till you couldn see his car no more.

Bear in mind, all that come to Mad after three years of what he called "explorin' the depth and substance of the multifold un-examined dimensions of love."

> Not True
> Monsters are
> Oddly absent
> In the middle
> Of the existential sea.
> We only fear
> That something dangerous
> Looks upward, hungrily,
> At our scissoring legs
> While we strain
> To chart the bottom
> Of a rising sky.

MAD OF COURSE WAS one of them kinda men that just don't ever seem to have his fist squarely up the ass of reality, but that is one of the things I liked about him. You could say that his nonsense made more sense in some ways than all the so-called common sense a lot of muthafukkas take so much pride in. Mad didn't have no common sense: He had UN-common sense. And that's exactly why he fell in love—though I always say "decided to fall in love"—with a Meffis nekkid dancer.

You have to understand, Mad had a theory. Hell, just about *every*thing he ever did have was a theory, but this one was this: True love was more likely to be found if you was loved by a so-called bad girl rather than by a so-called good girl, and that was, he had decided, because a so-called good girl couldn't really love nobody in actuality because she wouldna had no basis for comparison to nothin', if you're followin' what I'm sayin', but that a so-called BAD girl *was* able to love way beyond anything common opinion might allow for because of course bein' a bad girl and all, she had a whole passel of plus-and-minus sumbiches in her past—and present, too, I guess—she could sort through and size up by comparin' this muthafukka to another muthafukka; and *that*, theo-fukkin-retically of course, would finally guide her decision and enable her to choose the man of her dreams.

I could see the logic, natchaly; it's just that I wuddn too sure logic had anything to do with anything that made any sense, and that's one reason I ain't ever thought all that highly of logic in the first place. Fuk a buncha logic. I mean, just about any time something gets screwed up and don't turn out right, you can bet on one thing: logic is at the bottom of it.

Lord God, she was somethin', and she was destined to be Mad's temporary downfall. Money was just like those special women Mr. Brainsong loved to talk about when he'd tell that story about all them old-timey sumbiches in a boat tryin' to get back to their homes after that famous war, the one I mentioned in my first book—the war they named the rubbers after.

They, the women I'm talkin' about, was called the sireens, and Mr. Brainsong would say, "Junior Ray, those beautiful mythological creatures could," then he'd say, "I quote, 'sing your mind away!'"

Anyway, I reckon Mad was goin' to get *his* mind *danced* away. Money Scatters was a beautiful *Mempho*-logical creature.

> A NOD TO AARON COPLAND
> I like to dance
> The "Saturday Night Waltz"
> Deep down inside my skin
> I don't know where else
> Two step
> Or lambada dada
> Chacha cha.

He tried gettin' help at one point, before him and Money really took up together in their little apartment. Mad went one day a week to a church with a group of folks who were more or less in the same fix as he was, all upset about love, either because they had too much of it or else they wanted different kinds of it. Anyway, he said he didn't go no more after some sumbich got up and claimed he wuddn goin' to have no sex at all unless he had a "committed relationship," whatever the fuk that is, and that he wuddn goin' to do no more masturbation neither. And Mad said, "Junior Ray, that did it for me. Everybody was focused on the wrong thing and not on love itself." Personally, all I could think about was that if that muthafukka that stood up in the meetin' vowed he wuddn even gon' doodle his woodle, that was like turnin' your back on the one you loved the most.

But, anyway, I'll explain what Mad was talkin' about. Those dikheds at the meetin' was all boogered up about *not loving*, and Mad wanted to get a handle on how to do the lovin', the invisible part, not just with your dick and such. I'm just tellin' you what he told me. All of it is a yard or two above my head, but I can more or less get the idea of what he was after. And, even if I think it's crazier'n a geek in a carnival bitin' off chicken heads, I see the point—which is: *Don't just do shit every other common ordinary sumbich does.* Anyway, it wuddn long before Money was bringin' home on an average of around two thousand dollars a week, and that was really just from about four hours a day, four days a week, "payin' out days," workin' mostly in the afternoon, lapdancin' with her platoon of regulars and high-rollers, who come up from the casinos, down in Mhoon County, south of Meffis. Them high-rollers was like celebrities, and they more or less flew back and forth all the time among the casino capitals of America.

Money wuddn just beautiful. A lot of em was that. But she had something in her that must be older'n even creation itse'f, and whatever it was or is, she slid it right inside your eyeballs and down into your britches-balls. I'm tellin' you Money had a skill that ain't got no name and can't be taught or learnt. It's what all men want and don't know what to call it, and if they could have it all the time, they wouldn never go nowhere nor do a gotdam thing.

You have to understand, too, that the goin' rate at the time was something like fifty dollars every twenty or thirty minutes and that she was constantly snaggin' those men and carryin' em on back into the VIP Lounge, or upstairs, instead of settin' around like a lot of them girls, playin' solitaire on the computer and shootin' the shit with other girls about other girls. Money called them kind the Titty Commission.

The cash a girl made from actual dancin', nekkid, of course, on the main stage and in them little cages around it, off to the side, wuddn nothin'. The big bucks all come from her lapdancin' talent and skills. And ever' bit of it was profit, too, except she had to tip the bartender, tip the manager, and tip the bouncer at the door who walked her to her car when she got off work—and of course she had to do her "pay-out" to the club. "Pay-out/days" was only about thirty-five dollars; whereas "pay-out/nights" was fifty—and "mornings" was the cheapest of all. Money, however, mostly stuck to "days."

COURSE I THOUGHT MAD was always silly-headed when it come to love and google-moosh like that. If you ast me, he was just too serious about nothin'. I mean, you couldn't go a whole day huntin' rabbits with him without he'd be wonderin' what life and all that crap meant. I tol' his ass it didn't mean shit and to try to just concentrate on huntin' rabbits, but, oh, hell no, there weren't no stoppin' him until finally he'd be wonderin' further if it was right for us to be killin' them rabbits, so a lot of times I'd say, "Gotdammit, Mad! Gimme them things!" And I'd grab his rabbits and take em home and eat em myse'f.

But I liked him anyhow. I liked Mad a lot.

Anyway, there are some things sometimes a man thinks he's doin', but the real story is that it's the "things" that's doin' him. And that's how it was when Mad started goin' up to the Magic Pussy.

An awful lot of people turns up their noses at the idea of havin' clubs like the MP anywhere in the local area. Even some of these golfers that go there look down on the girls and call em trash, while they, them fat-ass, Sansabelt-wearin' muthafukkas, are slobberin' all over they cigars and th'owin' dollar bills at the girls, you know, stickin' em tween their tits, and fittin' em in their clits—well, gotdammit, you know what I mean!

That blows my beefalo. I just can't figure it. How can a sumbich look down on somebody that's makin' em happy? That's why I have come to believe all along: Not only are them coksukkas ass'oles, but they're not worth a sack fulla mule fruit as golfers. It's one thing to be your standard, ordinary ass'ole, but it's sumpn else to have a mean-ass heart as well.

Don't get me wrong. Mean is okay. Ain't nobody meaner'n I am. But meanness—in any way whatsoever—toward nekkid women is the lowest form of *in*human feelin' there is—especially if you got a bottle of beer in one hand, a fist full of paper money in the other, and a toesukkkin grin on your face. I ain't got no time for that—nor for any sumbich that does it.

WHEN YOU COME OUT of the parking lot and go inside the MP, it's like you ain't on Earth no more, and where you are is all there is or ever was. I'm not goin' to say I can't explain it, because *I can*. Any sumbich with one ball and half a dick for a brain can figure it out.

First of all, as a mammal, you are surrounded by a huge-ass dream, which, for a mammal is largely what you're always after at any given moment—just like it was when I was runnin' around after Leland Shaw wantn an opportunity to shoot him. If you're a *human* mammal, then it's like you've been wanderin', lost and searchin', in the fukkin woods, and then, blap, there you are in the middle of Pussy Paradise with all the tits you ever wanted to touch and all the poo-la-lah you ever wanted to look at, right there, all for you, and you didn't have to have eight hunnuhd million dollars and one nem little-bitty jet airplanes to get it.

Plus, once you're in there, there's no bills to pay, no taxes, no car notes, and not even no *pussy-ian* obligations of any kind; there's just you and the rhythm of the dark and the flash of snatches in the spotlights. And, it duddn matter if you're an ugly, fart-infested, green-toothed shit-head. So, hell, I'm for it. As far as I'm concerned, the Magic Pussy could put every psy-fukkin-chiatrist in the world slap out of business. I mean, when's the last time one of those diklikkers ever handed some sufferin' sumbich a *prescription* for a beautiful nekkid girl he could go up to the drug store, whip out his Medicare card, and pick up?

Never, that's when. Yet, that's really all any sorry-ass sumbich would need to lift his ass out of the ditch and get him over the blues. Listen, all you have to do is *touch* a pussy. It's like a shot of B12. And it's so fukkin simple. But, oh hell, no; them experts ain't lettin' you off that easy. They *know*, of course. *They know.* But they ain't tellin', and that's the shame of it.

Course if they'd just send every one of their depressed men to the Magic Pussy and say, "Listen, sumbich, you gon' *become a regular*, or your ass is gon' die," they wouldn need no more pills, and the po' sumbiches'd all be well as a muthafukka quicker'n you can flip your dick. Providin' you got one, of course.

THE THING ABOUT MONEY was she really liked the sex business, but that in itself didn't really bother Mad, because he liked it, too; however, he did not understand at all the full extent of Money's involvement in it, until one day of course he did. Overall, Mad was kind of innocent. Nevertheless, sex was the main focal point of his and Money's bein' together.

Once in a while some things would happen, like the time he took Money down to Pass Christian to visit his first cousin who was livin' down there and married to a big-time undertaker who was an ex-Alabama halfback, named "Killer," who'd in fact made a fukkin killin' in the funeral business—especially when the meningitis epidemic hit the big navy base down there at Buena Vista Bay. Mad's cousin said the numbers of dead sailors was un-fukkin-believable and Killer got to handle every one of em. She said it put him in such a good mood, she thought there might be somethin' wrong with him.

Anyway, what happened was that Mad's cousin—Annie was her name—she got Mad and Money a room in the Saint Stanislaus Motel, and everything went fine until after him and Money left and went back to Meffis. They had brought along some of their sex equipment with em when they went down there, and they left a nine-inch rubber dick under the covers at the foot of the bed, and it was found later the morning they checked out by the Mexican maid who took the fukkin thing to the office and gave it to the dumb-ass clerk who saw that Mad's first cousin, Annie Stone, had made the reservation, so he put the dick in one nem yellow envelops and told the nigga maintenance man to run it over to Annie and "Killer's" big house overlookin' the beach, cause he felt like that was the thoughtful thing to do and also believed it was always good public relations to return any kind of shit that people left in their rooms. Mad's cousin and her very square-ass husband, the "Killer," nearly had a gi-ass-gantic, double-fukkin cerebral hemorrhoid when they seen what was in the envelope.

They phoned up Mad, and he told me he told them he and Money didn't know nothin' about no rubber dick but that it was pretty fukkin inter-resting they should mention it because he had felt something funny that last night they was there, down at the end of the bed; only he'd just thought it was Money's big foot. That explanation smoothed out the whole thing, that was the end of it. But they was a lot carefuller after that and always made a list.

Mad said the "Killer" made the maintenance nigga carry the dick back to the clerk, who got upset and phoned up Annie who hung up on his ass, so he ast the Mexican maid if she wanted it, she said "Si" she did because the "Gringo burrito" would come in handy for her sister Lupe who lived in Bay St. Louis and who had just broken up with her boyfriend, and the motel maid said she believed that possibly the unclaimed rubber dick might well have been left in the bed as a gift for her sister from the Virgin Mary so that it could help, perhaps in a large way, to replace some of Lupe's loss. I just thought, "Got-da-um."

YOU MIGHT LIKE TO know this. Them college girls up in Meffis is sumpn else—and office-workin' girls are, too. Here's the way it is: The word is out—if you've got bills to pay and need some fast cash, go dance at the MP. See, a lot of them girls has had years of dance lessons and gymnastic stuff, so they're limber as a willow switch, especially when they ain't go no clothes on. I forgot to include housewives, them that's gettin' their husbands through the Podiatrist College and some whose husbands are way off outchonda drivin' a truck.

You got a tremendous selection up there at the MP. And that's just one of the reasons it's so popular with the golfers, and as you know, that's what I call em, the golfers, because you go in there and you won't find no trashy sumbiches standin' around. All of em is in there lookin' good in their eyezod shirts and their gold neck chains. Yet some of those fukkas actually are golfers, because whenever there's a big tournament in Meffis, real golfers come from everywhere and you can see em all over the place. But, son, when the sportin' day is over and the last swing is swung, and the sun goes down, the Magic Pussy is the hole they all want to put their balls in.

Course you got your Ole Miss college boys who love to come in there, too. They're generally just in shorts and a baseball cap turned around backwards. I don't know, maybe they're all catchers on the Rebels' team. Plus, from time to time, there seem to be a good many UT Dental students settin' around, checkin out some of the oral activity. Anyway, it ain't unusual to see all three of them categories in the Magic Pussy Cabaret & Club, wavin' dollars in the air, wild as a buncha Babylonians, and crowded butt to belly around the center stage like catfish gobblin' up Purina, watchin' two of the most gorgeous fukkin girls you'll ever see in your gotdam life nekkid as jaybirds, chompin' down on each other's shaved pussy like there wuddn nobody else in the room; and money is pilin' up beside em, and over em and under em, th'own in there by all them horny muthafukkas strainin' to get a look.

Then, the next day, them coksukkas'll go be golfers again, the

Ole Miss boys'll sleep late and drive on back to Oxford, the dental students'll look for wisdom in a tooth, and things will all get back to abnormal, which is what I think everyday life is anyhow.

That's probably what Moses didn't understand when he come down off that mountain and found all the Hebrews jumpin' and singin' and dancin' around that gold cow—you know the story, it's in the fukkin Bible—but Moses just didn't get the picture. He thought the Hebrews ought to be behavin' theysefs, doin' a lot of quiet stuff, prayin' and weavin' and findin' lost lambs and all such borin'-ass shit as that. And he thought they were actin' awful and were sinful and shouldn't be jumpin' around the gold cow, whoopin' and hollerin' and havin' a good time. And that's where he fukked up. What the Children of Israel was doin' was normal; they was doin' what human beings were meant to do, and the other way is really the true picture of Hell, which ain't full of sin at all, not one bit, and that of course is why it's called Hell.

I just can't say enough good things about the Magic Pussy. If it was a church, I'd be a preacher.

CHAPTER 9

A Survey — Mysterious Hot-Tamales — The Sportsmen's League
— Lapdance — Little Petunia! — Dyna Flo Sins — Mad Fails
at Love — Horn Island — The Importance of Sand — Mad's
Letter — Trip-Dik, Pussy for Men & The Clit-Mit

The only other woman I ever knowed named Money was a lady professor over at Ole Miss, Dr. Money Burns. She was a doctor of some kind of "ology" which I was never quite clear on, but it had something to do with one nem surveys you hear about, and in this case it was one about the South and about the muthafukkas who live in it. Plus, she was in a wheelchair.

Somebody had done give her my name, I guess, because of the first book and all. Anyhow, she called up on the phone and asked if she could talk to me and if I could come over to where she was, and I told her all that would be fine, so I drove over to Oxford and went to her office, where she and me talked for a long-ass time about everything there was to talk about, pertainin' to the South, of course.

It was something. I found out I knew stuff I didn't even know about till she asked me. That's the thing, I guess, about them surveys: They show you where the ketchup is on the shelf, and you was lookin' straight at it all the time but couldn't see it—till some sumbich comes up, points to it, and says, "Is that it?"

I liked her a lot—maybe it was because she was in a wheelchair and that made me think she'd done more with her life than a whole lot of muthafukkas I could name. I don't know. But I liked her, and I could tell she liked me, and, as you are aware, that's the whole trot line as far as I'm concerned. How many gotdam times do I have to say it: If a sumbich likes me, I like him!—or, in this case, her. It's the same as what those old philosophers all said, accordin' to Mad, way back in there, somewhere, around Bible times: "Ain't nothin' complicated once you understand how you'd like it to be."

Anyway, when I was fixin' to leave, she looked me square in the eye and said, "Junior Ray, do you like being a Southerner?"

And I answered, "Yes'm, I do, but an awful lot of people might tell you it's me and what I come from that's wrong with the South."

Then, quicker'n you could say Jack Robinson, she come back with, "You're not what's wrong with the South, Junior Ray: The South is what's wrong with you."

I come close to cryin', because I suppose I was so glad to hear her say it. It bout knocked me down. And that surprised me. But there again, that's the way it is with them surveys. Normally don't much bother me, but I have to tell you I have always felt the difference between me and those big shot planters was that the only field most of them sumbiches ever drug their ass across on a hot day is the golf course at the Meffis Country Club, and that little one down there at Clarksdale, too. And, as you know, both those places is made out of cotton. Fukkum.

DON'T MOVE, SUMBICH. IF you're hungry, when we get through talkin', we'll go load up on some of what I call muthafukka-yew-don't-wanta-know-hot-tamales: You just go to any fair-size broke-dick town in the Mississippi Delta, find the nigga there who makes the tamales, and you're on the road to some good eatin'. Get one nem big-ass metal popcorn containers full of em. Also, don't, for no reason, buy no hot tamales from a gotdam Mexican. They ain't as good as the real ones you'll find in the Delta. And don't attempt to make em yourse'f. You can't, and if you try, you'll fukkum up. Plus, unless you're a certified hot-tamale nigga, it's against the gotdam law.

Shoot, I used to go up to the MP off and on all the time, even after I had done took up with that woman over at Sledge. She was okay and all, but sometimes, like I said in my first book, I'd be afraid she was gon' crush my ass when she got on top of me, because, for one thing, she's a big woman, and for another, she moves like fukkin zippidy-doodah, and frankly that sometimes scares the woohaw outta me. So it's a real treat to sit up yonder in Meffis at the Magic Pussy, back in the dark with a teeny nekkid twenty-two-year-old nursing student straddlin' your lap while you got both hands on the prettiest pair of tits this side of Arkansas, and she's done grabbed onto your cock like she thinks that's the best thing she's thought of all day—that makes a muthafukka feel gotdam near forty-five again. Hell, I'mo keep doin' it even if I get so fukkin old I have to hire that worthless nigga, Ezell, to take me there in that ratty-ass taxi of his. That's right! Yeah, you got it . . . the gotdam Ohzeemoh.

For one thing I have discovered I am different in a lot of ways from these old whistle-poots around here I'm talkin' about. For-fukkin-instance, I don't want to go to no coksukkin deer camp and set around with a bunch of ugly-ass nosepickers all wrapped up in canvas coats and britches drinkin' whiskey and playin' gotdam poker. Fuk that shit. I want to keep on doin' what I'm doin' and that's goin' up to Meffis to the MP about three times a week. I'm gettin' to know all them girls and even some of them bouncers and managers and such. I even know the sumbich who owns it. Naturally, I do not tell him that I am in law enforcement—well, more or less, as you know I work security at one of the casinos, The Lucky Pair-O-Dice . . . which, naturally, I prefer to leave nameless. Not that I think any of them ass'oles I work for reads books, but you never know.

Anyway, I got invited by the Mhoon County Sportsman's League to go deer huntin' out across the levee and stay the weekend in the camp. In the first fukkin place if any of them muthafukkas is a sportsman, I am a Chinese-lady-cropduster. Hell, most of em is so fat they has to wear penny-loafers cause they can't bend down to tie their shoelaces.

Lord God, there was a day when I'da ate that up, but the glamour of hangin' out at the deer camp done wore off a long fukkin time ago, mainly cause I could see what was happenin' to those old farts. Just about all of em had give up on women, and all they wanted to do was sit around inside a over-heated tarpaper shack, drink, gamble, and call theyse'fs hunters. Fuk that noise. The only thing those fat-ass old buttheads have hunted for lately—and can't find—is their dicks when they go to piss, and I spect most of em wind up empty-handed. Their stomachs is so stuck out they ain't seen their own toes in forty years.

I had a gotdam spiritual awakenin'. That don't mean I seen Jesus out on Highway 61, but here's what happened to me: It was like all of a sudden I had a fukkin vision, and I saw them, and I saw me, and I was one of *them*, and I hollered, "Not today, muthafukka! I ain't like you coksukkas! I ain't some old bloata-belly that's give up on life—no sir, I said, in the vision, of course—no sir—you sumbiches can take every buck in these woods and stick em up your wo'-out, cigar-suckin', smoke-ring-blowin' you-know-whats, and then, in the vision of course, I added a final *muthafukka*. Why, I thought, would a grown man, or even one that wuddn, think more about gettin' his hands on some dumb, big-eyed, hunnuhd-dollar, half-ass goat than he would about the real, sho-nuff little "dears" up in Meffis at the Magic Pussy? It didn't make no sense.

I didn't know what that meant at the time, but I started thinkin' about it, and I realized I had to make some mighty big changes. For one thing I wuddn gonna keep just comin' home and watchin' TV and then spendin' the weekends, mostly, over there near Sledge with Dyna Flo McKeever, eatin' my balls off and fallin' asleep most of the time. Shit. I seen the fukkin light. And I saw how death comes without knockin' on the door and just lays down on the sofa beside you. And then after a hunnuhd thousand bags of Cheetohs and no tellin' how many cases of beer and buckets of chicken, your ass is planted outside of town in Oak Wood Cemetery.

I don't know. And right here I am tempted to ask what's it all mean, but the truth is I don't care about that. I just like what I'm doin' while I'm doin' it. And here's the deal: The Magic Pussy Caberet & Club is like dope. A muthafukka can get hooked on it because goin' there gives him something ordinary daily life cannot provide. And that's the feelin' that he can have it all, that somehow there is a point to ever'thing—and of course that's pussy.

That's it. And, look'a here: An old, ugly sumbich like me can come into that dark room in the afternoons and have young beautiful women come up to him and want to tweek his dick just like he was Clark Gable or Lash LaRue or something.

I mean, ten-four *this*, muthafukka: I wuddn about to get me one nem blow-up dolls, nor start keepin' a stack of magazines around, and I damn sho ain't buyin' one nem sponge-rubber, good-as-the-real-fukkin-thing, fake foam-rubber pussies they sell up yonder in Meffis at the Adult Super-*Teek*. Voyd had been tryin' to persuade me to get one, but I said, "Fukkew, Voyd, I ain't gon' get caught dead with my dick on one nem things, besides which, the last time I looked, all they had was black."

And he said, "Well, at least it won't talk back to your ass." I started to tell the sumbich them days was over, more or less, but I let it go.

"But," he went on, "You wouldn have to do all that drivin' over to Sledge all the time."

Fuk that, I thought. Distance wuddn really what bothered me, but destination did. I didn't mind the drivin'; the question about any kind of drivin' was what I'd be drivin' *to*. And that's when I realized the Magic Pussy Cabaret & Club . . . was for me.

And, yes, it can have a down side. Shitchyeah. I was up there at the MP one Saturday night when the golfers were so fukkin thick you couldn't stir the muthafukkas with a stick.

So there I was, in the smoke and the gotdam music and the crowd of men—and some of their girlfriends and wives—and the nekkid dancers, on the stage, and semi-nekkid girls prancin' around all over the place, movin' all through the gang of good ol' boys, lookin' for some sumbich to take back in the VIP Lounge and give him a lap dance.

And that's what I was lookin' for, too. So while I'm strainin' with the best of the golfers and the college boys to see the two buck-nekkid blondes up on the stage, some cute lillo thing come up behind me and reached around and grabbed me by the balls and whispered some of the gotdamdest shit in my ear you ever heard some sumbich lie to you about, so I, without, still, payin' no whole lot of attention to her, let her haul me off into the back where I plunked down in the dark on the couch, and she commenced to take off everything she had on except for her teeny-ass little G-string.

Then she stood up on the couch, straddlin' my legs, reached down with one hand and pulled that G-string way over to the side, and th'owed the cutest little pussy I ever saw—and I've seen a lot of em since I started goin' up to the MP—right smack in my face. Anyway, I flicked out my tongue like I was a big old lizard and just ever so softly licked her lillo whatchamacallit, you know, the love-button thing; then I raised my head and looked up at her, eyeball to eyeball, and she was standin' right there smack-ass over me, lookin' straight down into mine, and she said, "UNCLE JUNIOR!"

And I hollered back, "LITTLE PETUNIA!"

It was one of Voyd and Sunflower's granddaughters. So I said, "Gotdam, Little Petunia, what the fuk are you doin' up here!"

And, smartmouthed just like her grandmamma, she said, "I'm

givin' you a lap dance, you old dumb sunnavabitch. What the fuk are YOU doin' up *here?*"

"I come up here to get a lap dance," I told her, "but I didn't know it was gonna be from you."

And she come back with, "Well, then, I guess you could say this is just your lucky fukkin day."

And, bygod, it was.

> TEMPUS EDAX RERUM*
> Old Age
> Renders us
> To Glue,
> Unusable,
> To blobs
> And gobbets of goo
> Or to bones
> Whose joints
> Do not articulate
> The whatness of our was;
> Borne down by time
> In the crush of smelly rooms
> All alone and shouting about
> Some unremembered nightmare,
> We'll be units of disposable income
> Strapped in special chairs,
> Floppy and flat as empty shoes
> At the bottom of the stairs.

AFTER THAT I WAS a lot more careful and paid closer attention to

---

* "Time Eats Up Everything"—Mad made a "D" in Latin at Mhoon County High School. He did better later. He got the Latin motto, here, from a dictionary of foreign phrases.

what was on my lap. Little Petunia never said nothin' to nobody, and I sure as shit didn't. I mean it wuddn cause I was scared of Voyd. I could beat the crap out that little shitass any fukkin day in the week, but I didn't want to have to listen to Sunflower go on about it and get gotdam in-fukkin-dignant or something.

Plus, I mighta wanted to do it again sometime, so I didn't want to tear my jeans with Little Petunia. She wuddn really my niece, but she was a helluva lillo gal—smart as a crabapple switch and a sense of humor dry as a popcorn fart. She told me she was goin' to finish nursin' school but that right now, she liked what she was doin' and was makin' a lot of money at it, and unlike the majority of them girls, she was puttin' hers away, payin' her taxes, and learnin' about the stock market.

I never did know nothin' about that. I didn't understand it when I was young, and I don't know now, and I don't give a dog fart one way or another. As long as I got money in my pocket, I'm happy. And with my social security, plus my retirement from the county, and the little tad I make ever' week workin' guard duty in the parking lot up at the Lucky Pair-O-Dice Casino & Music Hall, which is over there between Hot Slots and the Temple of Fortune, both of which is slap up next to—and really part of—the biggest hotel in Mississippi, the Nebuchadnezzar, which is also the tallest building in the whole state, anyway, with all that comin' in, I'm in high cotton. Son!

But ir-regardless of anything else in this world, the Magic Pussy saved my life.

BEAR IN MIND, MEFFIS is different from other places, even New Or'lins, if you can believe that. I ain't been there but once, on account of Mad, and them clubs I went to wuddn worth a shit, kind of like bobakew in other areas when you're from Meffis and order it, say, in Nashville or Jackson; it not only ain't the same, it ain't bobakew.

Anyway, it ain't nowhere near as good, and the muthafukkas who sell it in those places oughta be prevented by the federal government from even tryin' to serve it. That's the way the nekkid clubs was in New Or'lins, like a flashy car with no fukkin gas.

But I got to stop here and tell you something I ain't gon' get too far into right now. You know that woman over near Sledge? . . . Well, she ast me to bring her ass up with me to Meffis not too long ago because she said she wanted to see what one nem nekkid dancin' places was like, and I told her if she could stop talkin' about Jesus for half a fukkin second, I would take her to the one I knew the most about, which was the Magic Pussy, So I did.

We walked in one Saturday night about eleven thirty. The place was stacked as usual with golfers and cowboys and high rollers and Ole Miss fraternity boys; and right smack in the middle of the room on the big stage, and just like you'd expect, there they were: two good-lookin' what I call aerobic instructors, chompin' away at each other's shiny little shaved coochies.

I thought Dyna Flo was gon' pee in her pants-suit. We sat down at a table some sumbich had just left to go have a "dance" in the back room with a Chinese girl, named Jasmine—hell, all them Chinese girls are named Jasmine—while me and Dyna Flo watched the two aerobic instructors continue to do their thing in, by then, a gotdam chef salad of dollar bills, and I noticed Dyna Flo was settin' there in her chair, still as an over-cautious squirrel, lookin' at the two good-looking' girls on the stage with the lids of her eyes not quite closed, and her left hand—she was left-handed—was down in her britches playing with her you-know-what.

Anyway, I leaned over and whispered in her ear that if she wanted to be with one nem girls, I could get her one, and she said she did, so I seen one I knew, named Adena, on the other side of the room, and I went over and brought her back to where we was settin'.

The long and the short of it is that we all three went back into

the VIP Lounge and stayed a pretty long time, and I could tell
Dyna Flo was havin' the time of her life, doin' almost but not quite
the same kind of stuff she had seen goin' on up on the stage. And
when we finally left and headed back toward Mississippi Highway
3 to drive back to Sledge, she didn't say nothin' till we crossed the
Mississippi line, and then she turned to me and said, "I'm ready
to get back to Jesus now." And she did.

"*MOOEY BONE EATER*," I had said to one of the girls, because it
looked like she was some kind of a Mexican. And I didn't want
her to think I was like all them other ignernt sumbiches in a golf
shirt and a pair of elastic-ass britches settin' there around that little
round, off-to-the-side stage, lookin' up between her legs and stickin'
dollar bills in her you-know-what.

    For the first time, I was inside the Magic Pussy, up in Meffis, on
a Sunday afternoon in the merry-ass month of whatever the fuk it
was, and here was the sweetest most beautiful thing you ever seen
in your gotdam life, standin' in front of me without much more'n
a stitch on, and gettin' ready to take that off, sayin', "Are you ready
for a two-for-one? I'll show you a good time." She meant, of course,
for forty fukkin dollars we could go off into the VIP Lounge to one
nem soft-ass di-vans back in the dark, where she would jump up
and settle herself down on my thang and straddle that sukka and
rub that no-tellin'-how-gorgeous little thingamawooba of hers all
over the front of my Meffis casual slacks for two whole long-ass
songs, if you could call em that.

    Plus, as you know, it also meant she might agree to a lot more,
and that's partly the reason the place was packed with golfers almost
ever' night. That's why, later, when I got to be a regular, I liked to
go there durin' the afternoons and on other off-times when there
wuddn as much of a crowd all up in there. It was kind of like it is
sometimes when you get to have a whole movie thee-ater near bout

all to yourself, if you know what I mean. It's real comf'table.

But here's how the whole thing began. It started on a Sunday. I had just got home from church—which I'd gone to just as a favor to a friend of mine whose twins was both gettin' awarded another rung on one of them Sunday school medals they gives out that has a ladder hangin' down off it longer than a night in jail, and for some reason, I just couldn relax.

That sorry-ass excuse for a preacher had laid it on thick about what a sinner everybody was and how we was all goin' to hell if all of us didn't repent, and I was spittin'-ass mad if you know what I mean. I don't have no intention of repentin' a gotdam thing—whatever of it I can recall—my only regret is that I don't get to go out and do ever' bit of that shit I all over again, plus a lot more, whatever the fuk it might be. Hell, I'd help all the jaybirds carry sand to the Devil on Fridays. It wouldn't bother me none.

Needless to say I was pretty restless, so I said, "Bygod, I'mo drive up to Meffis and go to one nem joints Mad Owens was talkin' about—especially the one he said was the tip-top best of em where the girls all dance buck-ass nekkid. Mad said a lot of em was workin' their way through school up there at one nem colleges or another and that they was, ever' one of em, real good-lookin', specially the nursing students, particularly without no uniforms—although, for some reason, I'd sorta like to see em keep on them capes they sometimes wear, and the little hats, too. That'd be sumpn.

So I decided to go. I remember when I was in Mhoon County Consolidated I always wanted to see them high school girls nekkid, and I never did get to, so I figured now was my chance to catch em on the college level.

Now that I've been there and am somewhat of a regular, you might say, I can tell you all about it. Bygod it was the damndest experience I ever had in my *en*-tire life, and that's why I decided to write part of this book about it—but, maybe more, about Mad.

The Magic Pussy had a neon sign out front that had a huge-ass purple cat on it that appeared and then disappeared in a gotdam shower of bright sparkly dust, what I call *fart* colors, all of which was part of the neon, of course. You can't miss it after dark, or even in the afternoon for that matter, and little did I realize what I was goin' to see when I got there, that first time.

I calls em fart colors because one of Voyd's other wild-ass grandchillun, Nasturtia, was goin' to the Junior College over in the Hills; she was takin' art, and she had a buncha paint supplies that included those same colors I'm talkin' about in a box that said it had come from the Dept. of F. Art. So, ever fukkin there-gotdam-after, I called em *fart* colors.

First, though, I stopped off at the fried chicken place on the south side of Meffis. It's in a bad-ass part of town, nothin' but niggas of course, so, you know, if I had'na been around em all my life like I have, I woulda been too fukkin scared to go in, but once you know em, well, bein' around em is just second nature. You just got to know em, that's all. Or, at least, think you do.

Anyway, I have to admit I had third and fourth thoughts about goin' in there, but I found myself pullin' into the ratty-ass parkin' lot and gettin' out of the car. And I 'member I was thinkin', "Damn, Junior Ray! You stupid sumbich." Neverthe-fukkin-less, I walked on over to the door of the place and grabbed the knob.

I pulled the door open, and a whole room-full of black faces turned and looked straight at me. I was about to haul ass when one nem big blue-gum muthafukkas way in the back of the room stood up, put his gotdam hands on his hips, give me one nem uppity-ass looks and said: "Hey, Junior Ray." Then another one of em piped up, "Come on in, you mean ol' white boy, lemme buy you a beer and a basket!"

It was that no good sumbich Ezell and his buddy, Sweet-tooth; plus, it looked to me like, half the gotdam male black population of Mhoon County, and Coahoma and Quitman counties, too, all settin' in there grinnin', eatin' their ass off and drinkin' beer—and every fukkin one of em, like me, was goin' to the nekkid joints—they, of course to theirs over on Brooks Road and me to what was gon' become *mine* out near the Mall and that big holy-roller church that looks like a gotdam orange squeezer.

Later I was to find out that there was some serious foodlin' and doodlin' goin' on over at their places, the major one of which is called, natchaly, the Booty Shop, whereas there was supposed to be only play-fukkin and an occasional handjob happenin' at the Magic Pussy—and also over at the number-two place, a fairly high-class joint near the Mississippi line called the Cuntry Club. But, as you know, *supposed* ain't always what *is*.

I have to say this real quick about Ezell. The truth is, worthless as he is, I have always liked him and, in some ways, more'n most other triflin' sumbiches, in one particular respect: He understands how gotdam incompre-fukkin-hensible it is to be devalued just because of how you was born, and by that I mean one time way back I was just settin' in the sheriff's office, and Ezell come in the side door with his stripedy britches on and loud-ass shirt he liked to wear when he'd go uptown to get the mail, which was only a fukkin block away, and when he come over where I was settin', readin' Lil' Abner, in the Meffis *Commercial Appeal,* he laid the mail on my desk and said, "You know, I ain't complainin' bout nothin', but I was just thinkin'—white people seem to love everything about us black muthafukkas except actually *us* . . . they can't dance unless they got a black band; they can't eat unless they got a black cook and a plate full of black food; they can't have no babies less'n they got a black-ass nurse; and they can't get upset about nothin' unless they got a nigga to blame it on, so why is it, Mista Junior, that white folks can't seem to live nor breathe without us niggas yet don't want nothin' to do with us at the same time?"

I just looked up at him and said: "I know what you're talkin'
about, Ezell; most of the coksukkas I got a bone to pick with is
white too. Fukkum." The sumbich was about half-way cross the
room by that time. I looked over at him; he looked back at me,
said, "Yassuh," and went on out where the patrol car was parked
to spend the rest of the day sleepin' in a chair he kept propped
up under one nem big ol' white oaks on the north side of the
courthouse, in front of the jail. And after that, that whole day, I
didn't have the heart to give him no "duties," unless of course he'da
wanted me to so he could go uptown to the City Drug where he
liked to get him a Baby Ruth and drink him a fountain Coke . . .
in a paper cup, natchaly.

Now A LOT OF people think the Magic Pussy is owned by a bunch
of Eye-talian muthafukkas. It is, but not entirely. What they don't
know is that it is partly owned by one of their own: Little Quitman
Tait. Only don't none of his planter kin know that. They think
he's just a student at Ole Miss. But I know the real story, and Quit
knows I know it—but he don't care because he knows I won't tell
nobody that counts.

Mad Owens knew it, too. Mad's his cousin. So, you might say
it's all in the family—and that turned out to be damn near more
true than even I could imagine that day I just told you about a
minute ago when I was holdin' on to the best-lookin' pair of titties-
lookin'-back-at-me I ever saw, and it turn't out they belonged to
Little Petunia. That gotdam Sunflower made sure all her girls and
any girls they mighta had was named for flowers. I say mighta
because with anything to do with Sunflower is a sho-nuff, solid,
definite-ass *mighta*. But that's another story, too, and another
gotdam garden as well.

I've given you most of it, but there's more of course, and I promise I'mo tell every bit of it, specially about the Quitman County

Bathhouse—plus God knows what all else, later, in my next book. Or I might get McKinney to do it. But, somebody will.

Anyway, I got *my* reg'lars up at the Magic Pussy. Plus, there's that old woman I speak about over there around Sledge, so as far as I'm concerned life is pretty fukkin good. Also, now I have time to think about a few things, and I guess you could say I have become a fukkin philosopher.

Mad said a philosopher was a sumbich that liked to think and some of em even made a livin' at it which don't seem like a bad way to earn a buck if you ast me, I mean, just sit around and think somethin' and get paid for it. I don't know that I'll ever see a dime from it myself, but it's good to know thinkin' ain't a total waste of time.

Mr. Brainsong one time said he believed I might be a philosopher, but I told him I liked law enforcement better. Back then I just couldn't see no future in philosophy. I couldna made no living as a coksukkin thinker. And I was convinced I sure as hell wouldna wanted to get up and do it every day.

I couldna been a philosopher when I was younger, but, as long as I don't over-do it, it don't seem like a bad-ass way to pass the time. Especially with a beer and a ball game on the TV. When you get tired of watchin' the game, you can just set back and think for a while, and then go back to watchin' the game.

For instance, the other day, I thought what if there wuddn no God and no angels nor no Jesus and shit like that. That would mean that all them churches up in Meffis and elsewhere, which are pretty expensive and are on every fukkin street corner in the whole gotdam city—and some of em has big-ass gymnasiums and places for divorced people to have parties so they can find somebody else to get divorced from—but if there weren't no God and no Jesus, then all that million-dollar real estate was built on illusion, just like love and the Magic Pussy, and so, in a sense, there ain't no difference

between church and the Magic Pussy, cause when a sumbich hollers
"Oh God!" there in the MP, that muthafukka means it.

> SEX PRAYER TO EROS
> Ohgodohgodohgodohgodoh
> Godohgodohgodohgodohgod
> Ohgodohgodohgodohgodoh
> Godohhhhhhgaaaaaa . . . . . d.

Mad of course had love involved in everything no matter
what the fukkin subject might be. He even knew, naturally, what
Shakespeare wrote about it and what the gotdam Bible and the
coksukkin Romans and the psy-fukkin-chologists and what every
other know-it-all Doctor of Bullshit that come down the road ever
said about it.

One nem experts was some Eye-talian sumbich Mad told me
about that died four hunnuhd years ago, or so, named Gazzocavallo,
and he wrote a huge-ass book, in old-time dago, of course, with a
fukkin goose feather, that goes on all about love, and part of it says
something about how love proves there's a God.

Wollaholla hu-hu. Love don't prove there's a God. It just proves
you got a pair of balls and a reasonably hard dick—because if
you didn't, you'd be happy enough just watchin' cable and eatin'
pigsfeet.

> THE GRAND DASEIN OF LOVE
> And
> What if
> I have learned
> A thing or two:
> That love and Being
> Can seem the same,

And being loved and loving
Are like water from the sky
And spaces in the rain.

Here I am talkin' about love, when, basically, I don't even know exactly what that is. Anyway, everybody pretty much has the same idea about what it's supposed to require, a feeling that you've got to be with some particular woman and not no other one will do and that, if she don't feel the same about you, you can't never be happy about nothin' the whole fukkin rest of your life.

Course, if there is anything at all to love, I'd bet Mad was the sumbich who really did it better'n anybody else. His whole idea was to love when it was hard to love and to try to love what the person you loved was and not what they done. That's way-ass over *my* waders. But that was his aim. And I don't understand none of it.

So when the break up between him and Money come about, Mad felt like a failure. And when I finally got off a fukkin shrimp boat, that somehow called itself a charter vessel, and drug my ass up the sand to where he was camped out on that gotdam hot-ass Mississippi island in the GuffaMexico, he said to me: "I've failed, Junior Ray. I've failed."

And I looked at him and said, "Failed? Mad, how could you fail? You ain't never even had a job for more'n a couple a years at a whack."

"I failed at love," he said. "I wasn't able to do what I truly believed in with the only woman who ever ignited in me the raging fire of cosmic desire coupled with an ineluctable yearning for one-ness even in the darkness that lies beyond the heat of the flames."

"What?" I said.

"And I wrote a book," he said.

"What's it about?" I ast him.

"It's about Money and me and other stuff as well," he said.

"Where is it?" I said.

"Right out there," he said, and pointed at the beach. "It's right out yonder there in the sand."

"Holyshit," I said. "It's all gonna wash away into the GuffaMexico."

"No, it won't," he said. And then he showed me he had it all wrote down on white butcher paper he'd gotten at the dock before he went out to the island. I ast him what he was goin' to call it, and said he had settled on *Organ Music*.

It was a pretty good book, just judgin' from what I know now about how books is supposed to be. 'Course he *wrote* his, and I *talk* mine, so there's some differences. But not a helluva lot.

Mad said he wuddn actually no writer. He called hissef a "dilet-tante," whatever the fuk that means, but it looked like he might be a real writer anyway because if you write a whole fukkin book, even in the *sand*, way out on the ass-end of Horn Island and on butcher paper as well, that's better'n most and sure as hell good enough for me.

He had a bad habit of low-ratin' hissef—and I might add—somewhat ever' now and then for good reason, but, then, that really don't make him much different from most people except that most people may not have what I call the "self-photography" Mad had.

I mean, he could thumb around in his mental scrapbook, as he called it, and say, "See. Look here. There I am. An asshole." And I would say, "Mad, you wanta talk about ass'oles, remind me some-time to show you *my* scrapbook." He was, overall, possibly one of the most innocent sumbiches I believe I've ever seen. Includin' a number of the ones I may have locked up from time to time.

But, hell, I always listen to crazy people. They might sound at first like they're just hollerin', but if you give it some attention once in a while, you find out they're singin'. And that's what Mad was doin'. Furthermore, only an R-tistic sumbich would ever do the things he's done. On the other hand, it ain't crazy to love a nekkid dancer. It'd be crazy not to, if you want my opinion.

Mad didn't want no "good Christian mother" to be his girlfriend. He said he'd rather be dead and in hell with his back broke than wind up with one nem women who's all wrapped up like a sausage in clothes you couldn pull off with the gotdam "jaws of life." And you know the kind I'm talkin' about. Chr*EYE*st! They never come down from the fukkin choir, and their hair is harder than long division or a datgum basket full'a coathangers.

Anyhow, what happened to Mad was that he went out one day to the Magic Pussy Cabaret & Club—and there she was. It wuddn love nor passion, nor none of them words at all—it was, instead, like he had gone out in space and had turned around to look back at the earth and he was like a burnin' ball of fire, a fukkin heavenly-ass body, like a star, just hissef, and all creation was rotatin' around *him*.

That's when he said he finally understood that love and passion and all the hoohah was really just the overlooked, absolute core of life, that what he felt when he seen her was: "Let there be light, kaboom," and he ain't never changed his mind about it since. He just knowed, when he had to break it up, that he wuddn able under the circumstances to keep true to his feelings and his beliefs. And that's why he felt like he'd failed—not as a man but as a star in the sky.

McKinney mighta had something to add, but I'mo leave that up to her. I did give some of Mad's book to her, and most of the poems, and she said, if she thought there was a place for some of em, she was goin' to use them somewhere in this new book.*

---

* At this point Junior Ray still had not seen a draft of the book. I debated whether to leave this graph in or to strike it, but, owing to the oral and primitive nature of the work itself—which indeed is the essence of its meaning and identity—I

I have to admit I wish sometimes I could have learned about writers and historians and all that back when I was younger and just wanted to shoot somebody, but, hell, what the fuk did I know? Nobody I growed up with knowed what any of them things were, except Mr. Brainsong, but I never did see him all that much, and I was too young and too mean for any of what he might have had to offer at the time to rub off on me. Besides, I tended to look up to older men who liked to hunt and spit, and, for that matter, I still do, only most of those tough, strong, tobacco-chewin', hard workin', tall, skinny, hard-as-nails and damn-near silent men whose faces looked like a wrinkled pair of briar britches is now dead. And that, I'mo say, makes me a lot sadder'n most people might ever think I could be.

> ALSO SPRACH ZARATHUSTRA TO DYLAN THOMAS
> Intelligence has "no dominion"
> And desire no tongue to speak itself
> Beyond a reaching after air.
> I clung to music of the past
> That pulled me into shadows
> And the company of ghosts
> Where drums are made of darkness,
> But the dancer is the light;
> Despair can't stand a dancin' man,
> Nor darkness ruin the night.

I thought about takin' Voyd with me down to see Mad, but Sunflower wouldn't let the little sumbich go—and I really don't think he wanted to anyway. He's gettin' to where he ain't inter-rested in much and tends to spend a whole lotta time down at the Boll & Bloom drinkin' coffee, smokin' cigarettes, and checkin' out the latest

decided, correctly, to leave the lines where Junior Ray spoke them.

waitress. The high point of his gotdam day is a free re-fill.

Plus he never seemed to give a crap about Mad one way or another. And, if you ask me, Voyd looks like he's on his way to where most of the old sumbiches down here are headed. Dumb-ass wo'-out muthafukkas. One day they're just gon' disappear into their socks. There's *some* things you can't re-fill.

THE CAPTAIN OF THE boat I got a ride on from the pier in Biloxi knowed exactly where Mad was. So he let me off right at Mad's camp and not on the "sound" side. I sure as shit wouldna wanted to walk through them evil-lookin' woods—I seen four or five wild hogs right there on the edge of em! Anyway, I didn't mind havin' to wade a few feet when I come off the captain's boat. He couldn take it up to the beach, or we'd all still be there.

My trip to the GuffaMexico come about because Mad had wrote me a letter invitin' me to come see him and tellin' me where to go once I got down to Biloxi. He told me to look up a sumbich right there on Highway 90 who was the captain of a rickety-ass boat that hauled tourists around. Mad said he had an "arrangement" with the sumbich and that the captain would carry me out to where he, Mad, of course, was.

Anyway, after I got off the boat an onto the sand in front of Mad's camp, and after Mad had waded out to the boat, where he and the captain talked about mail and supplies and such, the captain said he'd come pick me up in a week or ten days, and that suited me. I didn't have nowhere else I needed to be. Mad had struck a deal with the captain some kind of way so he, Mad, could stay up on all the things he needed in order to be a hermit, and the captain appeared to be a pretty good ol' boy, who talked funny, and was damn near burnt the color of a birdboot. But I liked him and didn't see no reason to distrust him.

BUT HERE'S WHAT I wanted to get into. In bein' with Mad there
on that gotdam island in the Guffa-fukkin-Mexico, I got to know
him even better, and not much to my datgum surprise I come away
with a lot to think about—not that I intend to think about none
of it all that much, but neverthe-fukkin-less . . . .

"Mad," I said, "Why in God's name did you come to this
place?"

And he said, "Junior Ray, I needed to go to the ends of the earth
or at least as close to it as I could, and the Mississippi Gulf Coast
seemed to fill the bill."

"Well," I said, "I still don't understand—I mean, you and I both
know you ain't the usual kind of sumbich, so it's not all that surprisin'
that you'd not do something usual, but this here place—though I
do see it has its good points as far as bein' able to look out over the
ocean and all, and not see nothin' except the fukkin sunset—this
datgum island is at the ass end of just about ever'thin'. Plus, it's fulla
mosquitoes and other shit I ain't never come across before."

"I know it," he said. "But somehow none of that bothers me.
Truth is I could stay here forever, even though I know I'll probably
get tired of it after a time."

Mad had plenty of whiskey and a couple of cases of hot beer he
had not yet drunk up but which I proceeded to help him do. That
helped me appreciate the environment a lot more.

And I have to say, I did some fishin' with what he said was a
castin' net. It was a lot of fukkin fun—I learned to see them mullets,
then I'd wade in the water just a tad and th'ow the net, and when I
pulled it in, it'd be fulla fukkin fish—mostly them mullets, which
Mad says is used mainly for bait but that down the road somewhere
they sells em in restaurants under the name of Florida Linda. Seems
people will eat a Florida Linda, but they won't gulp down nothin'
with a name like mullet; plus, a Florida Linda sounds like it ought
to cost more'n a mullet, and so it goes, just like Money's daddy's

one-stocking factory with the two boxes to sell em in.

Mad thought of himself as a hermit. Hermits, he said, was able to get a handle on how to live because they didn't have no worldly distractions, like phone bills, or the local googah-and-who-done-what-to-who goin' on in Mhoon County, or the daily need to go to Meffis. But Mad's main concern was not exactly the meaning of fukkin life. It was the "eidetic nature" of love, which he said, to get to he had to "bracket the dingin' zick,"* whatever the fuk that was.

"Junior Ray," he said, "love is not just a feeling or a kind of tickle here and there in parts of the body and in the mind; it's a genuine *thing*." I knew right there I was in for some philosophy.

"Love," he kept on, "is an actual thing. It's a natural—and sometimes, living—object, like a rock or a tree, or even a bird or maybe a squirrel. It can be a piece of glass or bit of metal—or water or just air! Love is a thing just like any or all of that, and I was determined to learn as much as I could about it, but more important than anything else, I wanted to to understand it. Well, to understand how to understand it."

A lot of times I didn't understand how to understand Mad. For one thing he was hipped on play-dough. He said there was stuff nobody could see or touch but was alive and well somewhere in play-dough. Play-dough, he claimed, was the *answer*, and then he went on to explain about how things we see ain't what's really there but that they *are* somewhere else, and he said, "See, Junior Ray, love is one of those things.

"Love," he went on, "can be seen—and clearly seen—and," as he put it, appre-fukkin-hended "in its thing-in-itselfness"—only a person's mind has to be trained to see it and after that to actually fukkin do it.

"It was," he said, and by then I didn't think the sumbich was

* *Ding an sich*, "thing in itself," which according to Kant is unknowable.

ever gon' stop, "my purest intention to love Money in spite of all the standard and predictable reasons I ought not to." By then I had caught on, so I knew he meant he had wanted to love Money for her-thing-in-herse'fness and not just for her looks and of course her pussy. Mad was real wound up by this time, and I hoped he wouldn drag it out and would go on and get to the punch line. Anyway, he was sayin', "I made up my mind that I was goin' to get at true love in a way nobody else had ever managed to get at it. Poets, Junior Ray, in the middle ages tried it and did not fully succeed, mainly because they mostly did not even *know* the person they were tryin' to love."

Right here, I thought: Who gives a shit?

"They," he said, "just mostly loved *their idea* of the person. And most of the time the woman of their dreams was totally unaware of those poets' existence."

"A buncha dumb sumbiches," I said. And I figured that's why it was no wonder there wuddn a lot of jobs for poets.

"Dumb sumbiches?" he said. "Well, sorta. But you might say those poets had a good idea, only that's as far as it went. And, frankly, all that hasn't changed much. Not really knowin' who we're dealin' with is pretty much the way it is today with most of us. There's a barrier, and my aim was to breech that barrier and discover the place where true love exists."

By then I had gotten into my third hot beer of the afternoon. But I got a memory like a fukkin Rolodex, and words people says just stays in my head and rolls around till I want to hear em again. "You mean you was goin' to overlook what she done at the Magic Pussy?" I said. "Even after you found out what she *really* done," I added.

"Precisely," he said. "That was number one on the list, but I couldn get past it to number two, which would have involved other areas of her character and intellect."

"I don't guess her bein' knocked-out beautiful had nothin' to do with it," I said.

"Oh, certainly it did," he said. "That was her honey that attracted the bee of my soul to the flower of her love."

"Your bee and a whole hive of others," I told him, "And, Mad, when it all started, I knowed you was bound to get the gotdam goatshit stung outta you."

"Haven't you ever been in love, Junior Ray?"

"Fuk no. I don't see no sense in it."

"You're right: there isn't any real sense in it at all," he said. "But for most folks there's just the odd necessity of it."

"Fukkum," I said, "I ain't never felt no gotdam necessity for anything, except maybe wantn to shoot Leland Shaw. Plus, love ain't never had nothin' to do with any kind of activities I was ever *inter*-rested in. For one thing it ain't got anything to do with guns or cars or pussy. I ain't never been able to see love bein' involved in none of that."

"It has to do with one-ness," Mad said.

"Fuk one-ness," I said, "It has to do with gotdam fun-ness, and that's the long and the short of it."

"No it's not," he said. "Love is like the sunlight and the rain and the night and the day and the earth and the stars all rolled into one. There cannot be a world without it."

"Yes, it can, too," I said. "And I been livin' in the muthafukka near' bout seventy years. Chr*EYE*st, Mad," I said, "All any sumbich needs is the Magic Pussy!"

Mad said he couldn agree with me on that, and he maintained love was right up there with religion. He said his failure was the failure to overlook the fact, as I put it, that Money was givin' blow jobs—and ever'thin' else kind of jobs—to her reg'lars at the club.

But Mad couldn let go the notion that all that shouldna made no difference to a person who was a "true" lover, and I said I didn't guess there was many of them sumbiches around. He did agree with me about that, and in fact he even said that there might not never have been any but, still, that possibility had not made him not want to try it anyway, which, right there, is Mad right down to the marrow bone, a gotdam philosopher. And of course a fukkin hermit as well.

ANYWAY, I STAYED WITH him for several days. He had a series of army-surplus tarpoliuns set up on poles and boxes and pieces of wood he picked up off the beach, so it kind of made a fairly big-size tent house. And there was a cool breeze a lot of the time comin' in off the GuffaMexico that blew the mosquitoes over to the back side of the island. Every now and then we'd have to adjust the tarps because the wind could get pretty stiff, and it loosened em up and that made em flap too much. But overall wuddn none of it a whole lot of trouble. The truth is it wuddn too bad, and I liked it. And that, when it comes to philosophy, is about the most truth I am inclined to want to handle.

Once in a while there was some little flea-bugs and other nit-nat things that would get to bitin' on us, but they really never did bother us none because every so often Mad and I would walk upwind and give the whole place a squirt or two of BugShot Double Oh-Oh! and that'd be the last we'd have to deal with any kind of them little bug sumbiches for a while. Mad did say it was not "ecologically" sound, but I told him I did not give a shit.

Horn Island is a long-ass piece of sand and some dark fukkin woods that runs more or less east to west. The back side of the island faces the whole state of Mississippi, but, in case you didn't know it, the water sloshin' around on that side between the island and the state of Mississippi, as it turns out, ain't really no ocean a-tall; it's just what they call the Mississippi Sound! Although, I have to own up, I listened, but I couldn't really hear nothin' unusual.

Mad, however, had his camp around on the true GuffaMexico side which was a whole helluva lot better and, frankly, more worth bein' at.

Back to the question of sand: It was sumpn I hadn't never faced before. Sand was the one thing I noticed the most when I was on the island livin' with Mad under the old army tarpoliuns. And one day I ast him if all that sand didn't bother him, because it was everywhere and up my gotdam ass at the same time, but Mad said, "No. It really does not bother me at all. I accept it as part of the furniture of my atonement."

"Your what? " I said. I could see him begin to get that "zoomin" look.

"My atonement."

"Where is it?" I ast. And then he explained to me that a atonement was, unlike love, not a *thing* but that it was a makin' up for something you didn't do right, so, in a way it was kind of like checkin' yourse'f into Parchman and pickin' cotton for a while in order to feel better about something you never should have give a shit about in the first fukkin place. That was what atonement was. Only he made it out to be something philo-fukkin-sophical, which I mighta known before I gotdam ast him. Anyhow, live and fukkin learn. That's my motto.

Real hermits, according to Mad, back in the old days used to wear kroka-sack* T-shirts and whup theyse'ves with little leather cat-o-nine-tails they called the flagellas, all of which, they figured, brung their ass closer to God. Mad, on the other hand said he wuddn tryin' get back closer to God; he just wanted to get back closer to his*sef,* which he believed he had sort of lost in his "failure" to keep on lovin' Money Scatters even though she was givin' blow jobs in the afternoon to her regulars at the Magic Pussy. Philosophy can be pretty fukkin confusin'.

---

* Burlap.

But, just like the Guffa-fukkin-Mexico, I am ready to admit there are probably some things that are over my head.

"Now, Mad," I said, "don't you just get wo' out with havin' sand in ever'thin'? I mean . . ."

And he come back with, "No, Junior Ray, I really do not, and I'll tell you why . . ." And then, Oh, Lord, he said I should think of the sand as "the primordial glass in the windows of the universe."*

And I said, "Holy gotdam shit."

And then he went on, like he does when he gets wound up on philosophy, "Think of it this way, Junior Ray: Every grain of sand is a basic particle of everything that is. Each tiny grain is a tiny laboratory of photonic energy, containin' the refracted properties of light, and light, as you know is what . . .?

"Light?" I said, without seein' any.

"Yes, but what is light, Junior Ray?"

I was about to get pissed off, so I said, "Light is fukkin *light*, gotdammit."

"You are absolutely right, Junior Ray!" Mad was rockin' and rollin' now. "Light is light, which is the same thing as sayin' that light is everything that is, one way or another, plus or minus, because light is the 'end all' and the 'be all' of existence. Indeed, it is light itself that defines the universe. The whole field of creation is mapped in light! And that very same light is in every single little grain of sand. So, even when that sand gets into my peanut butter sandwich, I love it; I love it because my peanut butter sandwich becomes more'n just a peanut butter sandwich."

"No, it don't," I said, "but I guess that's why you could call it a *sand*wich." That was a joke, but it went right by his ass, so I told him

* Before Junior Ray went to visit Mad, expecting to be "talking" another book that would have Mad in it, and wanting to be sure he got Mad's words right, he bought an inexpensive microcassette recorder at the drugstore in St. Leo. So the reader is seeing Mad Owens's words verbatim.

he answered my question and that I could see his point, although, I said, I guessed it would be more of a point for me to say that I could see where it *might be* a point to him but probably would not look nowhere even *close* to a point to very many other sumbiches out there, and he said, "Junior Ray, I appreciate your candor."

Hell, I didn't even know I had one, but I said, "Mad, you know, sometimes you are crazier than a Sugar-Ditch rat."

Then he grinned and told me I was "the jewel in the lotus."

I said, "Thank you," and ast him what was a lodus?

That's more or less the way it went for the few days I was with him on the beach at Horn Island, in the Guffa-fukkin-Mexico.

But unlike true hermits, I, personally, didn't have no visions or nothin' while I was there with Mad out on the island, and as I may or may not have mentioned, I sure as shit didn't come away with no extra wisdom, but I did get to see some of the world, and I guess that's good, though I don't exactly know for what.

Now I TOLD YOU about the letter Mad sent when he asked me to come visit him. Here's *some* of it:

Dear Junior Ray,

Long have I wandered in cloud lands of cumulative foolish-ness. But, frankly, I have found, if not peace—if not freedom from perpetual anxiety—I have bagged at least a watery view of the infinite. Indeed, I look daily in a line tangent to the Earth, bending not to any horizon, and though, perhaps, there may be nothing out there that I shall ever see, I know—or certainly from whatever scant information I have acquired over the years concerning my brief and not at all certain chronological Slot of Being—I remain convinced there must be much "out there" I cannot see, even with my glasses. Here, I was trying to make a joke, but I am not as good at that as you are.

Nevertheless, I had thought I could live like a good Buddhist, in the perfect acceptance of an illusion. The trouble is there are so many illusions. I've never been able to stand not knowing what's what; yet, whenever I find out what's what, I can't stand that, either, and cannot manage to let it all go down—and disappear—into the existential drainpipe. Thus, I can say with great authority that I know now how hard curiosity was on the cat.

And truth, Oh dear me, truth. I am afraid I can't stand that at all, and to my dismay I have discovered I have several sets of truth: one for me now and one for others now; one for me then, and one for others then—and of course the position and direction of the "sets" go both forward and backward so that I also have a "set of truth" for me and for others later. But that's not the end of it. The whole thing became enormous—For example, I discovered I have truths that could have been for me now and could have been for others now, as well as truths that might have been . . . and so forth, backwards and forwards in time, perhaps forever. And that's pretty scary.

But, enough of this; for one thing, most of it is in the subjunctive, and, worse, I can see that all of it would become extremely complex if I were to address the question of double and triple negatives.

I would give anything to be like you. So, you must come to see me here at the end of the world below the seacoast of Mississippi, a topographical phenomenon I have never gotten used to. Mississippi has always seemed born to be inland, isolated, cut-off, and relegated to a kind of chicken-fried savagery almost preferred and, I believe, highly enjoyed by the best of its inhabitants, one of whom I tend to think I am because my mother told me I was.

No more "love" for me, old buddy, just sun and sand, green surf up front and murky slosh behind, stingarees, boiled crab, red snapper, lemon fish, oysters in the summer, flounders on my "doorstep" and shrimp off the Slovenian Pier.

Then Mad went on to give me the instructions about how to get to him, and you know the rest.

LET ME JUST SAY one thing about Mad and about history and poems and litter-ture and shit like that. It's kind of like what McKinney says, that it seems like I have "become a magnet for the unlikely," but, fuk, that's just the way it is. It don't make no difference to me, and half the time I don't pay no attention to any of it—unless of course it has to do with history, then only, as far as I'm concerned, if it has to do with the Yazoo Pass!

Mad and McKinney tried gettin' me to read. I tried reading, but it didn't do no good. I tried, but I just could not get into it. Most of it didn't seem worth the time it was gon' take to do it, and some of that so-called litter-ture made my head hurt. Plus, I didn't want to know none of it nohow. And I feel a hunnuhd percent better since I give it up.

But I do like Seinfeld, which is, I guess, a little bit like readin'. Those little Yankee muthafukkas knock me out. I don't even know what they're talkin' about half the time, but that Kramer and that little goober-guy George tickle me to death. I swear, if they *was* ever to come down here, I'd show em a real good time. Son! They'd have a *big* time. But I don't think Jerry'd like it quite as much.

I'll say one thing for Money Scatters: she didn't let *love* interfere with *her* life. After she clumb down off the hood of Mad's car, that was fukkin *it*. She never did look back.

I kept up with her for a while because I was goin' up to Meffis to the MP all the time, but, after about a year and a half, she'd done moved out to California where I heard she really hit it big in the sex business. I guess she did always have her eye on Hollywood.

What she done was this: Money begun to have her name on a

whole buncha "products" like the ones you see in nem sex stores, which, yes, gotdammit, I *have* been in—I'd be lyin' if I told you I hadn't—but I don't go in em on a regular basis. I mean it ain't like, "Oh, shit, I'm all outta twelve-inch plastic dicks and black and white rubber pussies; dang, I reckon I'll just whip up to the sex store and get a few supplies."

I guess you prob'ly remember, from my other book, the first time I ever seen any of that outside a pitch'r was when I ordered off for that big-ass whang I was gonna put on Martha May Weathercraft's front porch durin' the time I was runnin' around tryin' to get a shot at that crazy sumbich Leland Shaw. But, hell, that's another kind of history, and that ain't what *this* book is about.

Anyway, it turns out Money didn't just have her name on that sex stuff I was about to tell you about; she invented it—and the imitation pussies was *hers*. But just to show you how smart she was, one of her inventions was a thing called "Trip-Dik for Women." It was a lillo doodad you could—well, a woman could—stick up between her legs whilst she was drivin'. Another hot-seller was a aftershave she called "Pussy for Men." You could even buy it in the restroom at the MP; plus, I seen it in some fillin' stations on the side of the road tween here and Teoc, just east of Greenwood.

I used to go huntin' down there with a crazy-ass half-Choctaw muthafukka that owned a little cotton land at Teoc, which is also near the edge of the Hills. There really ain't nothin' there but a buncha gotdam fee-larks. Anyway, I'd shoot them lil' sumbiches any time one'd fly up outta the grass; then I'd take em home, clean em, and put em in a pie. It don't matter what anybody tells you, tweety-birds taste just as good as all that official stuff. And as far as I'm concerned, "game" ain't nothin' more'n what some gotdam government-ass agency, like the fukkin "Gay Men's Fish Commission," decides to call it. To hell with waitin' around for a gotdam tough-ass turkey—or for some dumb-ass dog to sniff out a covey of quail—when you can just fill up your game bag with tweety-birds.

But let me get back to what I was about to tell you. The idea of that so-called aftershave was that it was supposed to get everybody excited, men, women, and whatever else, 'cept me, of course. I couldn see what all the fuss was about. I sniffed it, and it just smelt like privet hedge to me.

And then there was a thing called the Clit-Mit. I don't know right down to the letter how it worked, but the box it was in said it was designed to be "Handy for That Special Guy or Gal." I was stumped, and so was the sumbich who managed the sex store, but we figured anybody out there in California wouldn have no trouble gettin' it to work.

I'm not what you might call creative. I mean, when it comes to sex, I never did get much past the MoonLite Drive-In on the side of Highway 61 and them Milk Duds ol' Des got so pissed off about in the other book. However, I suggested to the manager up at the MP that they ought to have a special room done up with car seats. He said he'd speak to the owner about it, but the whole thing's too gotdam much to think about. I'm just thankful for the Little Petunias of this world. That's good enough for me. Although, I have to say I've been thinkin': It might be a helluva lot of fun to get in the bed with my girlfriend, you know, over at Sledge—Dyna Flo McKeever—and Little Petunia all at the same time. I know Mr. Floppy would go along with it. He'd be shakin' hands up a storm.

Money did get into the movies out in Hollywood. The first one she done was called *The Crack of Dawn*, and it didn't make much of a splash. But after that, she was in two more that I know of—and you've probably heard of em—because, as I understand it, they was both big-ass hits all over the country. Anyway, about a year after she was in the one I told you about that didn't do so good, she was the star in *Belle of the Balls*, which was about the South, of course, and then right after that one, she played a young woman from a small town in the Mississippi Delta who went to New York City where she met up with a sumbich known only as the D.O.D. That was short for the *Dick of Death*, which is what that movie was called.

And it was pretty deep. Her job was to keep the Dick of Death from fukkin up America by changin' us from a democracy to what was goin' to be called a *cock-ocracy*. In the movie Money was a superhero called—get this!—the Magic Pussy! Anyhow, at the last minute she traps the Dick of Death in her you-know-what; then, in a little bit the movie ends, and you see both of em grinnin' at the camera with her about to lay a karate chop on his pekka.

I DON'T NORMALLY TALK bad about women, but I do think I ought to mention that, in addition to her good qualities, Money wuddn what you'd call bad, but she wuddn good neither. And Mad of course just couldn't see it.

There was a time, when they took up together, when things seemed to go fairly smooth for Mad. She'd tell him she wanted to go off and live in the Rocky Mountains, or down in Florida somewhere, even sometimes over in North Carolina, wherever that is, or over in Arkan-fukkin-saw in the gotdam Ozarks with all them crazy sumbiches that live in the woods, have one license plate for life, and don't pay no taxes.

That kinda talk had a calmin' effect on Mad. And durin' those times when she'd go to work at the Magic Pussy, Mad would do his thing and run his errands and clean up the apartment, and then, when she was supposed to show up back home, she'd show up, and you'da thought they was just a couple of All-American muthafukkas.But, underneath the cosmetology, there was snakes in the brake. The good times wuddn gon' last.

Money was turnin' tricks and, I think, really believin', to herse'f, that wuddn what it was. She considered herse'f an entertainment specialist, as she put it one time when she was tellin' one of Mad's friends about her job. But the truth is Money was just a ho, though I have to say that didn't make her no different from a lot of those legislaychers down in Jackson or them politicians up in Meffis, a bunch of which finally got their asses caught by the law for stikkin' their horin' hands out, but there again in her case and in theirs, bein' a ho ain't the end of the fukkin world or maybe all that bad, cause bein' a ho is what has kept the MP open for business and available to me, and that is all I really give a crap about.

When you come right down to it, ho'in, not love, is what makes the world go round. Bein' a ho is fine as long as you don't try to call it sumpn else, well, like an entertainment specialist. But I reckon I'da been a ho, too, except most of the bullshit people woulda paid me to do, I'da done for free. I never was no good at business.

But I do get around as far as knowin' who's who and what the fuk is what. Plus, people tell me things. So that's how I knew what was goin' on between Mad and Money before Mad did. 'Course if it'd been me, I'da shot her ass and th'owed her off into the Mississippi River and let the turtles fuk her. But Mad ain't like me, and that's probably one other reason him and me is friends in the first place.

Anyway, Mad never knew the half of it. Hell, he didn't even have to go out of town for her to keep up her carry'in on. In addition, for example, to playin' with four thousand different dicks a minute in her job as an entertainment specialist at the MP, here's the kinda stuff she'd pull. One time she'd done met this high-roller at the club. He would come into Meffis from some shit hole like TexARkana, to play poker for three or four days at one of the ten or so fukkin casinos—the Emerald fukkin City, to be specific—north of St. Leo, in Mhoon County, in the Mississippi Delta, then

I suppose he'd crawl back under a pile of roadside trash back over in Tex-ass or Arkan-fukkin-saw. You know them pekkawoods over there th'ow everything they can get their hands on outta their vehicles onto the side of the road. I seen it. And I ain't never viewed nothin' like it. And, you know it must be bad, cause, Oh Hell-o Bill, I'm a pekkawood myse'f!

Let me clear sumpn up, I mean the fact that Meffis, Tennessee, is not in Mississippi, and it sure as hell ain't in the Delta. It's in the gotdam hills, and the west Tennessee hills at that. But I know sometimes it might be confusin' to people when I'm goin' on about something and switchin' back and forth between the Mississippi Delta and Meffis. What you've got to understand is is that Meffis— because of where the sumbich is situated—is the capital of the Mississippi Delta, and it's where people in the Delta, particularly the northern part of the Delta, all go to get born and to die and see the fukkin dentist and other such crap as that. Meffis is just settin' up there, actually, now, right on the state line just about half a mile after you come up out of the Delta at Walls on Highway 61.

Anyway, I hope this helps some in your understanding of where the fuk things are and why they're the way they are.

But back to the high-roller: Gold chain and all, that sumbich comes up to the MP on a break from the tables, and he meets Money. Money falls for his ass. For one thing he buys up all her time and hangs out with her in the VIP Lounge, her nekkid and all over him, on one nem big soft sofas. After two visits like that, Money decided she'd go out with him, so, on her off-night, she tells Mad she has to work, for some trumped-up reason, and here's what she does—it's slick as owl shit—she goes to the MP and lets the smoke and the "air freshener" and the smell of the baby wipes soak into her hair and into what little clothes she has on, then she meets up with Doc-ass Holladay and runs off to a motel with him for a few hours for free, then comes back to the Magic Pussy where she does some

more smoke and aroma-soakin' before she gets in the red Explorer
Mad got for her and goes home, smellin' of course like she's been
at the daily bump and grind, workin' hard, so to speak, at the club.
Plus, if Mad hada called her there, she'd done told her buddies in
the dressing room—the Titty Commission, which, as you already
know, was just a bunch girls who spent most of their time just settin'
around shootin' the shit instead of hustlin' the golfers—to say she
was with a customer. And that woulda been enough to have kept
him from gettin' in the car and drivin' over to the MP.

It was wilder'n a nigga baptisin'. Me, of course, I'da never been
in fukkin luv in the first gotdam place, so, truly, if I'da been hooked
up with her instead of Mad, I, personally, wouldna give a rat's ass
what she done. Hell, I probably wouldn't even have shot her.

But her trainload of dodges was just about endless. For instance,
she'd meet up with some sumbich for an afternoon of fukathonic
activity and tell Mad she was goin' over to the gym with her no-count
sister from Itta Bena. She'd pack her gym bag and, later, th'ow some
water on her gym clothes to look like sweat, then come home with
her tongue hangin' out, sayin' shit like "Whew! What a workout!"
Sumbich, you think I'm tellin' you a story, but I'm not.

THERE WAS ANOTHER LILLO girl up there from down in the Delta.
She called herse'f Rena Lara. That was her show name. And she possibly *was* the most beautiful little thing you ever did see, although
I do have a tendency to say that about almost every one of em. It
just depends, I guess, on who I'm talkin' to and how I feel toward
things in general *that* day. Anyway Rena Lara was about five-foot-
one, and she glided around in some of them huge-ass shoes a lot
of the girls was wearin' then. She had little-bitty bones and hair as
soft and delicate as you might expect to find among members of the
heavenly hosts. It was the damndest set of physical circumstances
I or any other sumbich I know ever coulda run into.

And when she'd take off that flimsy lillo top and strip down to nothin' but that G-string and straddle you in the dark at the back of the club, you felt like you didn't need to live a minute more in your en-tire life on this earth. She'd stand up on the couch right over you—just like Little Petunia—and—just like Little Petunia—she'd pull that G-string over to the side, and there you'd be, nose to whatchamacallit, lookin' cross-eyed at the sweetest-smellin', best-lookin' pussy the Lord God ever created.

One time she done it, and I tried to lick it—like I *did* do with Little Petunia—but Rena Lara backed off quick as a hamster, and I missed, and she said: "Junior Ray, I'm not ever gonna let you see it again!"

But she did, of course, only I never did try to lick it no more. I'd just blow on it, and she seemed to think that was all right. I mean, unlike some nem ass'oles who come up to the Magic Pussy, I ain't got no false hopes about nothin'. I know what the fuk I am. I'm a gotdam unit of income, and that's all. But, you know, sumneez dikheds think they've got something goin' with these girls when, natchaly, nothin' could be further from the fukkin truth. On the other hand, sometimes love does bloom, you might say, like it did for Mad and Money. Although that ain't necessarily good.

Me, personally, I admire them girls. If I thought for one gotdam minute a buncha these old ugly dumb sumbiches would th'ow dollar bills at me, I'd get nekkid and wouldn't wear another stitch as long as I lived. But I don't believe that's apt to happen.

Anyhow, Rena Lara told me she liked her job a lot but that what she really dreamed of was becomin' an algebra teacher, only she said, first, she had to get her GED. If that, plus X times Y, don't equal B for bullshit, nothin' does.

But I ain't gon' be the one to tell her. She has a good heart, and it'll just have to get broke some other way.

AND MAD? HE'S ALL right. I get cards from him once in a while, and McKinney, she keeps up with him real good.

Somebody ast me the other day where he was and was he still down on that island sleepin' up under them surplus tarpoliuns, and I told em the last I heard Mad had disappeared into the white space. You know, when you look at a road map there's all that white space at the bottom? Well, that's where that sumbich went. He left Horn Island and traveled west over to the other side of New Or'lins and hung a sharp-ass left at Houma. He drove south from there, right on down smack-ass into that white space on the bottom of the map, between one place called Cocodrie and another by the name of Theriot, where he took up with the Houma Indians, and now, he says, he has him a little house on the side of a canal that goes out through the middle of nowhere and finally empties out into the GuffaMexico, like ever'thin' else around here it seems to me.

Plus, Mad says the canal actually goes all the way to fukkin Alaska and that he might get a job on a tugboat and help haul something up there. That wouldn' surprise me one damn bit. Mad's a sumbich who can do just about anything he wants to. He's one nem kinda men; whereas, me, there's things I do and things I don't, but, with Mad, it's different; it's like he lives his life without no side-rails, and he don't think twice about doin' something he ain't never done before, and it's the same with him goin' places. It don't matter to him where them places are, because in a way, for Mad, the whole fukkin world's a road. So, whether it's the white space on the bottom of the map or in whatever's way up at the top—like the North gotdam Pole—to him it ain't nothin' more'n a ride to the levee.

Anyhow, Mad explained that these Houma Indians is what the experts and the ologists call "Tri-Racial Isolates," which he says is quite a special-ass thing to be because it means a sumbich is in one fukkin way or another a combination of the three major flavors of human being: namely, Black, White, and Indian. Plus, these Houmas speaks French, and Mad says it ain't that white Cajun French, and it ain't the Black French, neither. It's just plain fukkin *French* French.

Lu-ziana must be sumpn. Mr. Brainsong's nephew told me that's where the niggas in the Mississippi Delta got our word poontang.* Which, you know, means poo-lala.

McKinney told me Mad might go back to school and get to be some kind of doctor so he could spend the rest of his life studyin' and bein' with nothin' but Tri-Racial Isolates forever. That would be like Mad, to a datgum T. If anybody could do something like that, come hell or high water, it'd be him. Plus, I can just about guarantee you he wishes he was a Tri-Racial Isolate hissef. One time he told me he'd give anything to *not* just be what he called a Scotchy-Irishman, which he said, as far as he was concerned, was—and he said he read this somewheres—the "scum of two fukkin nations."

So there he is, and I guess he's pretty much got over his break-up with Money, although, the truth is it woulda been not breakin' up that woulda done most people in. And when I wrote him and told him about Money inventin' them sex toys and what a big success they was, he wrote back and said he wuddn surprised a bit; he said he always knowed she was one of the "most intelligent" people he ever had anything to do with, and he was glad to see her make good. That's the kinda sumbich he is, and always has been.

---

* Actually, from the French word *poutaine*, meaning prostitute.

CHAPTER 10

Gene LaFoote the Parrot — A Matter of Law Enforcement Protocol — And a Missed Opportunity — Back to the Pass — Wild Hog Supper

There's sumpn else I held out on you, too, because I wuddn sure I ought to bring it up. But this is it: When I got out of the captain's boat and drug my ass up on the beach and had went inside Mad's big wild-lookin' arrangement he'd made with the tarpoliuns, I looked straight in the face of a fukkin big-ass one-legged bird settin' there on a dry limb Mad had picked up off the beach and stuck in the sand, for the bird to roost on.

"*Fuk you, sumbich!*" the bird said said when I come up to him. It was some kinda polly parrot.

"Fuk you, too," I said. "What's your name, you gotdam bird?"

"That's Gene," said Mad. "But his full name is Gene La-Foote."

"Where'd you get the muthafukka?" I ast.

"*Sumbich!*" the bird said.

"I got Gene in Hattiesburg at a gas station on the way down. And he was already named when I bought him."

"Son!" I said. "He's damn near big enough to be a sho-nuff person."

"*Damn!*" Gene said.

"I think I'mo like yo' ass," I told the bird. "My name's Junior Ray."

"*Fuk you, Junior Ray,*" he said.

Gene was a helluva bird. And he was ever' kinda color you

could think of; plus, his hair, if you could call it that, puffed up in the front then slid down in the back where it kicked up a little and reminded me of Elvis.

Anyway, there we was, Mad and me and Gene, out in the middle of the fukkin GuffaMexico on a fairly large strip of sand, and except for the woods over to the east and behind us, I figured it was a lot like what those astronaut coksukkas run into way back when they went to the moon.

And the water. He'p me, Jesus! That was the largest piece of water all in one place this side of Sardis*—or, bygod, over that big-ass bean field down in Darling on the side of Whiting Bye-oh which, every few years or so, during the winter, when it rains a lot and the Coldwater rises, backs up the bye-oh, and floods all the fields south of Tom Dale Road and west of Beale Street,† and turns into a lake. When that happens, I call it the Sea of Darling.

Plus there was one other thing: I brung Mad one nem blow-up sex dolls with a face, which, if you wanted to, you could use to scare chillun on Halloween. You know the kind I mean, with the big eyes and the wide open mouth for some sumbich to stick his dick in.

Anyway, we blew her up, and Mad dug a little pit in the sand outside the shelter, and we stood her up in it and packed the sand around her feet so it looked just like another person standin' there near the doorflap, but out a little and over to the right as you went out of the shelter onto the beach. Things looked pretty homey.

All the info I gave you earlier about Mad's camp is the truth, but what I left out is this: One night a couple of days before the captain come to get me and take me back to Biloxi, I wake up in

---

* Sardis Reservoir, a lake made by the U.S. Corps of Engineers when they dammed the Tallahatchie River in an effort to control flooding.

† An unassuming gravel road in Quitman Country; not the famous one of legend and song located in Memphis.

the middle of the fukkin night, and, real low, I hear Gene sayin',
"Uh-oh, uh-oh, uh-oh," and I thought gotdammit, Gene, shut the
fuk up, but I never did get to say it because then I heard voices.
They was some distance outside the tent, to the west of us.

"Mad," I said. "Wake up, sumbich. Mad . . !" I was tryin' to
holler and whisper at the same time.

"What's the matter, Junior Ray?" he said.

"Listen!" I said. And Mad heard em, too. It sounded like there
was three of em. And they was comin' our way. None of the three
of us thought it sounded good, so I reached in my little satchel and
pulled out my .38 and handed it to Mad as he was easin' toward
the flap to take a look outside.

But before he could even get to the flap, it was flung open, and
we was blinded by three powerful-ass flashlights, all of which th'owed
us on our backs, and some muthfukka we couldn see said, "Aw-ight,
you coksukkas, give us ever'thin' you got and that means money as
well if there is any, or we'll blow your fukkin heads off!"

And that gotdam Gene pipes up with, "Fuk you, sumbich!"

To which Mad, calm as a cucumber and almost simul-gotdam-
taneously added, "Help yourselves." And he squeezed off four rounds
point blank at the light in the middle, and everything seemed to
explode and go pitch dark, but outside it was wild.

It all happened in just one or two split-ass seconds, kablam, all
of a sudden, the way it is when you walk up on a covey of quail.
There was two or three or maybe four shots outside the tent. One
was a big pistol—it coulda been a forty-four or a .357, and there
was two—at least—blasts from a shotgun. But only one of them
shots was pointed our way. And it was a slug.

That sumbich come hummin' end over end through the tent,
and whummed directly between me and Mad, and damn near got
Gene, because the slug hit his roost like an ax and cut it clean in
two, and Gene fell down on the sand behind Mad and me. Plus,

I have to say, by that time, Gene knew enough to keep his little beak shut.

I'mo admit to you that was the first occasion anything out of the barrel of a gun ever come close to me, and it may be the *only* sound I ain't ever gon' forget. If I hadna knowed it was prob'ly a slug by the way it tore up the air when it come by my ear, I'da thought it was a yellowjacket the size of a Stearman.*

Anyway, then it was quiet, more or less, and in a few minutes we heard a big boat motorin' away till we finally couldn hear nothin' no more. Nevertheless, we waited till mornin' before we went outside. We didn't mean to go back to sleep, but, of fukkin course, we did, and when we woke up when it was broad-ass daylight.

I opened the flap of the "tent" and had to squint because it was so bright, especially with the sunlight bouncin' off the sand on the beach. And then I saw it, and I said: "Mad, look at this here!" And he come out, and both of us stood there lookin' at the deadest muthafukka you ever seen, lyin' about ten feet out in front of the shelter, flat on his back with his arms spread out like Jesus. Plus his flashlight was there beside his no-count ass, both of which was all shot to shit. We next discovered there wuddn hardly nothin' left of our blow-up sex doll. It didn't matter, though. She was only for show and just to brighten the place up a little bit.

But now we had a huge-ass problem. Mad said we should lay him, the dead sumbich, over to the side and give him to the captain when he come to pick me up, and then the captain and him and me, and Gene of course, could all go report it to the "authorities." However, I told Mad that, as a law-enforcement professional, we ought not to do any such a thing.

"But what do you suggest, Junior Ray?" he ast. And by that time I had it. I knowed exactly what we was gon' do with the dead-ass fool.

---

* A cropduster bi-plane common in the Delta.

"We're gon' hand him over to the wild hogs over yonder on the other side of the island," I said. "That's what we're gon' do, and after a day or two there won't be nothin' left of his worthless carcass, and that'll be it. He shouldna been a gotdam robber in the first place."

"Well," said Mad.

"Well," I said, "let's you and me, and Gene, make us sumpn to haul his rotten se'f on."

But we couldn find any limbs or nothin' on the beach that was big enough or strong enough, or long enough, so that meant we had to use a couple of the poles Mad had holdin' up one end of the shelter, but it didn't matter a whole lot, because we could put back em up later, which we done.

We lifted up the robber and his shot-up flashlight and laid him on our stretcher. I got on the front end and Mad picked up the back. Gene hopped up with his one good leg and set on top of the sumbich's belt buckle, and off we went.

And, I mean, gotdam! It was hard walkin' through that sand! I hadn't never seen nothin' like it. "Ain't there no niggas on this fukkin island?" I said.

"No, Junior Ray, not a one," said Mad, "We'll have to do it ourselves."

"Chr*EYE*st!" I said.

"Chr*EYE*st!" said Gene. And then he said, "Aarrkk." He was a cute little sumbich. I swear, I never woulda believed I could think much of a bird, but I thought a lot of Gene. I truly did admire him.

We finally got over to the edge of the woods on the side of the island where the Sound was, and where the wild hogs appeared the day I come there on the captain's boat; and, sure enough, there was plenty of signs of root'n there, all over the place, so I knew we was where we needed to be.

I set my end of the stretcher down right in the middle of a buncha pig tracks, and Mad lowered his onto the ground too. He and I took ahold of the robber, with Gene still settin' on his buckle, and we rolled that shot-up sumbich off the stretcher so he could lay there amongst the tracks near the middle of the rooted-up area. Then, just to make certain them wild deep-sea swine would like his quickly spoilin' se'f, we poured a whole number-ten can of bobbakewed beans all over him and followed that with a big bottle of Brer Rabbit cane syrup. By that time, he looked mighty good, and I believe I coulda et him myse'f. Anyway, Mad and I and I guess Gene, too, knew them wild hogs would go hog-wild over what we had just fixed em.

"That's that," I said.

"Lord," said Mad, "I hope there's a hurricane this year."

"Go to hell, cow college!" said Gene.

"You ought to send this sumbich to Ole Miss," I told Mad.

"Fuk you, Junior Ray," said Gene. "Hoddy toddy!"

Mad kept Gene with him and has him to this very day. He was a helluva bird.

Two days later, we tied Gene's one foot to his new roost, and just Mad and me walked back over to see if the hogs had done what we had hoped they'd do, and they had. We couldn find no trace a-tall of the robber. And it was as if the whole thing hadn't never happened.

When the captain came to get me, Mad left, too. We folded up the tarpoliuns and threw them on the boat, and we gave them and all the rest of the supplies to the captain who seemed glad to get em. One thing about Mad, he did all he could to not leave no mess at the campsite. And me and Gene did our best to help him.

Plus, none of us never said one word about the robbers. Hell, no. And when we got to the dock at Biloxi and said goodbye to the captain, and after him and Mad did some more settlin' up, Mad

gave me the book he'd wrote, along with a buncha poems and some
other stuff and ast me to carry em back to St. Leo.

He knew I'd take good care of his writin' and that I didn't give
a shit about readin' none of it, but he said I could let McKinney
see it and that she could have the poems if she wanted em and the
book, too. I headed back up to the Delta, and Mad and Gene drove
on over to Lou-ziana where, as I told you, he disappeared into the
white space on the road map south of Houma. Later, though, you
know, he wrote me about all that.

He says Gene is fine and that the sumbich fell in love with a
gotdam cockatoo, whatever the fuk that is. It didn't sound good at
first, but, knowin' Gene, I'm sure it's a girl. I never had no doubts
about him.

As I indicated, I wuddn gon' tell you about *any* of this because
I was scared I could get in trouble, but then I realized Mad was the
one that shot and kilt the sumbich, not me, gotdammit! I mean,
on one hand it is a comfort to know I didn't kill the muthafukkin
robber, but on the other hand, I missed the only second chance I'll
prob'ly ever have to shoot a sumbich and get away with it.

Sometimes, I swear, I think maybe there *is* a God and that He
has it in for my ass. I'll never in this world know what made me
give my .38 to Mad, and I just keep turnin' it over in my head and
askin' myse'f, "Junior Ray, why, in the name of Jesus and Uncle-
fukkin-Sam, did you do that!"

Anyway, if the other two robbers is even still alive, they probably
ain't gon' buy this book. And if anybody, like the law for instance,
might try to do somethin' to Mad because of the book, I'd just say
I made the whole gotdam thing up.

So, fukkum. I think we're okay. Plus, I thought you might want
to know what really happened on Horn Island besides just Mad
and me bein' philosophers and talkin' about love. And, I have to
say, after dealin' with the robbers and feedin' that sumbich to the

hogs, love didn't seem to matter a whole lot no more.

But, now that all of it's more or less way in the past, I sure wish I'd been the one to shoot that coksukka.

Anyhow all that reminds me of a dish you could fix that, with a good bit of bourbon and Coke beforehand, would be a huge hit, with the right sumbiches. Here's the recipe for my Wild Hog Supper: Go down to the Kroger-store and buy a big-ass "fresh" ham—and don't do like one dumbass muthafukka and come back with a *cured* one . . . !!!

That's a joke.

IT'S SAFE TO SAY we didn't find no Yankee gold coins down there in the mud of the bottom of the Yazoo Pass from the expedition's paymaster's boat. But we did come up with something. While Harlan was chewin' Voyd's ass out in front of every planter and manager and nigga right there in the corner of three fukkin counties, Mad Owens come floppin' up to me in his scuba gear and handed me what looked like a big lump of mud, but it was sorta hard. He just handed it to me and walked on off toward his truck. I held the thing up and at first couldn't tell nothing about it; then I dunked it in a big mud-puddle between the gravel road and the side of a bean field and washed it off a tad. And then I seen what it was. It was a human skull.

My first reaction was that it belonged to an Indian or a nigga—or maybe a Mexican—but suddenly I knowed exactly what it was—hell, it couldna been nothing else! . . . it was the gotdam paymaster's head.*

Later on, I showed it to Ottis, and he wanted to send it to Jackson to have some "forensics" done on it, but I said, "Fuk that, Ottis. Them sumbiches'll keep it and stick it in one nem museums

---

* Probably not the paymaster's skull; most likely that of some, more recent, Saturday-night reveler who said "Good night" to the wrong woman.

or something." Ottis said I was probably right about that, so we just kept it and looked at it a lot, and the more we looked at it, the more we was convinced we had the real thing. Plus it really did look to him and me like the nose had been broke—even though there wuddn no nose there. Anyway, what we thought was really all that mattered, how we felt about it I mean, which is the way it is with everything in life.

It's the same as when some cock-eyed turkey thinks he has seen Jesus in a bean field. It don't matter whether he seen him or not; it just matters how he feels about it. I mean, truth is not a complicated thing, unless you go fukkin it up with a lot of facts. Then you're in trouble.

Well, one *fact* is we *did* show it to Dr. Knightly, who come in after Doc McCandliss had retired and went to live in Florida where he died pretty soon after he got there, and Dr. Knightly said it looked like to him the nose *coulda* been broke but that the thing had been settin' down on the bottom of the river so long that it was probably impossible to tell too much about it. He did say, though, that it wuddn no nigga's skull and that it was definitely a white man's. And that's the kind I like best. You don't find many of em around here, but there's plenty of them others.

BEFORE I GO ON, there is one thing I do need to mention, and that is that even though Lieutenant-Colonel James Wilson played a large role in that whole expedition, I did not focus on his ass, probably because he was so straight, and I don't have much time for anybody, historical or otherwise that don't have a few things wrong with em. It turns out he had a lot wrong with him but not in the kind of way that gets my attention. Wilson was a ass'ole. And I have a theory. There's a line that separates the straight from the insane. One side of that line proceeds from the goofy to the out-and-out fukkin crazy. The other side goes from what I'd consider just your average eagle sprout right on up to your top-of-the-line, totally intolerable ass'ole, usually the very sumbich you need to get the job done right, and that's the hell of it. Fortunately, though, there seems to be enough of them other crazy muthafukkas out there to gum up the works and make things interesting. I'd say, when you think about it, that's history in a nutshell. I oughta be a gotdam professor.

The truth is I get nervous around a sumbich who ain't a little bit squirrely. That may be for a couple of reasons, one of which is that if a sumbich is *sufficiently* squirrely, I can get over on him, and I'm in the driver's seat; the other reason is somebody that's got a few rips and tears here and there ain't gonna be no gotdam "takin' my measurements" like some straight-ass, always-do-it-right muthafukka would be doin'.

Anyway, apart from James Wilson bein' the guy that cleared the Yazoo Pass and apart from his hatred of po' ol' Watson Smith, I don't know where James Wilson is most of the time during the expedition. He don't always say what boat he's on; he just names a place on the land, like Moon Lake or Price's plantation or what have you. It's like he's makin' a point that he ain't in any way connected with the navy. However, I will say this: for a dikhed, he was a helluva good engineer. Plus, he went on to become a big-ass success after the war, but I'll say something about all that later.

Now, I GOT MISS Minnie MacDonald to type* all this for me, and she said, "Junior Ray, you've just got entirely too much sex here." And I said, "How can there ever be too much sex, Miss Minnie?

---

* I gave Miss Minnie the cassettes from my recorder after every session in Junior Ray's "living room," and Miss Minnie transcribed all of it onto a floppy disk. She had done the same thing for Junior Ray and young Brainsong II on the first book. The profanity's phonetics are hers, as Miss Minnie had once dreamed of doing graduate work in linguistics. Consequently, she had an enormous crush on young Brainsong.

Except for fightin' and drinkin' and tryin' to make a living, that's all there is. *Plus*, ever'body seems to be inter-rested in it."

And she come back at me with, "Well, Junior Ray, I thought this was supposed to be about history." And I said, "Yes'm, it is, and that's why there's so much sex." I tried to explain to her that even when there don't appear to be no sex in the shit that historical muthafukkas do, it's always right there, in the middle of it, behind it, underneath it . . . ever'where."

Miss Minnie went on about how she didn't believe it. She said she thought people were much more nicer than that and they didn't just go around thinkin' about such things much less doin' em. And I told her, "No ma'm, they do think about them things all the time, even the nice ones. And they does em too. It's just that we, as average citizens, don't normally get to see it when they go about it. And that's where I come in, as a historian.

But, besides, I told her, there ain't really that much sex in this piece of writing, mainly because I held it out . . . in case it mighta fell into the hands of a buncha fukkin teenagers or something.

You know, even with all the history that's available these days, people don't really learn anything. They're always discoverin' the obvious and wantin' to put a stop to their own natural ways. Take all this stuff you see in the papers now about seksh'l harassment and women and men in the military and fukkin adultery and all that crap. Nobody but a fool and a buncha silly-ass women believes *rules* can stop sex. And then when it duddn, they get all tweety-tweety about it and talk it all to pieces on the radio and on the TV, like it was some new discovery or something. It makes my ass puke. It's almost like the more advantages you have and the more schoolin' you get, the dumber you are. The bad thing about it all is that people get on the bandwagon and go along with all this hysterical claptrap.

Jesus, if a woman could know just for a fukkin second what it feels like to get on a hard, she'd be about as educated as she ever needed to be. But oh hell fukkin no. They somehow think that if, like in the army or on the po-leece force, men and women are not supposed to foodle and doodle with one another that they ain't gonna do it; and, then, when sure as shootin' they *do* do it and get caught at it, it's like this big-ass scandal and everybody's all shocked and ever'thin'.

My question is how can people be so fukkin ignorant and keep missin' the picture after all this time? I don't get it. But then that's always been one of the major differences between me and the rest of these muthafukkas.

Fukkum. I'm puttin' my money on history.

And something else: One thing I cannot stand is all this poopydoo about bein' a team player. That supervisor of mine up at the Lucky Pair-O-Dice—the casino where, as you know, I'm workin' security on the parkin' lot—is hipped on the subject of "team playin'."

In the first fukkin place, ain't nobody a team player and they never was. It's all nothing but a buncha googah. Hell, if it's one thing that makes me sick, it's some mealy-mouthed man or some tweety-tweet woman slobberin' all over the place about sharin' and cooperatin'. If people had had to do all that crap they'da never got nowhere. We'd still be lyin' around nekkid in the Garden of fukkin Eden, pootin' out cotton-candy farts and eyein' the antelopes.

There wouldna been no progress at all.

CHAPTER II

Blue Invaders and the Casinos — Water — A Submarine
Connection? — German POWs — Softening of the Brain —
Rear-ass Admiral Porter is Not Fat — The Pigtail Bandit
— The Value of High Water — Leland Shaw —
Junior Ray's "Nine-Step Fukkin Fish Soup"

I began my life with the best of intentions. Only I never knowed what they were. Things just happened, or they simply popped up, and I done whatever it was I done according to whatever I thought I could do and get away with at the time. And now I still have the best of intentions; only that's about it, they's just intentions, and I couldn't really say about what in particular. By now it's just kind of a principle if you know what I mean—namely, it don't mean nothin'.

Anyway, it is possible that one of the best things I ever got into was this business about the Yazoo Pass. I think if I had gotten some more education when I was younger, instead of me goin' into law enforcement, I mighta just gone into history—but not like that silly coksukka over at the univers'ty who wouldn't come over to see Ottis. The thing is, I have figured out why the Yazoo Pass expedition took such a hold on me.

It's the same thing I feel, in a different way, when I see all these casinos lined up here. They're the outsiders. In a sense, they're the fukkin Yankees, no matter if some of em do come from out West, cause, you see, that's where the Northern boys all went after they got through with the war. Most of the Rebs stayed here where they was. What the fuk did we want with *two* deserts? We was busy tryin' to clean up the one them Yankees left us with after we got finished beatin' the shit out of em. That's a joke. Still, I think there's somethin' to it.

I was out West once. It looked like a fukkin gravel pit to me. But, hell, that's Arkansas for you.

Anyway, it's this thing about the outsider comin' in here, particularly to the Delta. It all just seems otherworldly somehow. And now with these lit-up four-lane parkways snakin' out cross the cotton fields and a fukkin thirty-story hotel risin' up over behind the levee, it's just like it was when them six thousand Yankee soldiers and sailors was steamin' through the Delta on the Coldwater and the Tallahatchie in 1863. It's the same gotdam thing exactly, in terms of amazement.

Granted, a huge amount of the clientele is semi-local—Meffis, Arkansas, West Tennessee, the Hills of Mississippi over to the east, and the like—but the real direction of this thing is global, like Lost-fukkin-Vegas, which is what it is becomin'.

On the other hand, at least there was some bit of nobility to the reason them blue-suits come here in 1863; whereas, now, these gamblin' muthafukkas—from wherever they come from—are goin' to turn us, and I mean everfukkinone of us!: White, Black, and/ or Indifferent, all back into slaves and, I guess, little more'n just plain old whores.

But here's the nut: Like them Yankee blue boys back in the War of the Fukkin Rebellion, these present-day invaders are on water, too, more or less. Don't ast me why, but, like I told you way back, in Mississippi the law here says that gambling has got to be done on a *navigable* stream, which in this case means the Mississippi River and not none of them other little piss-trickles, like the Tallahatchie or, way down south of here, the Big Black or the Pearl and such—and especially not on no ditches or bye-ohs and sloughs, the way—at first—every frog-sukkin', greed-hog, foamin'-at-the-mouth, desperate-ass sumbich you could think of thought he and his family was gon' get theyse'vs a casino in their front yard.

I say "more or less" because, though these casinos is on the Mississippi, they really ain't. They're floatin' in a dug-out pond, tee-totally man-made and which you can't really see unless you know about it and make it a point to notice it. The way it is is that the foundation of the gambling part is built on a big-ass steel barge, several of em hooked together, which they brought in from the river through a canal they dug, and then they closed up the canal and the whole thing looks like it's just settin' there on dry land, which it is . . . but it ain't.

Only the gotdam gambling part of course has to be built on water—which in this case is not no more navigable than your fukkin bath tub—and all the other parts of the operation, like the hotel, the restaurant, the day-care center, and all the other convenient crap these ass'oles go for, can be slapped up anywhere—right smack-ass on the ground. And they are, and on both sides of the levee, too, which—as you know—the gambling part cannot be; it's got to be on the wet side of the levee, between it and the river.

Like I said, at first, every coksukka in the county who had even a drainage ditch runnin' through his land thought he was gonna have a casino on his property and that he'd be rich. Hell, whole families fell out about it. It was like the Devil had done come to town and th'owed a party.

Plus, there's something wild about it all. Maybe everybody thinks their part of the world is like the Delta here—intimately involved with craziness and high water. Hell, I don't know. To the best of my knowledge, I ain't ever been nowhere but here and Arkansas, and the Guffa-fukkin-Mexico.

I bet, though, don't nobody much up North, or between us and the gotdam Can-a-duns, think about those old times and all that shootin' and fear and sickness and death, and love it like we do down here. Hell, I bet they don't know the Civil War from the civil-datgum-service. Whereas here . . . you can see it. It makes your skin jump and puts your hackles up.

Just knowin' about people like po' Watson Smith and Mr. Foster and Lieutenant-Colonel James Wilson and the paymaster's boat and all that stuff can take up a large part of what goes on inside a sumbich down here, without, I might add, him even realizin' the half of it. But all of us are always chasin' something or runnin' from something we don't never find and maybe don't even never get to see, but we know it's here, and it's in the meat of our bones. It's always up the road in the distance and behind us in the fukkin dust, and it's in the darkness of them sloughs and in the slug-ass slowness of these coksukkin little rivers. You look down in the water, and it's lookin' back. You might think it's just a catfish, but it ain't. It's fukkin history.

Sometimes I wish those old invaders was back again. If they were, we'd know what to do and how to act, but with the modern world it ain't that simple anymore. You don't know who to shoot at. You don't know what's bad and what's good cause they both look alike, and you don't know which is which till you turn your head and find the outside world has done come in and fukked a hole in your house.

Well, it's not that we hadn't fukked it up, too, but at least it was us and we was what we was. Now we ain't nothin', and even the way we talk ain't the same anymore. Fukkum.

ANYWAY, HERE IS SOME of the info I put together on what happened after all them six thousand Bluebritches finally won the fukkin war and went on back to where they was from. Well, them that could, I mean.

Lieutenant-Colonel James Wilson—who I've been mentionin' and who put five hunnuhd men on a rope and cleared the Yazoo Pass—went on back up North after the war and became a general and then a big-ass businessman. He also remained a soldier, and when he was sixty, he served in the Spanish-American War and later got pissed off because they wouldn't let him do nothing in World War I. He even tried runnin' for public office, but, because he was such a disagreeable muthafukka, he never could get enough people to vote for his ass.

But, in addition to bein' a dikhed, he was also a very successful engineer. He built some bridges and some railroads and had a passel of children with a woman he met on a steamboat. It's strange how things like that happen. He had missed the boat he was supposed to catch a ride on, which was the *Sultana*, which he couldn't of gotten on nohow because it was so jam-ass packed with all them other Yankee muthafukkas goin' back home after the war—and as you know that sumbich blew up just north of Meffis and was the biggest water disaster in the history of the fukkin world accordin' to Ottis—and then he hopped the next one, and there was the woman he was goin' to marry.

She had been visitin' some of her Southern kin down around Rosedale, actually it was in Lushkachitto—and that's gon' telegraph what I'm gon' say—when the fighting broke out, and hadn't been able to get back to Pennsylvania where she was from. Then, after the surrender, she had done made her way back up as far as Helena where she got a on a boat bound for Cairo, Illinois, from which she was goin' up the Ohio to Cincinnati and then get a train to Philadelphia.

Well, you know the story; it's the same old thing; he met her, and they got to talkin' and later got hitched. But that's not the end of it. Her name was Merigold . . . Merigold Benoit. Her daddy was old Colonel Benoit's baby brother who had gone to the University of Pennsylvania and decided to stay on up there, mainly, they said, because he had learned something about economics and knew the South didn't have none.

NOW, JUST LIKE LIEUTENANT-COLONEL James Wilson, Mr. Foster couldn get rid of the South neither. After the fall of Vicksburg, he was put on the Mississippi River down there in that neighborhood to help get the port goin' again and to see that all them Yankee boys got back home. That was his job. He was appointed to it after some ass-hole stuck nine zillion of those po' wore-out bastuds on the *Sultana*, and the government didn't want nothin' like that to ever happen again—which it might well have if Mr. Foster hadna been put in charge.

The government was worried about what folks might think of whoever was runnin' the sumbich and wanted to make sure they could get more coksukkas to come fight a war for em if they took a notion to have one again. They didn't want to piss off the wives and girlfriends by havin' their boyfriends and husbands survive the war and then get blowed up and drowned on the way home. I tell you, to be as organized as them army guys are with all that fukkin stan'-up-straight crap and everything, it sure seemed like they went off half-cocked most of the time. But, I guess if you're gonna fuk up something, it's good to have the authority to do so.

Anyhow, after the surrender Mr. Foster hopped a train and was ridin' north but had to spend the night in Hernando* because the tracks needed to be repaired. And while he was there, at the hotel, he was invited to a little diddly-doo of some kind, and he met a woman named Amanda Owens who had swore she wouldn marry no man unless he had lost an arm or a leg for the South.

Naturally, she married Mr. Foster, moved up North with him, died in childbirth, and her older sister had her brought back to Hernando, and that's where she is to this day, in the cemetery, of

---

* Hernando, up in the Loess Hills and not far from the edge of the Delta, is one of the old upland towns, like Como and Carrolton, where many of the early Delta planters lived with their families before they eventually moved down into the malaria-plagued—mosquito, snake, and panther infested—bottom-land morass of the post-bellum Delta.

course. Later on, around 1944, Amanda's great-great niece run off with a German POW from the camp down at Pace, between Cleveland and Rosedale. The whole thing caused a helluva stir, but it worked out in the end, and they lived a pretty happy life, finally, with her German husband windin' up workin' for her daddy on his plantation near Como, over in the Hills.

If you want to know the truth, I always thought there was a connection between him and that German submarine Voyd and me found out over the levee in the woods around Hawk Lake. I can't prove nothing, of course, but it's a feeling I've had all these years, once I learned about that girl runnin' off with the German and all and him workin' on her daddy's cotton farm. You know, sometimes you just *know* things. Plus, it wouldna surprised me if that German sumbich had been a great-great nephew of Mr. Foster. I mean, hell, both of em was foreigners. There ain't a nickel's worth of difference between a German and a Yankee.

Besides which, he wuddn just no average German. He was an officer of some kind, and his people had had money, for a long fukkin time, over in Germany, so, later on in the minds of her people, it wuddn as though she had done took a step down or nothin', and the story was her mama and daddy and all the rest of em was real happy about the thing, once the war blowed over and we was friends again. Plus, he was *Baron* somethin-or-ruther, and her family especially liked that and all the string of long-ass names that went along with the baron part.

BUT IT'S WATSON SMITH I've always been the most interested in. For some reason I seem to be drawn to people who ain't right in the head. And in a way, I guess I was chasin' around after the commodore the same way I chased around after Leland Shaw, only I didn't want to shoot the commodore. And, if you want to know the truth, I am still hopin' Ottis is goin' to get me another z-rocks that'll tell me what the fuk, in the end, they said finally Watson Smith died with. Ottis said he might have to go up to Annapolis to get the information, or to Warshin'ton, DEEcee.

I know now that the pay-otey couldna killed Smith. He had something wrong with him in the first place, and the pay-otey just made him worse. I have mentioned that Admiral Porter said Smith had "softening of the brain." Well, in the old days, here, that was just a kind of polite term for syph'lus. But it would have had to be the third stage of it, and Mr. Brainsong said that takes a while to get goin', like ten years or so after you first catch it.

As a historian I did come across sumpn that said Smith was sent down to Brazil when he was a young officer, so, owin' to how long it takes to get up to your brain and all, he could have gotten it down there, but I don't think so, owin' to how available it was right here in America.

I don't know about up North, but, down here in the Delta, syph'lus was very, very popular. In fact, Miss Helena Ferry's brother-in-law died with it in the 1920s. The story was he had picked it up at a nigga whorehouse over in Arkansas, where he was from, when he was just a boy. The sores and the rashes went away, but them little corkscrew things swam out of his blood stream and up his backbone till they got to his brains and eat em up, and all that was happenin' after nobody could no longer catch it from him and he had done married and had a baby boy.

When the government come *back* around and give all those coksukkas whose Wasserman was positive a shot of penicillin, it knocked out the fukkin disease. I mean blammo. Just like that. But it didn't last. And the sumbich rose again and even got to where it didn't pay a whole lot of attention no more to the penicillin. Some people hooped and hollered about it bein' a curse of Godalmighty on us because of our sins. I never thought so. Fukkum. It was a germ.

Anyway, after a while, Miss Helena's brother-in-law started doin' really wild-ass stuff like not lettin' Miss Helena's sister leave the house and, later, not lettin' his son change his shirt. Plus, he did all that by wavin' a butcher knife at em. Miss Helena's sister had him committed, and then she divorced him. His mama and the rest of his family up in Meffis and over across the river never would acknowledge that anything was ever wrong with him, and, later, when he'd stagger nekkid down Union Avenue in the middle of Meffis, they'd pretend they didn't see him and would act all rude and pissed off with anybody who brought it to their attention. But, now, I ask you, who the fuk needs syph'lus to make em crazy? That whole brood was nuts. The syph'lus just made em *nutser*—which is what I'm talkin' about with regard to the pay-otey and Commodore Smith. It was just an extra.

On the other hand, a fellow who wrote a book about James Wilson said that Smith got sick "from serving in the pestilential swamps of Upper Mississippi" and that "He later resigned his commission owing to 'aberration of mind,' and not long afterward died of the fever he had contracted."* I can live with that, because the fellow seems to believe it was the place, the Delta itself, that drove Watson Smith insane, and as you know that is not hard for me to feature. But I'd still like to know the particulars a little better so I wouldn have to rely just on Ottis, and on what Mr. Brainsong told me—nor, bygod, on what Rear Admiral Porter said that time about Smith havin' "softening of the brain"—or even on my own natural historical skills, to piece it all together. The truth is out there, and I need to find the right hammer to hit it on its slippery-ass head.

AND HERE I WOULD like to change sumpn I misspoke about. I called Admiral Porter a fat-ass, but the fact is he was on the thin side. I do, however, think he was a little like me in that he could

---

* Edward G. Longacre, *From Union Stars to Top Hat*, p. 74.

get carried away ever' now and then when something important fired-up his interest. That's not necessarily the worst thing that can happen to a sumbich unless you get the whole fukkin U.S. Navy stuck somewhere in the middle of Tallahatchie County, which, I guess, technically he did and he didn't, because, next to General Grant, it was him, Rear Admiral Porter, who was the boss of the whole thing, and the one who chose Watson Smith to be the honcho in charge of the disaster. So Admiral Porter had one leg in and one leg out.

Bear in mind, however, that even though Admiral Porter wuddn on the actual Yazoo Pass Expedition, he absolutely *was* present on a similar operation up Deer Creek, lower down in the Delta. What happened was he and his boats got stuck good, and they was all lucky to get out of there alive.

In another totally fukked-up effort to slip in behind Vicksburg, Admiral Porter took one of his "flotillas" up Steele's Bye-oh, across Black Bye-oh, and into Deer Creek so he could come out into the Yazoo River and get the drop on the Rebs holed up on the high ground at Vicksburg. But, again, it was a mess.

Check out this z-rocks from a book about Porter:

> When the flotilla entered Steele's Bayou, it passed through a forest shrouded in mist and drenched with a dew that trickled like rainfall from dangling clumps of Spanish moss. Limbs hanging over the narrow banks crashed down on the decks of the iron-clads as they bulled their way through wild eglantine, briar, and grapevines. At midday the boats churned past Muddy Bayou, and thirty river miles later they reached Black Bayou, the four-mile link to Deer Creek.
>
> Porter entered the narrow bayou, found it rimmed with cypress and willow and ordered out saws, knives, and cutlasses. Details cut away branches and pulled up trees by their roots. Withes

dangling in the narrow bayou jammed the paddle wheels, and when slaves gathered on the banks seeking emancipation, Porter put them to work.*

The long and the short of it is he got up in there and couldn Get out because the Rebs moved in on him and his flotilla. The funny part of it is that the Rebs pulled out a whole brigade of soldiers from Fort Pemberton to go attack Admiral Porter down near Rolling Fork, on Deer Creek, at the same time old General Quinby had done made the Yazoo "blues"—then under Mr. Foster's command because Watson Smith had folded—turn around and go back to Fort Pemberton, which, let me remind your ass, was right there just outside present-day Greenwood.

And here's the kicker: Quinby coulda gone in there at that very moment and whupped the shit out of the Rebs at Fort Pemberton right then and there, but he didn't know the Rebs was all gone off to fight Admiral Porter—which just proves it's what you don't know that counts. Plus, there is such a thing as bein' too fukkin careful. And they didn't have no cell phones back in nem days.

I'm tellin' you. Porter had got his butt in a sling: "[T]he flotilla remained stationary, stranded in the willows" And "Every tree and stump . . . covered a sharpshooter ready to pick off any luckless [Yankee] marine who showed his head above deck." That was some bad stuff. The admiral's only hope was for General Sherman to rescue his ass, and "When no word came from Sherman, Porter drafted several hasty messages, one on toilet paper wrapped in a tobacco leaf." All them quotes is from the same book.

The reality of it is almost as good as the way I see it. And I

---

* *Admiral David Dixon Porter* by Chester G. Hearn, pp. 186–190. (Best regards to the MLA. Though our form may not be what it should, I labored conscientiously to ensure that Junior Ray gave proper credit to his sources. There is, however, little use in my trying to convince him a "z-rocks" is not sufficient.)

don't say that about everything. But when I hear about what went on or when I read a z-rocks of it, I just seem to know all the stuff that ain't been said. I know what's left out. I mean it's exactly like I'm lookin' at it all when it was happenin'—and I'm hearin' it too. Believe me—I know what those muthafukkas was sayin'. cause time and the world and the gotdam sunlight ain't nothin' but a tape, and every single-ass thing that was ever said or done is all still right there. You just have to tune in to get it. And I do. Otherwise I wouldn never be worth a shit as a historian.

Anyhow, it was General Sherman who saved Admiral Porter. And because Sherman's soldiers was comin' across some of the most godawful swampy-ass country in the world, all of em was covered in mud—and had so much buckshot* stickin' to their boots I expect they looked like gotdam mudskimos wearin' gumbo snowshoes when they finally got to Porter—but here's a z-rocks:

> Sherman, still far down the creek did not wait for Porter's messengers. That night, when he heard the distant rumble of naval guns, he urged his men forward. Being on foot himself, he led the men by candlelight down a mud-splattered road running beside Deer Creek. Crossing swamps hip deep, 'the smaller drummer boys had to carry their drums on their heads,' he wrote, 'and most of the men slung their cartridge boxes around their necks.'"†

More than twenty gummed-up miles later General Sherman was gettin' close to where Admiral Porter's r'nclad gunboats was stuck in the willows and about to be destroyed by the Rebs; somebody give him a horse which he jumped up on, bareback, and said,

> I . . . rode up the levee, the sailors coming out of their iron-

---

* Also called "gumbo," a clayey, very sticky soil type common to the area.
† Hearn, pp. 190–191.

clads and cheering most vociferously as I rode by and as our men swept forward across the cotton-field in full view. I soon found Admiral Porter, who was on deck of one of his ironclads, with a shield made of the section of a smoke-stack, and I doubt if he was ever more glad to meet a friend than he was to see me.*

I LOVE THE WAY he says his men "swept" acrosst a fukkin cotton-field. "Swept" my ass. It was all they could do to put one foot in front of the other, and I guarantee it. Hell, all you got to do to understand that is to go rabbit huntin' one day down there when the ground is wet, and you'll know it all.

I do love the way them sumbiches talked way back then. I can't figure out why people don't talk that way now, but I guess it has something to do with the fact that people don't talk much these days anyhow. And that's probably because of TV. I don't know what else to blame it on. Then, again, maybe folks don't talk much now-days because they don't know shit and don't have nothin' to say, unless it's about sports, and I, personally, don't give a crap about that. Talkin' about sports, to me, is the same as not talkin' at all. Voyd an' nem says that ain't true and somethin's wrong with me.

Fukkum. If they're *right*, Whooee Jesus! I'm gone! We got a problem. I'd just as soon watch a bug fuk as look at a gotdam pis-syanty ballgame. I don't care how big and tough them coksukkas are, it ain't nothin' but buncha lillo boys playin' with a ball. But, the real truth is I think my attitude has something to do with the fact that games is organized. If football wuddn organized and planned and if it didn't have no rules, then, son! I'd probably be glad to watch it—but not the way it presently is.

That's one of the reasons I like things about the War of the Fuk-kin Rebellion: Most of the stuff that happened was disorganized and/or unplanned. And I can't see a whole lot of rules involved;

---

* Hearn, p. 191.

although a few of them sumbiches was a little more gentlemanly about some things, though on the whole, and by and fukkin large, it was a gotdam dogfight. The whole thing was a total mess, and a whole helluva lot of them po' bastards died with nothin' more exciting than the gotdam flu.

They shoulda got a medal, called "the purple virus." One thing I have never, ever, understood is why a sumbich should win a fukkin medal for gettin' his ass blowed off. To me, it seems like the only time they ought to give you a medal is when you shoot some other muthafukka, not when some sumbich shoots you!

But I am totally knocked out by what Mr. Brainsong would have called "the whole mighty-ass pageantry of it all." Well, that's the way what he said come across to me; you know, Mr. Brainsong never did use no cuss words when he talked, but I just can't seem to he'p it. My daddy talked the way I talk, and so did my grandpappy and all my fukkin uncles. Now, my mama and all the rest of the women in the family never said nothin'. That's the truth. They was quiet as a cow. Just a-chewin' and never sayin' a fukkin word. I don't remember any of em ever talkin' at all. Mostly they just worked or stood back and looked on. That's the funniest thing. I guess I never thought about it much, but it's the god's truth. I never heard my mama say nothin'—nothin' at all. All the talking I remember come from my daddy and the men.

It makes me wonder what my mama would have said if she had ever said anything. But, I reckon from her point of view, there wuddn nothin' to say. What was was, and I know she never believed there'd be anything to change it. She probably never could have imagined that I woulda had a career in law enforcement. And I'm sure she thought people would be hoein' cotton till the end of the coksukkin world. She was a good woman, though. And she tried to do right by me and all of us. I just never knew her is all. Then, again, maybe I did.

Anyway, I grew up in what you might say was conditions similar to those at the time of the Yazoo Pass Expedition. We did not have no lights, nor no runnin' water, nor no telephone, nor nothing at-all which now people can't live without. We didn't have none of that, and until 1937 there wuddn but one paved road in the whole Mhoon County here in the Delta, and there *still* wuddn but one even after World War II. And that was Highway 61, which, when you got to Meffis, it was Third Street.

I doubt there was any kind of hard-top a-tall over where my daddy was raised and where I lived when I was real small, over near Clay City, in the Hills. Well, nobody with any fukkin sense wanted to go live there, and although most people should have wanted to leave, they didn't do much of that neither. Some sumbich who spoke at the St. Leo Rotary Club said what looked like laziness to the outside world was probably caused of the way those folks over there durin' that time in the Hills ate. He said their diet, which sometimes, I know, included dirt, spooned right out of the side of a gully, caused em not to have enough get-up and go—nor sense neither. Although he did say the dirt mighta been the good part of their fukkin diet on account of the min'rals.

Well, they didn't really know there was anywhere to go to anyhow. And, I guess because of all the hoecake and bacon grease, they didn't give a dam. And a number of the ones who might have known about places they could relocate must not have thought there was much use in it. But one day my daddy did leave and brought us down into the Delta.

Them planters sometimes would have to scramble around to find labor because a lot of the niggas was takin' off and goin' up North. My daddy, who was on hard times, heard about them Delta big shots lookin' for sharecroppers, so he packed us up and we come down to the Delta in my uncle Bigelow's old truck.

Uncle Bigelow took us out of the Hills and down into the Delta this side of Savage where he left us, my daddy and my mama and my sisters, all of us, in the middle of the fukkin woods at a place called Dooley Spur—which ain't there no more, and you can't tell it ever even was. Anyway, we walked just a little piece to the west of that gotdam semi-crossroads and stopped at a house that didn't have no doors, and that is where I growed up the rest of my young life and where my mama and papa died. We did put in some doors, though, one for the front and one for the back.

I have—or at least *had*—three sisters, and I only know where one of em is. She's in a growed-up cemetery—out at Little Texas, not far from where we lived. The others took off when they was barely fifteen and sixteen, and we never saw neither of em again.

One did write from Calumet City, and said she had become an entertainer and was soon goin' to reside in New Or'lins, but that was the last we heard. The other one must notta looked back, I guess. We never did hear from *her*. However, once I seen a picture of a woman in the Meffis *Press-Scimitar* they called "The Pigtail Bandit," and I coulda swore it was Wanda.

Whoever it was, though, they caught her and some dumb slicked-back sumbich at four in the morning inside Bobby's Bobbakew on South Bellevue, tryin' to prise the silver dollars out of the floor. Bobby's, as you know, was world-famous for the silver dollars it had there, all stuck in the fukkin floor, so people could look down at em and walk on em, and, I guess, talk about Bobby's. I don't know, though. The whole idea of it kinda pissed me off.

Anyhow, the article said the day before that "the pair" had "allegedly" been seen attemptin' to rob the ticket lady at the Princess Thee-ater on Main Street. After that I never did see no more about em. Fukkum.

THOSE TWO GIRLS NEVER would have believed I'da become a historian. Shoot, neither would I. But once I learned about all the

soldiers and sailors on all the big boats with the cannons and shit
steamin' around right where I am now not no more'n a hunnuhd'n
sumpn years ago, I was hooked, and I'll go to my grave thinkin'
about Anguilla Benoit and that weird-ass Mexican Indian of hers.
But mostly, I think about Watson Smith and how crazy he was
and how that po' sumbich must have suffered, slidin' his ailin'—as
it turns out—*syphi*-litic ass through this former gotdam slough I
call home.

The thing is, he was the one and the only one that coulda been
picked to lead that thing. Like they say on TV, he fits the profile.
He was the one, syph'lus or no fukkin syph'lus—pay-otey nor no
pay-gotdam-otey!—this place had the most effect on, and there has
to be one like that—because that is the way I see things, and I see
em thatta way because it is just the *nature* of this place that there
has always got to be some muthafukka in it who has gone round
the bend, so to speak, *because* of this place. It can be a Leland Shaw,
who never believed he was where he was, which was back home
here in the Delta, or a Watson Smith, who just could not compre-
fukkin-hend that there could even *be* such a place or, much less,
that he could be in it.

And I can't help but see the similarities in other ways. Leland
Shaw was hipped on the subject of high water. That was all through
his notebooks—which, as you know, was later edited and put together in a book by Mr. Brainsong's prissy-ass nephew. Anyway, you
remember Shaw thought the "high water" was his ticket home—not
understanding of course, because he was fukkin nuts, that he was
already at home. It's right funny. He was lookin' for the very thing
Watson Smith was tryin' to get away from, because as you know,
Smith and the six thousand gotdam blue-suited Yankee soldiers and
sailors was on the high water. *It* had found *them*. So to speak.

Not only was Smith on the high water but he, like Shaw, was
absolutely dependent upon it to get his ass out of the Delta so he

could go home to New Jersey where, though I'm sure he didn't know it at the time, was where he was goin' to die.

For Shaw, of course, all that high water crap was just a fantasy, just like the home he was lookin' for, which, I guarandamntee you, if you want my fukkin opinion, always had been. All them planters think the Delta is something more'n it is. It's the way those sumbiches are brought up. Plus, I guess they have to think that way; otherwise they'd all move. Probably, though, just up to Meffis.

And, another thing, Leland Shaw was so concerned about bein' tracked down by the Germans, and, as you remember, he seen em ever'where, all over Mhoon County, but I guess he didn't know anything about the six thousand Yankees that had invaded and was floatin' around all over the high water a little less than a hunnuhd years before the time he had done run off from the rest wing of the county hospital and I was out tryin' to catch the sumbich while he was holed up in that gotdam silo—which me and Voyd didn't figure out about till it was too fukkin late to shoot his ass.

I guess he woulda really fell off his log if he hadda been more of a historian, like me, and known the de-tails of the Yazoo Pass Expedition and somehow in his crazy head hadda thought them Yankees was still splashin' and bobbin' around out there lookin' for *him*.

But, it's funny, Leland Shaw was looney and seein' things and worried about bein' chased by the fukkin Germans, who of course in a way was here, too—a bunch of em, and some Eye-talians as well, durin' the 1940s, penned up in camps down in Clarksdale and at Rosedale, and, though it's close kin but not actually in the Delta, also over in the Hills at Como; and some of em even come here by that submarine me and Voyd found over the levee—and ain't nobody really sure where *them* coksukkas went—but, anyway, they, and all them other German soldiers in the camps, all of em, come here in a boat durin' the high water, just like ol' Watson Smith and the fukkin *flotilla* full of them Yazoo *blues.*

Speakin' of water, you and your mama and nem might like to try out my recipe for fish soup. Here it is:

🦪 JUNIOR RAY'S NINE-STEP Fukkin Fish Soup 🦪

1. Do not go catch the gotdam fish. Buy the muthafukkas up in Meffis at the grocery store.

2. Get two cans of chicken noodle soup, open em up, put it in a saucepan, and add some water. Stir it all around, then get out a big-ass pot, and pour what you've got into it through a strainer, so you there won't be no noodles and other crap in the pot. Or, screw the chicken and just use the juice in a can of vegetarian vegetable soup. It's probably better for you cause it won't have no fat, and, once the fish are in it a few minutes, it'll taste exactly the same as the other. Take it from me.

3. Put the fire to it, and add a can of pureed tomatoes. Turn up the heat . . .

4. Then get out your fish—halibut, salmon, shrimp, lobster, scallops, squid, and if you can find them, some really, really, fresh, shucked oysters, but, unless they are squeakin' fresh, don't use em. I'm tellin' you. Don't do it! I don't care what anybody tells you. If the sumbiches are not just right-out-of-the-shell fresh, you don't want em in your fukkin fish soup, which is what some ol' boy told me was called "a kind of boo your base." And he claimed saffron was good to put in it, so th'ow some of that in too, along with some basil, some thyme, some garlic, some rosemary, and, that's right, some gotdam cayenne.

5. Next, get a skillet, cover the bottom with olive oil, and

commence to saw-tay (just a very little bit!) all the fish-fish and shellfish you've got. Put a lot of garlic in there with em, and do em all around. The reason you don't want to cook em much in the skillet is because you're goin' to th'ow it all into the big-ass pot with the chicken soup in it, which has now come to a boil.

6. Dump what you got in the skillet into the pot. People may say you got to have a fish stock to make fish soup, but what they don't tell you is that, whether your pot is full of water or full of chicken soup, it's the fukkin fish that'll make the stock. So fuk tryin' to boil up a bunch fish heads or pou-rin' a bottle of clam juice in the pot to made a fish stock. It don't take a gotdam fish rocket scientist to clue your ass in to what I just told you.

7. Let all your stuff simmer-ass along in the pot—so ever'thing gets a touch of ever'thing else, and you especially want the squid to cook a long time so they'll be tender and not taste like a piece of rubber hose, like they do in all them communist Chinese places. I don't trust them sumbiches.

8. Warnin': If you do use oysters, wait till just before you get ready to dip the stuff out before you add em to the pot, because if you cook the muthafukkas too long, they'll shrink up to nothin' like your dick. If you got one.

9. Anyway, after a while, grab your bowls, and stick a big piece of French bread in em. Then, ladle out your "Nine-Step Fukkin Fish Soup" for you and your company. And that's it, Chili Dog.

CHAPTER 12

The Romans Was Wrong — The Truth Is Unimaginable — The Ease of Research — Miss Sadie Hamlin — Them Planters Is Dying Out — Chinamens — History vs. Philosophy — Sex, the Magic Pussy, & the Law

The trees ain't as big now or as numerous as they was back then, and I look at em all the time when I'm ridin' along the Coldwater and around where the Pass goes into it out there north of Birdie, east of Rich. I even go over to the left of Lambert every now and then on the sixth of March* just to look at the spot where the Coldwater runs into the Tallahatchie. And, God knows, I could set there in front of Uncle Hinroo's and look up and down and out across Moon Lake all day long and think about all that carryin' on, all them soldiers and sailors and especially the gunboats, and all that trouble they all went to mostly for nothin' whatsoever. History'll tear your ass up if you let it.

One time I said that, and the liberrian, Ms. Pursley, said, "Oh, Junior Ray, you're so sensitive!" And I told her, under my breath of course, "Fuk you, you silly-ass cow cunt. If you ever say that again where anybody can hear you, I'll piss on your gotdam encyclopedia." I don't know why that come to me thatta way, but I know I couldna thought it up beforehand if I'da had to.

Anyway, I don't do none of that historical shit because I'm *sensitive*. Gotdam. Gag my ass with a fukkin rat. Jeee-zusss ChrEYEst! That *sensitive* crap *really* gets away with me. I go look at all that

---

* In a sluggish span of time roughly between the 5th and the 7th the naval vessels and the army transports had all steamed out of the Coldwater and into the Tallahatchie.

stuff because, as I have already said, them soldiers and sailors is *still* there. Hell, if I don't know nothin', I know that whatever happens never goes away—even though Mr. Brainsong claimed he believed in what he told me them old Romans used to say, "*Tempus Exdax Rerum,*"* which he said means time eats up ever'thin'.

Well, it don't—and them fukkin Romans was wrong. They was probably just thinkin' about houses and other regular doowah such as that. I'm talkin' about events. Things that happen—if they're big and powerful enough—can make a kind of imprint in the air. Just like when you slap your hand in wet concrete.

And fuk you. Don't be tryin' to say I'm like that gotdam Leland Shaw! Cause I'm not. But just because a sumbich is insane don't mean that he's wrong. At least not about everything.

So when I see things, like the trees and the water the way they is now, I also see em as they was back then. You might say it's like lookin' at a footprint and hearin' a sound comin' from a hole in the air. Whatever happened once is in the vacancy, if you know what I mean. In other words, it's still there—*because* it once *was*. And if you're any kind of historian a-tall, you can find the hole, and you can see the shape of what was there and hear the fukkin noise that was part of it at the time. Otherwise there wouldn be no point wastin' your time tryin' to fuk around with history. It's a good bit like bein' a tracker over at Parchman.

But, hell, when it comes to sound, if they can get a song out of a piece of plastic and a fukkin needle or a radio program or one on the TV right out of the muthafukkin air—well, what I'm talkin' about is the same gotdam thing, but just on a bigger scale and without no special equipment. But, Jee-zuss Chr*EYE*st! Electricity is ever'where. So, I mean, there you have it: a Hollywood-size, natural-ass color TV and stereo system just right there in the fukkin

---

* See earlier note on Mad Owen's use of this maxim as the title to his poem on old age.

scenery! Personally, I don't see nothin' strange about it one bit. And I don't think your average historian would either.

Nope. I just like what I like, and I like the *parts* of things that I like—cause I don't much like *all* of anything—such as history, for example. I don't give a shiverin' shit for any of it except the part about the Pass. And that ain't ever goin' to change. The rest of the "War of the Fukkin Rebellion" don't mean doodly to me.

Funny thing, though, except for me and Ottis, I cannot see that any of the other historians out there care much about the Pass one bit. Personally, I think it's because they've been educated too fukkin much. And that's the shame of it! Hell, I don't need no buncha books as long as I can get hold of a few z-rockses.

I'm on up in years, and bein' a historian is probably a natural thing. Most people, it looks like to me, become real inter-rested in the past about the time it becomes clear they're about to become part of it. That's why it occurred to me that some of the real young history professors over at the University look young, but they're rotten-ass old on the inside, unlike, say, a fukkin sign-tist. Now, those muthafukkas is always workin' with the future—because half the shit we're gonna have ain't been discovered yet. Bear in mind I ain't talkin' about them sign-tists that dig up old bones—well, I don't want to get into that unless it's to piss off a preacher . . . which, as you know, I never like to miss a chance to do. I just can't stand a sumbich that has everything *solved.* And it's the truth, too. When them sumbiches write, they don't never use a question mark. Fukkum. Well of course I do know one or two good ones, and they're all right, bygod; but I ain't got no use for the rest of em.

Beyond what I've already told you, there's not much I want to add to what I think were the most inter-restin' facts concernin' the Yazoo Pass Expedtion. I mean there's always more if you want to go into it, but I don't—at least not now.

So, I'll just say this—and it's the point of the whole thing, and that is: If you can imagine six thousand blue-suited Yankee soldiers and sailors crammed into ten warships full of cannons, trailin' two coal barges, and twenty-two other steamboats, all anywhere from 150 to 220 feet long, comin' across Moon Lake and hangin' a left at Uncle Hinroo's where they proceed to twist and turn their way through the woods and swamps and flooded cotton fields of the upper part of the Mississippi Delta, and doin' it all on nothin' more'n a buncha big-ass bye-ohs a hunnuhd and thirty-four years ago where, with half of them ol' boys sick with killer colds, the malaria, typhoid, and everything else, including the *Smilin' Mighty Jesus*, not to mention gettin' their two r'nclads shot to shit in the middle of fukkin nowhere, and then havin' to turn 'round and come back-ass out again, plus also havin' worked like dogs and CPA's at tax time just to NOT accomplish all that, you've got the picture.

A swamp is a swamp no matter whether it's summer or winter. In one season you're hotter'n a muthafukka day and night and drove outta your gotdam mind with bugs buzzin' in your ears and up your butt, and in the other you're just colder than shit and God he'p your ass if you get wet! Cause, sumbich, there ain't no relief available.

Those miserable sumbiches chuggin' through the Yazoo Pass on that fukked up expedition got a taste of both. First they begun it in February and wound it up in April—I say wound it up; I really mean "gave it up" and had to come on back outta there and say to hell with it, cause they couldn get past Greenwood. They never even got into what you might call the full Yazoo of the thing, cause they got stopped on the Tallahatchie before it hit the Yalobusha.

BUT WHAT GETS ME about history is that a lot of the stuff that happened back then, right where I'm settin', so to speak, is just plain un-fukkin-imaginable. Just look at the difference between then and now. We got a four-lane, air conditioning, color TVs, and a Sonic drive-in right at our fukkin fingertips, and back then there wuddn nothin' but snakes and bobcats. Shoot, where I am right now the vines and the oaks and the cypress was so thick there prob'ly wuddn even no sunlight, just a buncha woods and brakes.

So the idea of six thousand Northern-ass soldiers and sailors in—I would say boats, but them things was ships—*ships,* bygod, longer'n a night in jail, sportin' every kind of cannon just about that there was at the time—Parrott* guns and Dahlgrens and such, both rifled and smoothbore—but the very fukkin idea of them sumbiches even considerin' doin' what they did in that godawful wet-ass wilderness is why I got so caught up in needin' to understand it and to see in my mind the way it probably was.

Now, in my re-search, some of which I done at the liberry and a lot of which I done just talkin' to folks—largely Ottis and Mr. Brainsong—I figured they'd already took care of most of the re-search theyse'fs, so there wuddn no sense in me goin' in behind em when all I had to do was ast em what I wanted to know. Fuk sittin' in a gotdam liberry when you can just set your ass around Ruffin's Bait Shop, have yourse'f a cool one, and shoot the shit about history and come off learnin' just as much as you would have if you'da done it right. I know you've probably noticed like I have that people always talk about re-search bein' so hard and all, but I never could see what all the fuss was about. I thought it was pretty fukkin easy, if you ast me. I mean it ain't like a sumbich was workin' or nothin'. And I was good at it.

But even though I gave it my best shot I couldn find much out about Anguilla Benoit in the liberry, but I learnt a helluva lot about her from Miss Sadie Hamlin—who was way up in her nineties, maybe god knows even older, and loved to drink beer and fish off the pier—and who remembered seein' Anguilla long after

---

* A rifled "cannon" invented in 1860 by Robert Parker Parrott.

old Snake Frontstreet had done sipped his last silver julep cup of "Jack" over cracked ice. Plus, if you remember Dundee Hamlin, who I mentioned earlier in the book and who was the sumbich who called up Sheriff Holston when Mr. Flickett blowed up Slab Town, he, Dundee, was Miss Sadie's baby brother.

Anyway, Miss Anguilla was a real old lady then and used to come down from Meffis to St. Leo in a special railroad car to visit Miss Helena Ferry's mother and drink what Miss Sadie called "absent drips," whatever the fuk those were. Miss Sadie said you was only supposed to drink "absent drips" in the morning and that that's what people did in New Or'lins, but that Anguilla and Ol' Miss Ferry done it all day long and whenever they fukkin well wanted to while they set there on Miss Ferry's side porch and talked about all the po' dead muthafukkin rich-ass, hard-drinkin', high-rollin' cotton men they'd knowed in their lives, and had probably kilt one way or another and, I expect, had had theyse'vs a helluva good time doin' it, too.

Anyhow, Miss Sadie said she was about eight or nine, and she recalls bein' over there and meetin' Anguilla. Miss Sadie said she even remembered the show boats that used to come and tie up on the river out at O. K. Landing. Plus, she also told us she used to roller skate on the second floor of the old empty courthouse that stood by the levee at what was left of Port Tubby, one of the early-ass county seats of Mhoon County, and which the river run off from and left high and dry after the channel changed during one of the big floods back in the1880s and left the town a mile away from the Mississippi River so it wuddn a port no more, which didn't make no difference no way because it wouldna lasted due to the fact that, about that same time, the railroad had come through and was suckin' everything away from the river towns faster'n a rabbit can fuk. So, the gotdam point is, a sumbich don't need a liberry if he's got Miss Sadie.

Plus, all that and a lot more ain't gone with no wind; most of it, most of what was here, went with the Mississippi River. Well, the heavy stuff anyway.

And I'll say this about Miss Sadie: I never held it against her that she was part of them planters, because she fit into the Bait Shop just fine like the rest of us. I liked *her*, and she liked *me*. And that's the long and the short of it and of course mainly why I liked her.

THEM PLANTERS IS DYIN' out. First of all there ain't as many planta-tions no more and ain't none of em that's left is run the way they was before the *changes*. In other words you won't see fourteen-zillion niggas, or any of my raggedy-ass kin, all pickin' and choppin' in the fields which some sumbich at the Boll & Bloom Café said now look like a pitch'r he saw once of Kansas, and, from what I see when I look out across em now from Highway 61, I guess he musta meant there wuddn no end to em and that they had done got so big the rows just disappeared into the fukkin sunset. If it wuddn that, then I don't know what the sumbich was talkin' about.

Anyway, bein' a planter nowdays don't really have a whole lot to do with plantin' anything. It's mostly what's planted in nem sumbiches. I guess you could say it ain't exactly an attitude; it's more like a gotdam assumption: "This is who I am, sumbich, cause this is who I was, and you ain't never been nothin', so fukkew."

But, hell, you can't touch em. Ever' one of em went off to school somewhere with, you know, a senator or sumpn. Still, I say those ass-holes are sound asleep. Only a few of em ever wakes up and goes their own way, and, when they do, all the other'ns call em crazy.

It'd be educational here to say something about the gotdam Chinamens, but I'm goin' to save that. Those little fukkas called us Bockgways, which Emerald Hoh told me meant "White Devils." I bout fell out laughin'. Those little fukkas, you couldn never tell what was on their minds, and I always liked em. Hell, they worked harder'n any sumbich in the Delta, and every little Delta town had some—they was a Chinaman's grocery store in ever' lillo town, and you could always get what you needed, cause them sumbiches never rested. My hat's off to em.

Oh, they called the niggas Hockgways, "black devils." Well, I don't know, white or black, the truth is, I guess, to the Chinamens in them Delta towns—and over in the Hills, too—we was all devils. They was squeezed in the middle of the whole mess and had to walk a narrow road. They was smart and worked hard every minute of the day and never knew where they was gon' fit the next or what was gon' happen to em, and I knew how they musta felt. I'll get into all that another time.

YOU MIGHTA HEARD I thought about goin' into rilastate. It's true. But I said fukkit I'm stayin' in law enforcement. I've always been in it, and I believe one way or another, as I have said before, I was meant to be in it.

Plus, lately there's a good chance they'll give me my pistol back up at the casino—well, it's *their* pistol of course; I carry my own, but don't nobody know it. It would be good, though, to get the one they issues you up there so I can put it out on my hip where a fukkin pistol gotdam ought to be. The thing is there's been so many robberies lately, up in that area of the county, that my supervisor come to me and said I might not have to be a ambassiter of goodwill no more and that I can prob'ly just act natural. That suits the shit outta me.

Course don't none of that interfere with me bein' a historian. And if you think about it, for a law enforcement professional like me, bein' a historian is a natural sideline. For one thing, findin' out about historical stuff changed my fukkin life because now when I look out across Moon Lake, I see the flotilla, and I know for certain, now, that what Mr. Brainsong told me was true, that whatever was never goes away. It can't—just like the track of them old traces and trails and early roads! And that's because it's the past, and the past can't go nowhere. It's here forever. I see it—and don't tell me I don't cause I do. Plus, it matters to me more'n what's just got here. Anyway, all that made me realize, next to law enforcement, I was born to be a historian.

To some people history is just information. To me, though, it's part of everyday life, only it don't never end.

Now, I know, at one point, while I was gettin' into becomin' a historian, there was, at least for a second or two, some question about me considerin' takin' up philosophy as my sideline. And I guess it looked like I coulda gone either way, but I was just naturally drawn more to history than to all that fukkin thinkin'. It wuddn zippy enough.

Philosophy, as far as I could tell, didn't have enough sex and violence involved in it—except during that little bit of time I was in the middle of all that doololly with Mad and Money and on Horn Island with Mad when me and him and Gene LaFoote had to fight the robbers and th'ow that sumbich Mad shot into the hogwallow.

Whereas that's all history is, sex and fukkin shootin' and violence ever'where you look. And that's what I love about it. But I ought not to talk bad about philosophy, even though most of it is *more or less* like some tweety-tweet woman tryin' on hats—dyin' to find the right one, only this one's got a feather, and that one don't. Hell, you know what I mean. Course you may not have had as much experience with it as I have. Shoot, Gene LaFoote was more of a philosopher than most of those old real famous-ass philosophical muthafukkas that all had names that ended in "eez" and "knees," and I don't even know who half of em were. So I say fuk bein' a gotdam philosopher.

Life is a gotdam slough. And it's bein' a historian that has taught

me the most. You might not be a dumb-ass blue-suit Yankee soldier
in the Civil War, steamin' out across a flooded cotton field, or just
floatin' around in the middle of a seven-thousand-square-mile cane
brake in a two hunnuhd-foot-long r'nclad battle ship, and you may
not never fall your ass in love with a Meffis nekkid dancer from
Tchula, Mississippi, or own a one-legged parrot.

But, Buddy-Ro, sooner or later, you and every swingin' dick I
know—hell, *all* of us—one way or a-fukkin-nother, out there in
the everyday swamp, is gonna step into a stump hole and come up
with our own rendition of the Yazoo blues. Yet, it's the same song
no matter where you sing it.

THERE IS ONE LAST thing you should know. At 1:45 A.M. on the early
morning of December the 9th, 2006, the Magic Pussy Cabaret &
Club was raided and closed. The Meffis Po-leece, the FB-fukkin-
Eye, the IR-gotdam-S, the A-T-F'ers, and—hell, for all I know—the
coksukkin Baptist Youth Group—all them sumbiches—busted in
and carried off ever'thin' and ever'body they could get their hands
on and padlocked the datgummed door. The authorities claimed
there was drugs bein' sold and other stuff goin' on. I never did see
no drugs sold, other'n beer from the bar. Anyway, I was glad I
wuddn in there when it all come about. Chr*EYE*st.

The prosecutor said the club was a nuisance, which tells me
the sumbich ain't never been there. If he had, he'da said the Magic
Pussy was a public service.

Anyway, it's a shame they closed the club, and I'm goin' to
miss drivin' up to Meffis to be a regular. But I believe what's right
will win out in the end—and that sex and the Magic Pussy will
outlast the law.

POST-ASS SCRIPT

I never did believe that snake crawled up inside that sumbich voluntarily. Some people might disagree. Fukkum.

Anecdotes, Observations, & Bon Mots

John Hayes Pritchard III, David Womack, Will Long, Nan Borod, Bard Selden, David Shands, Blackjack, Jimmy Lewis, and Lucia Burch.

Actual Historical Sources

James Truslow Adams
Shelby Foote
Chester Hearn
The Fukkin Internet
The Liberry of Congress
Edward G. Longacre
William T. Sherman's Memoir

Junior Ray Appreciates, For-fukkin-Ever

John Pritchard's beautiful, smart, perceptive, and highly risible wife who gives morning and evening and mortality a new and better meaning; . . . and Carol DeForest, who is absolutely responsible for Junior Ray's inclusion in the history of American Literature because she laughed at and validated every syllable of the first book, *Junior Ray*, over meatloaf at a near-by Meffis cafeteria; further, also, and always: NewSouth Books and all NewSoutherners; plus,

the People of the fukkin Delta and the Loess Hills, especially the
gotdam Planters, syphilis, and the Niggas, the Mississippi Guffcoast,
poagie boats, and the blood-guzzlin' Cath'lics; Moon Lake, Queers,
Meffis, the Magic Pussy, Mhoon's Landing, Beaver Dam, the levee,
Highway Sixty-One, Dead Nigga Slough, Highway One, Helena,
J. L. & the Northern alligators, the Irish Travellers, the Yellow Dog,
Michael T. Kaufman, Richard Houston, Linda & Layng Martine,
Corey Mesler, John M. Willcox, Alston Purvis, Carl Middleton,
Peter Formanek, Mr. Floppy; and everybody Junior Ray has ever
known, seen . . . or listened to.

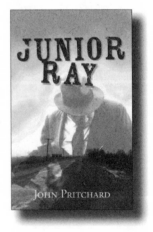